BLACK
BAMBOO

V J Stevenson

Bamboo: A symbol of flexibility and strength.
When the storm comes, bamboo bends with the wind.
When the storm ceases, it resumes its upright position.

A catalogue record for this book is available from the National
Library of Australia Cataloguing-in-Publication

Print ISBN 978-0-9943420-1-0
eBook ISBN 978-0-9943420-0-3

Cover design and map by Deranged Doctor Design
Formatting by Polgarus Studio

Darkness withers the heart.
But kindness
is like a refreshing drink
from a mountain stream…

Contents

Chapter 1.
The Wounded Man

High in the mountains late at night, the old man named Sharian sat still and silent in his log hut. The silhouette of his weathered face was like a rock statue while he watched the last flames flicker in the fireplace.

Far away in the next valley, Sharian heard a sound over the noise of the wind. He tilted his head to listen. It was the howling of a wolf, which was not unusual in these mountains, but tonight there was something different about the call. Instinctively he knew someone was coming, though visitors were rare.

"*Is there danger approaching?*" he asked himself, then closed his eyes for the answer.

In his vision he sees the drawing of swords, blood on the snow, deaths of strong warring men, and the escape of one lone man who comes his way. The man trudges on through the night, weary and wounded.

After a few moments Sharian nods, *"Not by chance does any man come this way. I hope the wolves don't get him,"* he thought sighing to himself.

The next morning the old man was up at sunrise as usual and stoked the fire. After making breakfast, he prepared a large stew and left it on the edge of the fire to cook slowly during the day, then went out into the cold, clear morning.

Sharian lead his woolly black horse from the barn so it could graze on sparse blades of grass that poked up through the thinning snow. He pottered in his vegetable garden and hummed to himself while digging over a bed in preparation for the spring planting. Occasionally he looked up for a sign of the approaching visitor.

Across the other side of the valley a wounded man stumbled down the steep hillside, struggling to keep his footing on the icy slope. The man noticed a barely discernible movement in the distance, and with fading energy he stopped to focus on what had caught his eye.

"Had danger followed him? Had the attacker preceded him here?" His head reeled when he tried to concentrate. He was hardly aware of his own wounds, but winced inwardly when flashes of memory brought back the screeching metallic sounds and the fierce screams. His own wounds had weakened him, though he had struggled on for two days and two nights to get away from the danger. He must keep moving or he would surely freeze to death if he lay down in the icy snow to rest, or the wolves would

finish him off. Either way, he knew, he would not get up again.

The wounded man saw the movement again in the distance. He could just make out a dark coloured animal moving slowly, about halfway down the side of the next mountain.

Keeping his eyes on the dark shape, his right hand slid instinctively to the knife he wore, not that the weapon would be much use in his present condition. Just as his hand touched the hilt a bird called out overhead.

The bird seemed to signal the white-haired old man who stood in the distance and turned to face him.

The old man's clear eyes went directly to his as he stood there shakily looking back; eyes squinted against the glare of the snow.

The wounded man had great difficulty keeping his numb legs from buckling under him, as he desperately struggled to assess the situation. "*Was the old man a threat?*"

He looked across the snow at the old man ... then a calmness spread over the valley like a blanket covering him. He felt a peacefulness in that calm, observing look of the old man who watched in the distance.

His body was numb and exhausted, but he lifted one foot and then the other, trudging on through the snow with heavy mechanical legs, throwing any caution of danger to the wind. Finally he stumbled and fell down in the snow, aware of a white light all around him, then nothing. He did not get up again.

Sharian sighed and nodded slowly to himself. He put his tools away and went about hitching up the shaggy black mountain horse to the rig he used to carry firewood out of the forest.

It took awhile to reach the other side of the next valley, but he found the fallen man easily and noted the gash on his head. He nudged him a couple of times before rolling him onto his back. Sharian could see that it was a young man lying before him, but when he saw the man's face, his eyes widened at the resemblance to an old friend of his. He had known this man's father once, and also knew that the old friend was no longer with the living.

"Hmmm. It has begun," he murmured to himself, and then quickly rolled the injured man onto the log carrier behind the horse, placing a blanket and an oilskin hide over him to prevent rain and snow from falling onto him.

The horse stood patiently. Its dark coat contrasted against the white snow as a cold morning breeze fanned its long dark mane and tail. Without any direction but a couple of clicking sounds made by the old man, the horse obediently turned and proceeded to pull its load back up to the other side of the gully in the direction of the hut.

Walking behind the horse, Sharian turned often to look and listen for any pursuers.

The horse continued forward, knowing exactly where to go – straight on to the wooden barn next to the old man's hut.

When they eventually reached the barn, Sharian went to get blankets, throwing a log on the coals to build up the fire as he went past. He untied the unconscious man and dragged him onto a thick bed of straw near one wall of the barn. Sharian examined and washed the wounds before applying healing herbs which he pounded into a paste. He covered the man with the blankets and sat back against the far wall watching and waiting, though he knew the wounded man would not wake for some time.

Sharian got up and went outside to chop wood and tend the small garden, keeping an eye on the direction from where the stranger had come, and staying alert for any danger that could be following.

When he went back to his hut, he boiled water for tea, and started to prepare food for himself. He knew his visitor would probably sleep till well into the night.

The buildings had been purposefully designed so that the heat from the fireplace in the old man's hut would permeate through to the adjoining barn, giving the animals warmth in the freezing winters. Throughout the night Sharian got up to put just enough wood on the fire to keep it alive. Each time he silently opened the front door, a cold wind blew wisps of his white hair back. With his chin slightly lifted like an animal sniffing the wind, he stood listening and scanning the escarpment for danger, but could sense none.

Over the next couple of days, the head wound started healing thanks to the medicinal skills of the old man. The visitor still experienced headaches and dizziness, especially if he sat up too fast, but these lessened after a couple of days. It was his inner grief and pain that would take much longer to recover from, and would torment him for years to come.

They had exchanged only a few words; Sharian sensed the young man's mental wounds and knew not to ask questions of him yet. All he had told the visitor was that he was welcome to stay as long as he wanted to.

At night the young man woke from nightmares where he saw the agony on the dead faces of the men he had known, the charred bodies of his mother and the rest of his clan, and the red blood spilt over the battlefield he had left behind. He panicked and struggled painfully within himself at having to face the harsh reality. He was now utterly alone in life without family, friends or home and knew not what direction to travel next.

Until a few days ago, he had never had to look at his own life or make such choices. His life had always been mapped out for him by his family and by the customs of his village.

Daily tasks and duties were performed alongside the people in his clan, with rituals and celebrations set out by the generations that went before him. One day he was to have taken his father's position of clan leader. All of that was gone now, wiped away in a single day by an unprecedented dark force that killed with no mercy.

The wounded man squeezed his eyes shut and shook his head trying to remove the painful and raw memories. In the end, they could not be erased.

He staggered out into the night and the dark shadowy forest, not caring that the cold air bit into his numb body.

Eventually he stopped near a large tree and squatted down on his haunches, leaning his back against its trunk while holding his head in his hands. He breathed heavily from the exertion, but before long great racking sobs shook his body and tears rolled down his face to land on the snow. He wailed and shook his head at the futility of his loss and all the grief he felt, not caring how cold he was or what happened to him, as he faced the dreadful reality of what had occurred. The storm of his emotions poured out and tears rained down. Anger burned white hot in him when he thought about the senseless waste and destruction of the recent events. He cursed the Creator for taking everything he loved away from him and did not understand why he alone had survived.

He stayed out there for hours letting his body get cold, almost welcoming the numbness and oblivion of the dark forest, breaking down again and again in despair.

Finally, he expressed his goodbyes and sorrows to his parents and friends. The tears continued to fall till there were none left. He was left with no choice but to face what had happened and, like it or not, he had to accept his situation. The previous events were irreversible and final. His father had saved him so that he would live on. He had to face life itself, as it was, and he had to go on living. He did not really know what he was doing staying with a stranger, but he felt he could trust the old man. It gave him time to try and make some kind of plan for himself and decide what to do next.

Sharian looked out through the window and watched

him disappear into the darkness that night, not knowing if the wounded man would come back, but knowing intuitively to let him go. The visitor needed to face his grief alone.

In the early hours well before sunrise, Sharian heard a slight noise of the barn door closing, then sighed deeply before going back to sleep.

The next morning when he went to the barn he found the young man sitting up against the rock wall watching him. He could see some of the anguish and turmoil had now gone from his face and was replaced by a hollow look of resignation.

"Who are you?" the wounded man asked shakily.

"I am named Sharian," the old man replied. "And you?"

"Navek," said the young man in a sombre tone, offering nothing further.

"I was about your age when I first came here," said the old man. "I was born in a village to the north-east of here in the alpine country like you, but I've lived up here now for over fifty winters."

Navek looked up at him, "How do you know where I am from?" he asked incredulously, not quite wanting to approach the subject of his father and his village, though curious about this man who knew of his clan territory.

"I have been to your Videha village years ago with my father, but you were not born then. I even knew your father Hatchiman in his younger days," Sharian answered simply, "and I could see his making in you as soon as I rolled you over in the snow the other day".

At hearing these words Navek looked across at him with unfeigned surprise.

"Come on next door and we can talk. I'm cooking porridge and have water boiling for tea," Sharian said before walking over toward the horse stall to lead the horse outside, leaving Navek to come at his own pace.

Once inside the hut, they both sat near the fire where the old man stirred the porridge which was suspended over the coals on a steel tripod stand.

"Why are you living here alone?" asked Navek.

"It's a long story," he replied looking over to the young man briefly to see if he really wanted to hear the answer. "My father was once the village shaman, a healer of men and animals. He would roam the forests gathering the traditional medicines of nature, communicating with the spirit world for guidance. He was often called upon by the elders to foretell the future of the village. Anyway, it was my father who first forecast that a dark age would come over the land, an ice age, the Great Freeze he called it. He said it would spread first from the north then down through to the south, and all in our lifetime. During some of his ceremonies he saw terrible visions of the death and destruction that were to come over the people and the land. His forecast is now manifesting it seems. Sometimes I would travel with him through the mountains to try and warn other clans of the pending danger, though some thought him a fool and didn't listen."

Sharian paused to put the porridge aside and get the

9

bowls ready. "Hatchiman was one of the few who believed the warning and remained ever vigilant against its approach. In the end nothing, it is now evident, would prevent it coming. So against my mother's tearful wishes, my father sent me away to protect me from what was to come, and for awhile I used to travel back to see them each spring, but not anymore. You see sometimes, I too can see things, visions or foretellings," the old man went on, "so I know that my village has since been wiped out by these dark spells and my clan are all gone now, as are yours," he added, glancing at Navek.

Navek stared into the coals, frowning, but listening intently, wanting to understand the conversation as it helped make some sense of his own circumstances.

"Here, visitors are rare, and I have lived a solitary life up here in the mountains ever since. Alone, but not lonely," he added. "Occasionally I would travel east to the port town of Jenolan to get supplies before winter, but it is a long way and I don't go there now."

Sharian reached over to poke around in the coals before serving the porridge into bowls, and then poured boiling water onto herbs in a teapot. He sat back from the fire as they ate in silence, observing Navek churn the information over in his head.

"Where does this darkness come from?" asked Navek.

"It comes from one man," Sharian replied solemnly, "one man's mind". He paused before continuing on: "Just as there is good in this world, there is also evil, as sure as sunlight will cast a shadow, though we humans always have the choice of which to follow."

Knowing Navek needed answers he continued on. "One night years ago, I was dozing off here in front of the fire when I was jolted awake from a terrible dream. It was then that I knew my family were gone from this world. I saw the image of a skinny, unkempt boy, a very angry boy with smouldering eyes who looked to be about thirteen years old. I recognised him as a boy from the outskirts of our village who was named Jackyl, Jackyl Nazarak."

He went on nodding to himself slowly at the recollection of the strange boy. "I feel shame now at how my friends and I had bullied the outcast boy. He came from a poor family who treated him cruelly, and sometimes they didn't or couldn't provide enough food for him. His father would beat him badly and often kicked him out to fend for himself, even in the winter. Some of the mothers would feel sorry for him and leave food out for him; others shunned and bullied him because he seemed different. But he would never cry out or make a sound when they beat him. Anyway, in the dream I saw him crouched in the darkness outside my father's hut, looking in through the window just watching. I had the feeling the boy had been there before. My father was busy with something on the table and had his back to the window, when all of a sudden he turned and looked the boy straight in the eyes. They both stayed like that for several moments, and I sensed my father was looking past the anger, deeply into the boy's soul. He held the look a few moments longer before turning to go back to what he had been doing. The boy entered the hut and extended his arm toward my father – three fingers pointing at him like a trident. I saw a visible force radiate through those fingers which took my breath away – even in a dream. My father turned to face the boy with a look of resignation on his face, almost as though he was expecting this to happen, then he fell to the floor. The boy stepped forward and snatched the stone amulet that my father had always worn and some old books, then ran out into the night. In my panic, I woke with my heart pounding and could not shake off the dream. That same night the spirit of my father visited me telling me not to worry. 'Practise the skills and help those who will come to you in need,' he said to me. He assured me he would always be with me, just as your father and all your ancestors will remain around you Navek. You can always talk to them."

Sharian looked at Navek who avoided his eyes by fixing his gaze on the fire, but he was still listening, so Sharian continued.

"In previous days the reputation of my father had spread far, and I can recall many coming to see him. Sometimes they came from other villages at night so as not to be seen by their neighbours, trusting him to heal them and set things right. He would help whoever came to him no matter who they were. Some would bring him gifts of food as payment, others had nothing to give, but he helped them nonetheless. You see my father was truly gifted. Not all shamans have the true gift of healing and some use their position for selfish gains or their intentions are not for the good of mankind. It is a tradition usually passed down through families, and in my family, there is a long history of healers.

"The amulet he wore around his neck was an ancient and magic stone, a Dragon's Eye it was called. It enhanced his powers, but in the wrong hands it could magnify the worst of intentions too. I remember marvelling at its silky deep brown lustre. It had bands of gold which shifted with the slightest change of position, and if you looked into it the wavy bands resembled a scenic view. For generations it had been handed down to the apprentice son from the father. If called upon, it was said to enable the transfer of information between the wearer and the spirit world and thereby heighten the powers of the one wearing it.

"Unfortunately, it has strengthened the dark spells of its current wearer, enabling Jackyl Nazarak to wreak his sorcerer's revenge on us all, and he has plans to continue Navek. He has started to spread his sinister manipulations further southward with each passing year. He has killed both our families and many others, and we must stop him."

"We?" Navek repeated, angered to hear the suggestion it was up to him to do something about this vengeful killer of his people. He had no strength to fight anyone and felt weakened and vulnerable. He just wanted to run as far away as possible from the mountains and the memories and the grief.

"Yes it will be you. You and two others will bring about his undoing," Sharian paused before adding, "and I can see you being saved twice more my friend, before you face this enemy".

The old man spoke the words quietly, not wanting to inflame Navek any further. He knew he had said more than enough for the young man to cope with, but he needed to introduce the foretelling to Navek. Even though the young man could not know it now, the forecast would one day affect his future.

The weight of these last words seemed to echo loudly around the room for long moments afterward, then as though realising he had said too much, Sharian said, "It's a lot to take in. Let's talk again later; I have to check on the horse now," and he stood and went outside into the sunlight, leaving Navek near the fire to think over the information.

For the next couple of days, Navek kept mostly to himself in the barn, still weak and recovering from the head wound and feeling numbed to all hope in life by the trauma of losing everything. He could not stop thinking about the shocking recent events and could find nowhere to rest his head in peace. The days passed with few words spoken between them, and nothing more was said about the wayward sorcerer. Navek pushed the conversation away, not wanting to acknowledge the subject again.

He would get up early and go straight out from the barn to roam around in the forest nearby, so that he would not be overwhelmed by anguish and angry thoughts which were ready to jump on him as soon as he woke.

He occupied himself by looking for firewood in the

pre-dawn light, sometimes pulling up branches that poked up through the snow or breaking timber with a sharp strike of his boot, before eventually returning to the hut carrying or dragging the damp wood.

Once he heard Sharian was up and making breakfast, he would cut some of the drier firewood and bring it into the hut, grateful for something to do with himself – and also wanting to help the old man who was giving him shelter. During the day, Sharian would potter around, tending the animals and the garden, occasionally talking to Navek about practical matters, but otherwise knowing to give him plenty of space, aware that his visitor was facing an unknown future in an unknown world.

However, in the evenings around the fire, they discussed all kinds of subjects. Sometimes the depth of the old man's simple wisdom would transform Navek out of his turmoil and into an experience of calmness. He came to welcome these words that offered him some freedom. At times, he glimpsed that there truly was a sanctuary of the soul; when the mind was still enough to accept it.

Sharian found it refreshing to have Navek's company and enjoyed their nightly conversations. Though his visitor was a man of few words, he knew how to listen, and drew out Sharian's inner wisdom. His eyes would twinkle when deep, forgotten treasures were uncovered and awakened.

"Life can be ruthless my friend," Sharian said one night. "I've been there believe me, and more than once. It can deal out some heavy blows at times, and sometimes our whole world can be changed in just a few moments. But life boots us along whether we like it or not, and sometimes we have no choice but to move on because life's very nature is to change. If we can be like the willow tree that has its roots anchored deep in the ground, but with branches that are flexible and bend in the heaviest of storms, we can survive without breaking."

He leaned forward and added more water to the teapot, and then there was silence for a while as the sounds of the fire crackled gently. "Remember that the shadow can never be more powerful than the sun."

Navek listened in silence at the words as though he was the student again learning from his elders; hearing truthful words that sounded familiar and seemed to strum chords within him.

"If you find you are facing the shadow, then you have your back to the sun, so turn and face where light comes from, then the shadow of confusion will not exist. Light the flame of peace my friend and the darkness will go away."

The old man stared into the fire, transfixed on the lapping flames, then after awhile the wisdom flowed on.

"If a person can go back to the source and strip away all else till he is left just breathing and existing without thoughts, he can find the path to follow. Really, it is incredible that life gathers itself into us as a breath, and it is the greatest challenge for a person to simply exist moment-to-moment. Not many have achieved this, but that is precisely where true freedom lies my friend. Peace seems hidden away, but just as the myriad of background sounds in the night can go unnoticed, they can also come to the forefront and become a loud cacophony of music for those who choose to listen."

That night Navek lay on his bed in the barn and felt a welcome clarity in himself. He smiled when he recognised the sun had briefly emerged and dispelled the shadows of his mind. He put his attention to the noises of the night and heard the symphony of sounds, just as Sharian had described. The longer he listened, the more magnified the sounds became. He felt connected to all of life then, and understood the meaning of Sharian's words even more deeply.

Chapter 2.
Turning Over of the Seasons

"To forge a strong sword my friend
It takes many blows to the steel."

Winter turned to spring, as snow thinned and melted into a brown sludge that covered the mountains. Navek's wounds were mostly mended thanks to the healing skills of the old man, but restlessness grew in him. Sharian had welcomed him to stay on, but it was fear that made him restless. Fear of stepping out on his own and facing the uncertainty. Soon he must leave the relative safety and familiarity of the mountain hut and face life again.

He could not go back to his village – nobody was left. The only other place he had travelled was the port town of Jenolan. He had been there only twice before with his father and two of the villagers, when recent harsh winters depleted their stored food supplies. They had made the treacherous journey to the coast and traded dried mountain herbs for grain, so they and their animals could make it through till spring.

In the town they had seen strange sights. People rode inside noisy mechanised vehicles, light somehow came from wires and shone inside the shops and houses. Many other objects and activities also pointed to a more developed or advanced community than he was used to.

Both times Navek was drained by the unfamiliarity of being in the town, and had felt out of place around some of the traders in the marketplace. They seemed to mock his father and friends. Both times he had been glad to get back to his simple village life and amid familiar territory.

Sharian planted the seeds of vegetables and herbs into the tilled soil, as Navek dug over the garden beds ahead of him.

"Thinking about leaving?" Sharian asked casually, surprising Navek who had been occupied with his thoughts.

"Is it that obvious?" he replied, then after awhile added, "It is hard to know what to do next Sharian. As much as I appreciate all your generosity and help, I must go on, though it is with much trepidation and fear. I know not where to go or how to survive. Apart from two trips to Jenolan for supplies, I've only ever known my simple village life in the mountains."

The old man stood up and leaned back to straighten his back. He recognised the need for some practical advice and looked over to Navek, weighing his words before speaking. "These days in the cities you won't last long without money. To start with you could head toward Jenolan, which is about three- and-a-half days' walk from here. You could look for work; even ask around on the way to see if the farmers need help during the spring harvest. If you get to town, the steel factories sometimes need workers, or talk to people down at the wharf where they unload the ships. Look at what you *do* have Navek. You are young, strong and fit, and sometimes you can barter your labour for money or food or a roof over your head. If you do go, watch out for thieves and shysters because not everyone is honest. Some wouldn't think twice about slitting your throat or robbing you, so you can't be naive either."

Navek mused over the words while they continued gardening, then Sharian added, "Perhaps you could find work, and then see where life takes you next. It would be difficult at first, but being busy can be a good thing. Working will keep your mind occupied and give you a purpose for awhile, until you know what to do next. A change with new people and new ways of thinking may do you good, but of course you can come back here anytime".

Navek never wanted to leave the shelter of the old man's house and did not want this time to end. He had forged a lasting bond with Sharian and felt safe in the remoteness of the mountains, but they both knew he would be leaving soon.

Two nights before the planned departure, a light

tapping at the window startled Navek, who had become complacent with the evening routine. Unperturbed, the old man stood and opened the door to find a young boy standing on the doorstep, dressed in a rough oilskin coat.

Sharp, dark eyes went directly toward Navek, who recognised the high cheekbones and olive skin of one from his homeland region. The lad looked to be about twelve years old with cropped black hair, strong body and a healthy glow to his face.

"Ah, come in from the cold," Sharian said, but the boy remained in the doorway checking out Navek. The boy glanced at Sharian and found no sign of tension or fear. He stepped inside and closed the door to the icy wind that blew in behind him, all the while keeping his eyes on Navek.

Sharian turned toward Navek and said, "This is my young friend Jake. He'll be staying here".

Navek responded with a nod.

"Navek," he replied.

Jake remained near the door and removed his coat and gloves before sitting at the table. He continued to eye Navek, somewhat intrigued by the rare visitor, while Sharian busied himself reheating food leftover from the evening meal.

Jake ate ravenously then joined the others around the fire, where, for a while, few words were spoken as they stared into the flickering flames, each thinking their own thoughts.

"Jake knows the way and can travel with you as far as

Jenolan," Sharian said. At hearing these words, Navek and the boy looked in surprise at each other. As though reading Navek's thoughts Sharian added, "Don't be put off by his size. He can take care of himself and knows the way well".

There was something about the boy Navek liked, but these were dangerous times and surely he would only hinder his progress through the mountains.

Jake must have been tired and had trouble keeping his eyes open. Eventually, he went over to some shelving on the far wall, where the middle shelf had a mattress with blankets thrown together on top. He rolled himself onto the shelf, covered himself and, without a word, closed his eyes and fell asleep as though he belonged there.

After awhile, Navek saw the boy was asleep and asked, "Where are his parents?"

Sharian looked across at Jake to ensure he was asleep. He sat forward in his chair and stoked the fire before answering quietly. "Ah. Everyone has their story. Now here is another tale of rescue. I seem to have done a few rescues eh," he chuckled as he added more wood to the fire. "They were killed years ago by the remote Raghasse tribe. It was further to the north-west of your village. As you would know, the Raghasse are a warring tribe who still keep to their old ways. They would not agree to the keeping of peace and have caused a lot of trouble and grief to people of the highlands over the years." Navek knew well of the primitive and brutal clan who, just weeks before, had been the ones pursuing them on that last tragic

22

day. His eyes gleamed in anger at the memory. Images flashed through his mind of the alarming pursuit and the eerie feeling that had intensified before the attack. Navek had caught the odd look of alarm on the enemy leader's face before the brute had veered off and retreated without attacking. He would never forget that magnified sound as though angry bees swarmed over them, but shook his head not wanting to think of such odd occurrences that could not be explained. It had not been the enemy Raghasse clan who had dealt the final blows that day. He shifted his position and sat forward toward the fire to avoid the raw memories resurfacing again, and busied himself pouring tea as Sharian talked.

"When Jake was about six years old, the brutes raided his village looking for food – killing, looting and burning the huts of the people. His mother ran with him trying to escape but they were captured. She died a terrible death soon after while living in the enemy camp. Jake was raised by a cruel woman from that clan who treated him brutally and used him like a slave, even at such a young age. He lived an oppressed and futile existence tied up day and night with a chain around his neck like a dog so he wouldn't escape, and she would drag him from place to place to work during the day.

"At nights he ate what the dogs ate and slept chained up with them in all weather. He had some rough leather boots, a few clothes on his back, an old cowhide for a blanket and the heat of the dogs to keep him warm. Some of the dogs were savage and could kill him, but a couple of the pack leaders that were smarter than the rest would defend the boy. He developed an affinity for these dogs and considered them his friends. He knew instinctively how to communicate with them and they understood each other, sometimes just by eye contact or with small sounds or by an invisible sixth sense. Anyway, the tribe treated him like a fool, but he was no fool. He watched and waited for a chance to escape.

"It was toward the end of winter when he found a sharp piece of metal and threw it over unnoticed into the icy mud where he slept. At night he would use the point to poke around inside the lock, practising, till one night the crude lock finally popped open. But with a smile, he closed it again.

"Preparing for his escape, he collected some scraps of food to take with him, and then a few nights later waited until after dark to open the lock. He communicated to the animals that he was leaving and not to make a fuss, but some of his favourite dogs had already sensed his plans. They whimpered as he patted and hugged them goodbye before watching him escape into the forest. A couple of dogs barked in an attempt to warn the tribe of the disturbance, but were hushed by the lead dogs who growled in a low threatening tone to show them their place.

"For most boys of that age, being alone in the forest at night would have been frightening, but to Jake it was freedom. The strange noises and the solitude didn't scare him at all. Anything had to be better than the dog's life he had endured. Even the threat of attack from hungry animals in the mountains didn't scare him. He just wanted to get far away before the morning light, which was when the clan would come looking for him with the dogs. Instead of heading south toward his old village where they would have expected him to go, he headed south-west into higher mountain country; then south in a bid to lose them. He knew of a cave some distance from his village where he would stay. He guessed that his dog friends would lead them back to his village to the south, but occasionally he would walk up icy cold creeks with bare feet to throw them off the trail.

"Soon after all this, I had a vision of a young boy who was alone and needed help. I was charged with a strong compulsion to get up in the night and go far from here into those mountains, to a particular area where I would find him in a cave. He is special that one and I couldn't ignore the quest for I was being pushed by his parents from the spirit world to help him. I knew more or less where I would locate him, not so far from his old village. He was in a cave where his parents took their goats to feed during summer. So in the night I took my old horse from the barn, loaded it with blankets and food and set out. It took four days of trekking through the mountains on foot to reach the cave, and when I got there it was almost nightfall. He behaved like a wild animal with a fierceness in his eyes like a cornered beast, but he could see I was not one of his former captors.

"Imagine that, a six year old able to find his way to the

very cave he'd been to with his parents, then surviving out there in the freezing mountains. He was a tough little fellow who had spent many a night sleeping outside in all kinds of weather with only dogs to give him warmth. He was a miserable sight though – big hollow eyes, purple lips, skinny and hungry when I found him, and he wouldn't have lasted much longer."

Reminded of the sorry details of their first meeting, Sharian glanced over to the sleeping boy with a look of kindness.

"So I just ignored him and set about making a fire and cooking some food. While the food cooked, I went out and brought my old horse into the shelter of the cave to protect it from the cold, and from any wild animals that could be roaming the mountains at night looking for a meal. Jake's sharp eyes watched my every move, but I suspect he was exhausted and weak. After I unhitched the saddle, the food was cooked and I set it near the fire and beckoned him to come over, then sat back to eat.

"At first it was like taming a feral animal, but he eventually edged his way over, grabbed the food, then hurried away to gulp it down. I'll never forget the look of relief in his eyes – of having hot food and a fire for warmth. A boy that age shouldn't have to be on his own like that. When he finally looked up, I threw him another thick crust of bread which he caught effortlessly with one hand before engulfing it. He closed his eyes as he ate at the sheer pleasure of having food after days of hunger. Later I tossed a woolly hide in his direction and took another hide myself. "Tomorrow morning I'm leaving early to travel home, about five days to the south-east. You can come with me if you want and I can give you a place to stay as long as you choose. If you live with me, I will need some help around the house that is all, but you are free to come and go and your life is your own." Then I put a log on the fire and lay down to sleep, as it had been a long journey for me too.

"In the morning the boy was sitting up against the wall of the cave with the hide wrapped around him just watching me. He was waiting and ready to go with a look of resignation on his face, but at least the hollow look had gone from his eyes. I wanted to be away early; I didn't want to meet his enemies who may still be out looking for him.

"But several days had gone by since his escape, so why would they spend much time looking for a young kid who they would have given up for dead. After I hitched up the horse, I walked it over next to a large rock and said, 'Come on, let's go. You can ride on the horse if you want. Get up on that rock to get on.' The boy hesitated for a moment, but knew he didn't have a lot of options and quickly got on the horse."

The story went on into the night, not unlike Navek's own miserable tale of death and loss, till eventually Sharian looked over again to make sure Jake was still asleep.

"He keeps all this to himself and has rarely talked of it, but for the images I have seen I would not know most of this. Like you, he comes from a strong peacekeeping family who were wiped out."

Navek felt his heartbeat quicken as the old man continued. "I told Jake if he helps me around the place, he can live here as though it is his own home; I'm glad to give him a roof over his head when he chooses to come. He learns quickly too. I teach him about the basic healing herbs, edible roots, their medicinal purposes, and where to find them in the forest."

Sharian leaned forward and stoked the coals, pushing all the unburnt ends of wood into the centre where they ignited easily.

"Sometimes he goes away for months at a time, leaving just before winter and coming back in time for the spring. He told me once he goes to live with monks at a monastery built high on the side of a cliff near the southwest coast. He learns their fighting arts and trains with them through the winter. He comes back with his head shaved, body strong and the light of truth sparkling in his eyes. He absorbs their fighting skills as easily as a fish swims and has natural potential. I think the training and the lessons help to purge the suppressed anger he carries from the hard life he has been dealt.

"In my visions I have seen the boy stick-fighting barefoot in the snow and swimming in icy seas with the monks. They push him hard but he thrives on the discipline and the learning of new skills."

Sharian glanced over to Navek before adding, "It takes many blows to the steel to forge a strong sword my friend".

A few long moments of silence passed before the old man stood and lifted the screen across in front of the fire for the night.

"Don't forget my friend, you are always welcome here."

"Thank you Sharian," said Navek sincerely, "for everything you have done". "It is a good feeling for an old man like me to be useful," he replied. "Come on, it's getting late and time to sleep. I've done more talking in one night than I would normally do in a year!" he chuckled.

Later when Navek went out and lay on his bed, he thought about the conversation long into the night, wondering about all the deaths and waste of lives, unaware and astounded that this had gone on for so long in the north. With reluctance he thought about the far-fetched forecast – that it would be he and two others who would be the ones to end it all – before pushing such thoughts aside as nonsense. He decided he would accept the boy's sullen company to guide him to the town, as at least he knew the way. It helped to know that they had both been cast from a similar mould.

Chapter 3.
To Town with Jake

After leaving Sharian's hut, Navek and Jake walked for two full days, during which the boy hardly said a word. He proved to be a tough little travelling companion though, and kept pace as easily as any man. He showed Navek the quickest way through the cold mountain range was by keeping to the high ridges.

Being active again invigorated Navek, but by the second day when he anticipated they would stop for the night, Jake pressed on further.

The sun had gone down behind the mountains and the air temperature was dropping quickly. Jake led them to an outcrop of snow covered rocks, where they sheltered under an overhang which offered some reprieve from winds and unpredictable rainfall during the night. Jake set about making a fire from a stash of sticks and logs, and Navek saw the boy was familiar with the place and had stayed here before.

Navek slumped down against an icy wall and closed his eyes. Though recovered from his injury, he was still not quite back to his former self and was grateful for the rest. Eventually, he hoisted himself up and went to find more sticks and dead branches to ensure the fire would last the night. Evening settled around the two travellers, as they sat and watched the fire flicker and dance. They ate some of the salted meat and bread Sharian had packed for them, and after a long, arduous day of walking, they savoured the taste. That was followed by a handful of small dried berries, which tasted both sweet and sour, and was washed down with mouthfuls of snow.

Navek was thankful to the kind old man, who had provided them flint to start a fire, and food, as well as all the other help given.

The young man and the boy sat in their own silence, thinking their own thoughts.

Navek understood why Sharian let Jake share his solitary life in the mountains; the boy was self-contained and did not require a continual response from others like many his age. This made him easy to be around, and allowed others to keep their own focus.

Navek felt for Jake, as the boy had also lost his parents and came from a region near his own village. There was probably only about six or seven year's difference between them.

"You know I came from a clan from the north like

you," Navek said as he poked the coals with a stick.

"Which clan?" the boy asked.

"The Videha," Navek replied as he watched the dancing flames, and considered whether he would add anything further. "They were all killed recently. I was the only survivor," he added in a dour tone.

A long silence followed till the boy nodded almost imperceptibly, keeping his eyes on the fire to hide an old pain of his own from his past. Though Navek was not much of a talker himself, he sensed the boys' thirst to know more about his own origins, and the people of his homeland, though he would not ask directly for such information.

Navek continued on, telling Jake how one of his friends had found a pair of hungry wolf cubs whimpering and alone in the woods. The elders had not allowed him to keep the pups in the village for fear of other wolves coming around and eating the goats. He kept them further away in another valley, hidden in a narrow crevice in some rocks which became their home. He told Jake how almost every day his friend would hunt and bring the cubs food and water, later even teaching them to hunt for themselves as best he could.

One day the friend found the pups gone, so he followed their tracks for hours until he saw they had joined other wolf tracks. Though his friend loved those pups, he was glad that they had been accepted into a pack of their own.

"Did he see them again?" Jake asked, dropping his

guard.

"No, he didn't," Navek answered, "but he would hear them at night, howling in the distance and knew they were alright".

Navek saw the boy was listening, so he told a few other tales often heard around the fire at night when he was growing up, making himself nostalgic for all he had so recently lost.

That night they sat up late talking as they watched the embers burn down. As though in another realm, they became unaware of the world around them; uncaring of the icy wind blowing, or the animals that may be hunting nearby.

Jake found that the tales reminded him of his home country, and it was much later when they both pulled their long coats up around themselves, and fell asleep.

The next morning Jake was keen to be away, and Navek hurried to keep up with him for the rest of the day.

Late in the afternoon the village of Ripolin appeared far below them. By the time they came down from the mountains and neared the outskirts of town, a late snow started to fall and nightfall was upon them. Unnoticed in the dim evening light, they continued toward the few scattered houses on the edge of town, where they hoped to find somewhere to eat and stay the night.

They passed one old house, and could just make out someone chopping wood at the side. A woman's voice cursed when the axe missed the mark. Sharian's advice about bartering came to mind and Navek turned toward the woman, nudging the boy to follow. "Need help?" Navek asked.

"Who's there?" replied the startled woman, unable to see them clearly in the shadowy light.

"We are travellers going to the coast, just looking for a place to stay for the night and some food if it is offered."

The woman eyed them suspiciously, peering through squinted eyes to see them as they stepped nearer. But when she saw it was a young man with a boy she relaxed a little.

"Where have you come from on this cold night?" she said, able to see them now and looking up and down at their rough mountain clothing.

"We have no money to pay, but can chop your firewood or help with other work if need be," said Navek. "All we need is somewhere to sleep for a night and some food if you can spare it. We'll be gone in the morning."

The woman's eyes softened when she looked at Jake. She looked back at Navek, staring directly into his eyes, weighing up whether she would trust the pair, as not many strangers came this way – even in spring.

A long moment passed. Finally she said: "OK. Chop me a few days' supply of this wood and I'll make you some dinner, but you'll have to sleep in the barn with the animals".

"That would be just fine and much appreciated. Thank you," said Navek, happy his first attempt at bartering had been successful.

He set about chopping the wood while Jake went to the barn with their bags. Jake returned and carried an armful of wood into the house, setting it down next to a kitchen stove.

Potatoes, carrots and cabbage were cut up on a chopping board and the aroma of food cooking wafted throughout the small house. He went back out and carried several more armfuls of wood into the house before the woman said, "Tell him that'll do with the wood. There's a tap near the door to wash up, then come in and get warm".

Navek chopped a few more logs while Jake stacked the wood up against the house, till finally they both came in.

The woman may have been in her late fifties, it was hard to tell as her face and hands were weathered from years of hard work and surviving in the semi-rural conditions.

"Heading east to the coast you say?" she asked as she added vegetables to the pot.

"That's right. We're heading to Jenolan city," said Navek, offering no further details and feeling a little uncomfortable in a stranger's house. "We appreciate you taking us in like this," he said politely, suspecting that the woman lived alone.

"Looks like you're on your own here, must be hard doing everything yourself?" said Navek kindly, as he thought of his own mother who had always worked hard.

After a few moments she said, "I had a son once. He was a bit younger than this boy when he was out hunting with his father and they were both killed. They crossed a frozen river and fell through the ice".

She busied herself with the cooking then added, "It was a long time ago, so I'm kinda used to it now. But you never forget".

Jake, who had been quiet the whole time, looked over to the woman when he heard this. Their eyes met briefly before he looked out into the night through one of the windows.

He was restless and had a worried look on his face; Navek noticed that something disturbed the boy.

Finally Jake asked the woman, "Why are those animals barking and yelping like that?"

Navek listened and sure enough, far in the distance the sounds of yelping animals in distress could be just heard above the sound of the fire crackling and the stew boiling. He was surprised he had not heard it earlier.

The woman frowned and hesitated before answering, "Hmm. Every year it is the tradition in this area, for some of the town's men to trap animals for their skins to sell to the fur traders. Tomorrow will be the day of slaughter and skinning. It's a brutal day of death, where all kinds of furred animals, including dogs that have been trapped, are all kept together in a big shed over in the next valley. The poor creatures are jammed into small cages and not fed for days, and you can hear their terror and misery as they await their cruel fate. Tomorrow they will all be killed. Some even skin them alive. Have you ever heard of such an atrocity! The hunters say the skin comes away easier if the animal is not dead. Hmph. I hate the vile practice and have been trying to have this cruelty abolished for years.

Many of the townsfolk shun me for my views, and a lot of people around here are unaware the animals are being skinned alive. But most villagers live out of earshot and can't hear the poor souls crying. I am glad of your company tonight, but tomorrow I must go from here or I'll be haunted by the tortured cries for days after".

She went about setting out the plates on the kitchen bench.

"What is wrong with people," Navek said shaking his head in disbelief.

"Sorry to tell you this," the woman said, "I am ashamed people from around here partake of such a sickening act, as though wild animals are a commodity to be traded and feel no pain".

Jake went back to looking out the window, into the dark night in the direction of the sounds, looking more concerned than ever.

She went on, "Of course since our ancestors' time, we all use the hides of animals, but hunters have always killed the animal quickly. None of this live skinning business. Ah, don't get me started. People can be truly heartless".

The woman realised the conversation had become grim and tried to lighten the mood, "Anyway, enough of all this". She brought out some homemade mulberry wine and three glasses, and then poured them each a shot of the brew. She held up her glass and toasted, "Better days ahead".

They both agreed and sipped the sweet potent brew which hit the bloodstream quickly, helping to relax them all.

Later they sat down to eat, and even though Navek and Jake had walked all day and had not eaten much, they had lost their appetites.

The suffering of the animals in the next valley affected them all, and the woman understood well the cause of the sombre mood.

After dinner they helped clear the table and wash the dishes, and then Jake went outside to the barn. Navek thanked the woman for her hospitality and stood to go also, but she insisted he stay for another small shot of her home made wine. He stayed to talk a little longer to keep her company, more out of politeness than anything else, as the strong wine had a relaxing and warming effect on him.

"He's a good boy that one," she said, "He cares about the animals. Even though he's hardly said a word I can see he's had a hard life, but he's not a brute like many of the others".

Navek replied, "He's an orphan who is used to surviving on his own," realising as he said the words that he too was an orphan now. "We're only travelling together as far as Jenolan city," he said, feeling loosened up by the effects of the wine.

"You are both welcome here anytime you are passing through. Tell the boy won't you," she said with compassion in her voice.

Navek smiled to himself, as he had deliberately given her this small piece of information about Jake so that she may offer him a place to stay on his future travels through this area. The woman and the boy could both be a help to each other.

He didn't even know the woman's name, but he knew she was a good person who would be grateful for the boy's company if he chose to stay.

"I'll tell him," said Navek. He stood and picked up the blankets she had given him and headed toward the door.

"Wait a moment," she said, and went into the adjoining room where Navek heard the sounds of drawers sliding open and shut. She came back with a bundle of clothes and handed them to him. "These belonged to my husband and they're about your size. It'd make me happy if you use them."

Navek looked at the woman in surprise and saw the offer was quite genuine, so he accepted the clothing with gratitude, aware that his current attire was rough and worn. He remembered the stares from the townsfolk last time he was there.

"We are both grateful for your kindness on such a cold night. Thanks again," he said.

When Navek got to the barn he found Jake still wide awake sitting on the straw which had been gathered up as a mattress. They were both tired but remained awake for a long time huddled under their blankets, uneasy at having to listen to the caged animals in the distance; the cries contrasted against the quietness of the night. Though they had both hunted animals before, they found it abhorrent that in the hands of men, an animal was left without hope and without a second thought. As the cold night set in, the howls and yelps quietened till only an occasional sound was heard. Navek fell asleep, still feeling the effects of the wine.

About two hours before daybreak, Navek was woken by the creaking sound of the barn door closing. Alert with eyes open, he remained lying there, just able to make out the silhouette of Jake slipping in under the blanket in the darkness. A breeze of cold air brushed past from Jake's body, and Navek knew from the chilliness of the breeze that the boy had been outside in the cold night air for quite awhile. The boy sighed and went quickly to sleep. Navek lay there wondering where Jake had been, and listened to snow falling on the roof.

It seemed Jake had just closed his eyes, when Navek shook him gently to get up so they could be on their way early. A reluctant and yawning boy got up and folded the blanket, gathered his things and headed out again. They walked through the sleeping town and out to the north-east toward the coastal city of Jenolan, while snow continued to fall lightly in the pre-dawn light.

Once they were on their way, the boy was in better spirits, and Navek again had to walk quickly to keep up.

Navek passed on the message from the lady; that Jake was welcome to stay with her anytime he travelled that way, and that she would be happy to have the company.

The boy took in the information but gave no acknowledgement, as was his way.

Later that morning, there was a lot of commotion along the road leading past the woman's house. At first she thought it was the noise of the town's men going to the shed for the slaughtering, but the voices were angry and loud and there was something odd going on. She went out to her front gate and asked a passer-by what had happened.

He told her the shed had been burned down overnight and the hunters were angry. The entire winter stockpile of skins had burned with it. Charred cages were all that were left, but the cage doors had all been opened. Not a sign of any of the animals, not even one burnt carcass could be found in the ashes. The man hurried on toward town to spread the news, as such an event had never occurred before. It was big news!

Light snow still fell on the woman who stood at the gate a few moments as she took in the information. She turned and went inside the house, unable to keep the smile from her face or suppress the happiness.

She went straight out to the barn to find the blankets folded neatly on the straw and the two travellers gone. She picked up the blankets and hugged them, then spun around in a circle. Once back in the house she could not stop smiling and sent them a silent blessing for their journey.

Chapter 4.
The Monks of Jenolan

Snow fell lightly for most of the day and though spring should have arrived by now, it was turning into another long winter. By late afternoon they had easily followed the road to reach the coastal town of Jenolan where the travelling companions would part ways. Daylight started to fade from the grey sky and they were both tired and hungry.

"Let's find somewhere for the night," said Navek, "then we'll go our separate ways in the morning".

The boy nodded in agreement but kept on walking along the street, pointing impatiently ahead toward shops and places to eat.

A fear of the unknown crept over Navek. Though he had been here before, the town seemed unfamiliar; he felt trepidation and uneasiness start to weigh on him. He could see that Jake knew where he was going, so he followed behind not asking questions of the boy who seldom spoke.

The travellers walked right on past the main group of buildings and shops, and kept going toward the dockyards. They passed by rows of older, double-storied wooden buildings that stood back from the water. Some of the buildings were joined together with verandas and balconies across the front of them. In front of one of these buildings Jake stopped.

"Wait here while I go see someone," he said, indicating with his chin for Navek to wait on the veranda while he disappeared around the back.

Navek looked up at the old building, weathered from years of salty winds and harsh conditions. Only remnants of paint were left on the weather-board cladding; most had peeled off long ago. The building held a certain fascination to him after the simple mountain hut he was used to. With no sign at the front, it looked more like a private residence than somewhere to stay for the night.

He wondered if he should follow the boy this far, and was thinking he would rather stay anonymously somewhere in town, when the front door opened. A monk with a shaved head stood in the doorway, and behind him stood Jake.

Dark shiny eyes on a jovial face peered out, and Navek noticed at once the solid stance and strong body of one who trains in the fighting arts. Navek saw a new brightness in Jake's face, reflecting a pride the boy felt from his association with the monk.

"Welcome. Come in, come in," he said to Navek. "I am Mancel. Our friend Jake tells us you have both come far and seek shelter for the night. Come in."

Navek felt no apprehension or danger from the well-spoken monk, so picked up his bag and entered the house.

Once inside, the monk asked Jake to take Navek upstairs and show him where they would both stay and where they could wash up.

It was obvious Jake had stayed here before, and upstairs Navek nudged him playfully saying, "You have a bed in every port, eh?"

The boy didn't look up, but Navek saw the youthful pride and a brief smile before Jake quickly covered it over with his usual serious face.

The upstairs room overlooked the port where fishing boats and dinghies were tied to the wharf. One larger vessel, a rather gloomy looking wooden ship with three tall masts, stood out from the rest.

Navek quickly washed and changed into clothes the woman from Ripolin had generously given him, grateful for the upgrade to his current wardrobe.

When they went downstairs, they saw there were seven other monks staying at the house, all physically fit and strong. The monks greeted the pair warmly and Navek saw that most already knew Jake.

Two of the monks went back to the kitchen to continue cooking, and soon the aroma of food wafted throughout the house. The monks happily shared their simple meal with the two visitors, their minds focused as they ate in silence.

Later they gathered around the living room fire together. Some sat around on the floor and others lay stretched out on mats while they chatted among themselves or calmly watched the flames in the fireplace.

It was all very new to Navek. He appreciated that none of the monks asked about his past or why he was in town; they seemed content just to be in their own company.

Relaxed by the warm room and dancing flames, it was not long before a yawning Jake slipped upstairs to bed. Navek felt glad now that they had not stayed at some inn, where strangers were often looked upon with distrust or judgement. He liked being among these men who were friendly and had a pleasing outlook on life. He was also interested in sharing the company of those skilled in the fighting arts.

The monks told Navek they had come across Jake quite happily surviving in a cave not far from their monastery on the west coast. They had seen smoke coming from his campfire, then one day out of curiosity, the head monk decided to take a group on a gruelling training run past the cave. They told Navek of their surprise to find a young boy sitting there, calmly watching them and unperturbed by their approach. The head monk had stopped the group for a rest, and went up to introduce himself to Jake. He liked the boy's bearing and invited him to come and visit them anytime.

What the monks did not know was that Jake had been

aware of them well before then, and had already ascertained they were no threat to him.

In moonlight, Jake had crept up close a few times, marvelling at the structure of the monastery built precariously onto the side of a cliff face and wondered what went on inside. Occasionally, he watched in fascination from a hidden vantage point while they trained outside their building or near the sea. He had even memorised some of the techniques to practise on his own.

About three weeks later Jake had turned up at the monastery, asking to see the head monk, who warmly welcomed him in.

The head monk told the visitor a little of how all the monks had chosen a life based on achieving inner tranquillity, and each day they practised sacred and ancient principles to achieve this. One of the younger monks was called to show Jake around, then the head monk asked Jake to come back to see him before he left.

A few years older than Jake, the young monk had chatted away as they toured the kitchen and dining area; a large hall where they meditated; and the sleeping quarters. Outside he was shown a well-kept garden of herbs, vegetables, an enclosure of goats and another one for chickens. When they reached an open courtyard, they stood awhile to watch several monks participating in a rigorous training session.

Stripped to the waist, agile monks parried hard against each other with long wooden staffs, sweat dripping from their shaved heads and muscular bodies. One teacher wandered serenely among them, occasionally making minor corrections. It had been hard to tell if the teacher was young or old, but at one point, Jake realised with a start that the teacher was watching him from across the courtyard. When their eyes met, it was a timeless moment. Everything stood still. An unexpected thrill coursed through Jake, as though those dark eyes had seen into his soul. The teacher had bowed slightly to the boy before going back to his work, and the sharp clicking and clacking of the wooden sticks continued to resound around the courtyard as it had before.

During the tour Jake hardly spoke or asked questions of his guide. He was taken back to the head monk but could not forget that timeless glance and those dark knowing eyes of the teacher in the courtyard. A spark of new possibilities awakened in him. A small excitement called him, a calling that he had not experienced before. He knew then he wanted to join these men and learn their skills. Not for the sake of fighting to maim others, but for his own interest and growth.

The head monk had seen the transformation on Jake's face and asked if he was interested to learn more. He described the daily schedule and what would be required of Jake. To join, there would be a two week trial period where each day he would be required to rise early with the others to learn doctrines and meditation. They all had daily disciplines and tasks which included domestic chores and cooking, then training in the ancient martial skills that had been passed down for generations by great masters.

Jake would have to train hard and there would be no sparing him.

The monk had added, "But the rewards are many on the path of light".

A few of the monks had gone to bed, and Navek was about to go himself when he noticed Mancel watching him through half shut eyes. Eventually the monk spoke.

"A dangerous quest is ahead of you brother, and one not of your own choosing. You will travel beyond death's door, and more than once."

The others in the room looked over at them and fell silent to listen.

"Accept your path and life will flow more smoothly, as it was written before your birth. But its success will depend upon your outlook."

Navek looked away from the monk toward the coals, reluctant to listen for the second time to the forecast about a difficult future, but Mancel continued.

"You will embark on a journey to the north and face many dangers and perils yet." He was silent awhile, then leaned toward Navek and added with compassion, "A heavy burden has been placed on your young shoulders my brother, a burden which has rarely been asked of any man. Help will be given if you remember to ask, and you will not travel alone. Remember though, determination and need were born together".

Sitting back the monk watched the coals for awhile, and then said on a brighter note, "The journey will be a success and you'll return home in the end".

Navek sighed after hearing the monk's insight. "I hope so," he said blandly. Unwilling to accept the words of others who attempted to outline his future, he suddenly felt tired of hearing about some invisible path he was to follow to the north. He just wished he could belong somewhere, have a purpose, or live simply like the monks around him.

The next morning Navek woke just before daybreak, when the unfamiliar scent of incense wafted up the stairs. He scrambled to get his bearings at first and forgot where he was, till he saw Jake sleeping across from him. Now that he was awake he had to face the horrible truth again – that his parents were gone, and he had no purpose and no work. He shook his head in an effort to stop the thoughts from weighing down on him, as they did every morning when he first opened his eyes. Deep reverberating sounds of chanting and sticks clacking sharply together started downstairs, and he turned his attention instead to the strange droning music. It had a nice effect on him and calmed his mind. Navek had never heard such a deep sound, earthy and ancient, and left the sleeping Jake to go downstairs to investigate.

In the lounge the monks stood with their backs to him, all chanting in unison to create the fascinating deep music. He listened for awhile before continuing outside into the chilly morning air.

Fastening his coat, he gazed around at all the buildings in apprehensive fascination. The smell of the sea air, the paved roads, the ships, everything was strikingly different to his simple life back in the village. Doubts started to grow as he wondered what he was doing here and how he could survive. At that hour only a few people hurried about the streets. From his conversation with Sharian, he would have to find work to survive.

He walked around for several hours, taking in the new sights, almost welcoming the distractions which gave him something to think about other than his predicament and his grief. Vulnerable, alone and surrounded by strangers and new surroundings, he eventually headed back to the monks' house.

Breakfast, consisting of a large bowl of porridge made from some unfamiliar grain, had been saved for him. Though it tasted fairly bland, it filled him and he appreciated their generosity.

Navek talked to the monks about finding work in the town. One of them suggested he could enquire at a new storage shed being built along from the docks. But they reassured him he was welcome to stay as long as he needed.

Later he strolled down to the waterfront and found the construction site where he enquired about available work.

It happened they needed a worker and were willing to give him two days' work if he came early the next morning to start.

By lunch time he found the work more relentless and laborious than anything he had done before.

"*Work surely is hard here,*" he thought to himself. "*They have a strange way of working and don't seem to work together to help each other. They prefer to pay each person to work like a dog."*

He thought about how all the men from his clan would work together at the various tasks to lighten the workload and make it easier. Everything got done and everyone benefited.

Though he was normally fit and strong, by the end of the second day his body ached and he was glad when the work finally ended. Pleased to collect his first ever pay, he pocketed the strange coins before heading down to the salty sea to wash the grime from his face and hands.

During the day he had overheard two of the workers planning to find a cargo ship that would take them to Welpecca. It was a harbour town to the south where work was supposed to be plentiful.

Navek went down to the wharf where only a few other people lingered, including some fishermen preparing their boats to go out to sea. Two dock workers were opening a large metal roller door on one of the warehouses, so Navek asked them about the wooden ship that was moored and where it would sail to. He found out it was a supply ship named the *Sea Snake*.

It sailed along the eastern seaboard, dropping off and picking up supplies from Frozia in the north, down to Welpecca in the south. It was the only ship that would sail south and was due to depart the following morning. The ship would stop at the island port of Mazzara before reaching its destination at Welpecca.

"They're a rough bunch though. Thick as thieves, so

watch yer back if yer travel with em," one of the workers added.

Navek thanked the men and headed toward the wooden ship. It towered above him, looking eerie and sinister now that he was up close. The ship's name was painted on the bow in faded black letters, and as he neared the vessel, he felt apprehensive about seeking travel on the unfortunately named ship.

Navek stepped onto the gangplank and was almost aboard the ship, when a big rough brute of a man with arms covered in tattoos, blocked him.

"What do ya want?" the man asked roughly.

"I'm looking for passage to the south," said Navek.

Several of the crew on deck eyed him suspiciously as they prepared for the forthcoming trip. The big man remained looking Navek up and down, till finally he signalled one of the crew to go get the captain.

A tall dark haired man with narrow shifty eyes appeared at the rails and looked down at Navek.

"I'm the captain," he barked impatiently, "what do you want?"

"I'm enquiring about travelling to Welpecca. I can work for my passage. Will you take on a passenger?"

The captain scratched his head noting Navek's strong body. "Hmm, the kitchen boy disappeared on shore and I don't think he'll be back, so I'm short a hand in the galley. You'd have to help the cook and do other jobs around the place," he said, glancing at the crew with leering eyes as they sniggered among themselves.

Navek had never come across such a small minded wily bunch. He sensed there could be trouble if he naively put himself in such a situation, but he was following a reckless impulse to travel south and away from his so called destiny.

Navek paused before answering. "Could I see the job first, you know just to make sure I'd be up to it?"

The captain hesitated. Finally he snapped at one of the deckhands called Pete to show Navek the galley, telling the hand to hurry up then get straight back to work. Below deck Navek asked the deckhand, "What happened to the last kitchen hand?" "He absconded into town and hasn't come back," was the reply. "Couldn't hack it here I guess. Pity, cos some of the boys really liked him," Pete added with a leer.

They came to a small kitchen where five tables stood with bench seats either side. A large man looked up at Navek, not bothering to hide his obvious dislike for the newcomer as he went about preparing food for the crew. He had a shaved head and tattoos on both arms. Under a white singlet stretched over an ample stomach were more tattoos spreading across his chest.

"Where would I sleep?" Navek asked Pete, who continued past the kitchen to a small cabin with narrow beds and swinging hammocks.

"That was the young fella's bunk," Pete gestured to a corner bunk crammed in among the others.

Navek had an uneasy feeling about having to sleep in such a cramped cabin, and sensed what had gone on here before.

"How long will it take to reach Welpecca?" he asked Pete.

"Just over two weeks if the winds blow true," said the deckhand.

"OK, take me back to the captain," said Navek.

Once back on deck, he was taken to the captain's cabin. He knocked on the door and entered when the captain's gruff voice called out.

"I'll do the work in the kitchen, and whatever other work is required," Navek said, "but only if I can sleep on deck somewhere. I can't sleep down there," he gestured toward the lower cabins.

Busy at his desk doing paper work, the captain looked up at Navek contemptuously, with a mean look in his eye. Navek could see the man had no moral integrity and could become dangerous if rubbed the wrong way. Impatiently the captain said, "All right. You're lucky I'm busy and happen to need an extra hand. Find somewhere on the deck and look after yourself, but you'll freeze at nights. What's yer name?"

"I'm named Navek," he replied.

At hearing the name the captain looked up at him with a look of disdain "Pfft," he hissed, "What kind of name is that! We leave tomorrow at the crack of dawn. Get out of here," he said, waving Navek out of the cabin without looking up from his papers again.

"I'll be here," said Navek, closing the door behind him.

Navek disembarked from the ship and returned to the

monks' house with an uneasy feeling about the shifty captain and his crew.

He had never been to sea before, but the idea of getting away to follow unknown possibilities in the south lured him somewhat. It would take him away and distract him from his past. At least he was making some kind of a plan, he justified to himself, albeit with an element of rebellious determination involved. He wanted to get away, and not be influenced by far-fetched predictions of perilous journeys to the north and rogue sorcerers. He did not want to think about the impulsive choice he was making or the dangerous situation he could be putting himself into.

When Navek stepped inside the monks' house, he was drawn to sounds coming from the back yard. Jake and the monks trained bare foot on the cold paved surface, displaying a magnificent array of skills. Watching in awe, Navek found it a stark contrast to the villains he had just encountered on the ship. He pushed aside doubts about going on an uncertain journey, and also leaving these good men who had become familiar in just a few short days.

That night, Navek told Jake and the monks he had found passage on the ship that would sail south in the early morning. He said goodbye to the kind hosts who had treated him as a brother. When he tried to give them some coins as payment, they insisted he keep the money for his journey ahead.

Mancel had a sense of foreboding when he heard this news, but mentioned nothing. Instead he welcomed

Navek back anytime he was in the area and put his strong arm around Navek's shoulders.

In the background Jake sat with a sullen expression listening to the news, then without a word went upstairs to bed.

Chapter 5.
The Stowaway

The next morning before daylight, Navek left the house with his few possessions in a bag slung across his back. Some day he hoped to come back and spend time with them all, and see Jake again.

Once aboard the ship, he went downstairs to the galley. He stashed his bag out of the way, and then remained working under the cook's gruff instructions till well after they set sail.

Floating on the sea was a strange sensation; it was hard work to keep balanced when the boat leaned and rocked.

Following instructions was easy for Navek after working at the construction site, but it wasn't until much later in the day that he was allowed to sit down for the first time. He managed to eat a late lunch and drink tea before the big cook named Elroy, urged him to get up and scrub dishes. Soon after, they prepared food for the evening meal.

This was to become his daily schedule for the next eight days. When they reached the island port of Mazzara in the Parrot Islands, they would stop for one night to deliver and take on supplies. After that, they would sail for another six days to reach the southern settlement of Welpecca, where Navek would disembark and start looking for work.

For the first few days the crew were all busy with tasks, and no one paid much notice of Navek. After dark, he found a place to sleep at the bow of the ship. Glad to be out of the stuffy kitchen and on his own, he climbed under a pile of canvas covering some crates to sleep.

Days of relentless and thankless work went by. One day over the sounds of the ship, Navek heard an unfamiliar sound outside. From down in the galley he listened closely to the distant call of a bird. It was a bird he had not heard before, but by the urgency of that call he knew a fierce storm was blowing toward them.

By the end of the day, wind whistled through the rigging and heavy rain started to fall. It wasn't long before the ship was heaving up and down huge rolling waves. With gale force winds blowing hard against them, they struggled to keep the ship steering to the south-east. Frantic crew ran around, yelling over the din of the storm to shut the hatches and take down the sails that flapped and whipped about.

Down in the galley Navek felt vulnerable in the

wooden vessel when its timbers creaked and groaned under the great pressure. Several times the ship tipped completely over on its side before righting itself while huge waves broke over the top of them. Tossed around on the vast wild ocean, just how much pressure the ship could take? He looked to Elroy who seemed unaffected by the commotion.

Elroy sent Navek running to secure pots, food and kitchen implements from flying around the room. Cooking was put on hold during the turbulence. The big man sat on a bench seat with his back to the wall and one foot up on another seat. He rested on an elbow with a smug look on his face – this was one of the few times he didn't have to be busy cooking.

Navek was sent to the engine room to help shovel coal into a giant furnace which fuelled the engines. Down in the engine room it was noisy and hot; the two other men glowed from the reflection of flames on sweat covered bodies. Strong muscles rippled as they shovelled coal like machines into an open furnace.

"Here," one man yelled to Navek, tossing a long handled shovel through the air toward Navek, assuming he would be slow to catch it. Navek's reflexes were sharp however, and he caught it in mid-air with eyes not leaving the other man's.

Navek noticed the two men glance at each other in surprise. One stepped aside for Navek to take his place, while he went behind the pile of coal to push some forward. Standing steady and shovelling at the same time was not easy in the rolling ship, but Navek learnt fast and managed to do the work.

All night the storm raged outside; all night Navek and the men shovelled coal into the furnace. They stopped only to drink water from a hanging bucket with a wooden lid that swung near the door. With sweat rolling off, all three were stripped to the waist, tired of being tossed around at the mercy of a huge swell. Strong and fit as Navek was, by morning he was tired and his arms and back ached tremendously.

About mid-morning the storm finally abated and the heaving and rolling eased. They rested awhile leaning on the shovels, and then Pete appeared halfway down the steps.

He yelled over the engine's noise that Navek was wanted in the kitchen. Relieved to be out of the engine room, Navek straightened his aching back and drank some water. He could feel the nerves in the muscles of his arms and back actually stinging from over exertion.

After a quick nod to the men, he headed up the steps toward the kitchen. He thought he noticed a hint of respect coming from the pair – after all, he had kept pace with them all night.

On the way he stopped to ease his muscles and catch his breath. Ignoring the hurry to get back to the galley, he looked out through a porthole and saw dark clouds departing across the sky, while rain continued to fall from them. His thoughts went nostalgically to the people he had met recently – Sharian, Jake, the woman who had given them shelter, the monks. He had put himself in this situation and he was glad they could not see him now, floating precariously on the ocean like a piece of flotsam.

The crew were busy pulling on guy ropes and hauling sails back up to catch the wind. Navek hoped the two men downstairs would get a well-earned break.

Once back in the kitchen, a chaotic scene awaited him. Tin plates, pots and other items were spread over the kitchen floor and Elroy, reeking of whisky, was in a worse mood than usual.

Navek replaced items to their rightful places while the cook ordered him around, working him nonstop. No breaks were given, but Navek managed to drink some water and grab a bite to eat when the belligerent Elroy wasn't looking his way.

After Elroy fell asleep, slumped over one of the tables, Navek went out on deck to find a new place to sleep. The canvas that had previously kept him warm was now saturated from rain and seawater.

He breathed fresh, salty air into his lungs, and looked up to see a clearing sky with sparkling stars, then clouds moved to reveal a bright yellow half-moon. Dead tired, his body ached in the chilly night air, but the vision brightened his outlook.

On deck he searched for a dry place to lie while avoiding guy ropes and rigging that hung everywhere. Finally, after finding nowhere dry, he decided to go down to the storage area in the hold of the ship. Navek found some wooden crates and heaved himself up onto one, then crawled over against a wall and stretched out. He pulled his coat around himself and closed his eyes, breathing a deep sigh of relief after such long, hard work.

Drifting off to sleep came easily, until Navek became aware he was not alone. Someone else was there in the hold. His eyes flew open but he did not move. Though he could not hear breathing, he sensed a presence not far to his left. His hand went instinctively to the short blade inside his coat pocket.

"Who's there?" he asked simply.

"It's me Jake."

"What! What are you doing here?" said Navek incredulously.

"Comin' with you," was the matter of fact reply. "Got any food?"

Navek groaned at the unexpected burden of Jake being on the ship, but was too tired to think about it now. A long moment passed. With great effort, Navek cursed and heaved himself up to sitting position.

Sighing heavily in exasperation, he jumped from the crate and hurried back up the steps to the ship's kitchen. Slipping past the snoring cook, he grabbed a container and stuffed it with leftover food, then filled a jar with water. Luckily, most of the crew were asleep and no one noticed as he hurried back to the storage hold. He shoved the container and jar into Jake's hands and climbed back up on the boxes. Navek was soon fast asleep.

The day before the ship was due to moor at the Parrot Islands, the crew saw dark storm clouds gathering.

Another storm was on the way and the weather was about to get rough again.

It was then that one of the crew discovered Jake down in the hold. He was hauled up on deck by the scruff of his neck and thrown at the feet of the captain. Navek heard the jeering and followed the cook upstairs to see what was going on. A frightened Jake sat in a heap on the deck looking dirty and scruffy. He squinted from the glare of daylight and looked nervously around at the crew who were suggesting he be thrown overboard. Some yelled other more lewd suggestions, which disgusted Navek – he had already heard what they did to the previous kitchen hand. The captain and crew seemed to find entertainment in the boy's anxiety, till finally Navek stepped forward to address the captain.

Navek proposed that the boy would be useful to him once they reached Welpecca. He said he would be looking to hire someone anyway to help carry supplies, and the boy looked strong enough to do the job. More lewd remarks were made, but the captain grew tired of the entertainment and became impatient knowing there was an approaching storm to think about.

As the captain turned away, he kicked the boy hard. "Put him to work and work him hard. Nobody rides on this ship for free," he said to the deckhand Pete. As an afterthought he turned and kicked Jake again. "And only feed him scraps. He ain't gettin' any food."

To Navek he said, "He's all yours when we get to the mainland, but you'll have to chain him or he'll run on ya".

Navek and Jake glanced at each other. Navek noticed a relieved look on Jake's face as the boy rubbed his leg where the boot had struck and a dark bruise would follow. But they both knew this was a dangerous lot and the boy would have to watch his back.

While on deck, Navek noticed the warm breeze. The further south they sailed, the warmer it became, and in the sweltering kitchen, sweat poured from his body. There had been times when he did not know if he could endure the long hours, the relentless workload and the oppressive heat.

In his village he had worked hard, but neither he nor the men of his clan had ever worked like this. The work conditions on board the ship bordered on slavery.

The day started off warm and sunny, but a change was in the air. Dark turbulent thunderclouds rolled across the sky behind them and a strong north-westerly blew at the stern. It was not long before the whole northern and western horizon darkened over, and grey rain fell in torrents beneath some of the darker clouds in the distance.

Torrential rain started falling, making the deck slippery and visibility poor. Strong gusty winds increased and streaks of lightening flashed and crackled nearby, lighting up the turbulent sea. Long rolls of thunder boomed across the skies overhead, as tempestuous conditions enveloped the ship, catching it in the midst of a heavy swell.

On the way to the engine room, Navek saw the captain at the helm shouting and barking out angry orders at the crew to take down the sails, batten down the hatches and tie things down. Navek quickly looked around for Jake but saw no sign of the boy, then continued to the engine room where he joined the same two men on the shovels.

This time the worried looks on the men's faces did not bode well, and Navek felt he was at great risk down in the bottom of the ship. They staggered and swayed around trying to maintain a footing, while joints groaned and fasteners creaked under the intense pressure pitted against them. It was a miracle the vessel even held together in a storm so fierce.

All his life, Navek had had his feet on solid ground; he hated the idea of drowning at sea. He could not think of a worse way to go, but nothing could be done about it now. He feared the fierce electrical storm that showed no signs of letting up and regretted ever stepping onto the ship and putting himself in such danger. His father would have scorned such a foolish choice.

For hours the ship struggled through ocean swells. Huge grey waves loomed up and towered over them, lifting the ship before crashing down over it. Each wave caused chaos as everyone hung on tight to anything they could to avoid being washed overboard. The vessel leaned over dangerously at times, and the helmsman struggled with all his might to steer them through. Every wave threatened to snap the wooden ship apart and spill out all on board to the bottom of the sea.

"Never seen one like it!" Navek heard someone shout.

Over the roar of the storm, everyone felt a shudder go up through the ship, and heard a terrible metallic scraping sound. In the night, the bottom of the cargo hold had hit something and timber was rupturing and splitting apart. Masts snapped and crashed down onto the decks, and then the bow lunged downward into the sea before a large wave lifted her up again. The ship was buoyed forward for a distance before it came down again, heavier now as she took on seawater.

The metallic scraping sound reminded Navek of the eerie screeching he had heard before the death of his clan, and he rushed upstairs with panic pulsing through his veins.

They were going down fast and soon the whole ship would tear apart and go under, taking all the men with it. He thought of Jake who should never have followed him onto the ship, and knew the boy would be scared, but he was nowhere to be seen.

Terror spread throughout as a large crack opened in the hold, while men frantically scrambled to untie the life boats amid the chaos. The ship lurched forward and several of the crew went overboard. Navek rushed forward to help with the boats, but could not hang on when a huge wave came down on top of him. He was swept overboard.

The ignoble prospect of drowning filled him with dread as he went through the air into the water. Suction, caused by the boat sinking, pulled him down into the depths, and then somehow the churning motion of the water propelled him back upward. Navek struggled back to the surface and was aware of debris nearby in the water. He could not swim but managed to grab on to a couple of splintered planks, hanging on for his life in the darkness as great avalanches of waves crashed over. Navek called out to Jake, but even if Jake was in the water nearby he would not have heard over the deafening roar of waves and rain.

In the darkness, visibility was almost nil. Occasionally, broken debris from the ship hit against Navek, and twice in the darkness he pushed away the drowned body of one of the crew. The night seemed endless. Incessant crashing waves pounded him and he shook from cold and fatigue. Each wave churned him into the sea and held him under till he would eventually resurface, still gripping tightly to the wooden planks which were his only lifeline. The storm eased overnight though smaller waves still pounded his shivering body. Navek felt small and hopeless floating out on a vast ocean, but managed to hang on till the light of dawn broke on the horizon.

Once daylight had broken, he lifted his head and looked around. In the distance, the green peak of a mountain stood out above the waves. Was he imagining it? He looked again to make sure. Yes, he could see one side of a mountain lit up in the sunlight. A chance of survival mixed with extreme relief filled him, though land was still far away.

As the day wore on, breaking waves and the current pushed Navek toward land. Occasional sightings of debris floated by, but with no sign of survivors. Once, in the waves as they lifted up around him, he thought he saw large grey shapes and thought of sharks. But the chance of reaching land drove him on. Exhausted and thirsty under a hot midday sun, Navek lost sight of the mountain altogether and thought despairingly it may have been his imagination.

Later when the waves subsided, the mountain reappeared in the distance. A bird circled high overhead and called down to him several times. Navek became aware of the sound and tried to look up, but the muscles in his neck were aching and too stiff.

Eventually nightfall came and settled all around him. He was alone again in the dark. He drifted off to sleep but would be jolted awake, gasping and spluttering for air when his head had gone under the water. More than once during the night, he was sure something nudged against his legs and the dread of sharks startled him awake. He could only haul himself up onto the wooden planks as best he could and was now at the mercy of the current and the rolling waves.

Chapter 6.
The Island

Navek groaned and flinched involuntarily. His father Hatchiman ran behind, breathing hard and cursing as he stumbled on the rocky slopes. Warriors from his clan raced toward the shallow creek as a diversion tactic to keep the pursuers away from camp. As they ran, they ducked and weaved with crossbows and other weapons hitting together.

Navek had grown up in the Videha clan, with Hatchiman being their brave and responsible leader, as was his father before him. As highland warriors the Videha were not afraid of the pursuing Raghasse tribe, though they were not to be taken lightly. The Videha were far more agile on these familiar rocky slopes than the Raghasse, who came from further north where the snow rarely melts from the mountain caps. The Raghasse lived with their dogs and goats for warmth, and were a foul smelling clan who wore tunics cut from the shaggy pelt of bison.

Across the shallow creek, Navek turned to see their attackers come over the ridge in relentless pursuit toward them. The Raghasse leader was a large hairy brute of a man with dark slits for eyes, and looked half animal. He was an age old enemy. Navek was surprised to see him blow through a bull's horn, signalling his clan to veer away from the pursuit. Surprise turned to alarm when an ominous purple fog rose up over the ridge and hovered there.

Hatchiman saw the look in his son's eyes. Though his son was coming into his manhood and was trained to fight, the father had never seen such a look of alarm. Hatchiman turned back as he ran to see what caused the alarm, just as a huge bruise-coloured fog rose up and bore down on him and his men. The shape shifted and changed to form a giant arrowhead which emitted a sound like a frenzied swarm of bees.

Hatchiman sensed something gravely wrong. He tasted sulphur in the air while a strange atmosphere of malevolence and impending doom came over him.

The spear-shaped cloud cast a shadow over the valley, as though a dark storm had blown across, descending on them with the swiftness of the wind.

"Look out!" Hatchiman yelled to his men. "Go the left!"

"What trickery is this," he growled under his breath at

an unknown assailant armed with weapons not of this world.

Navek smelt the foul smell of sulphur in the air, as the high-pitched buzzing became a screeching metallic sound. The strange phenomenon was gaining ground and was almost upon them.

A sudden blow from behind struck Navek between the shoulder blades, and threw him forward and off balance. He wheeled to the right and fell, though he heard the others crashing through the creek to the left. After landing on his right hand, he rolled forward in a full somersault, as he had practised in training many times before. Barely skimming the top of the water, he sprang immediately back up to a standing position before running to join the others. He thought he had been struck by a weapon, though the ensuing tribe had veered away and were not within throwing range.

He felt a fleeting feeling of shame at falling before his mighty father, but paid it no heed.

Hatchiman and the others came crashing through the water at full speed. Already across the creek, some from his clan were ascending the banks over thickets of twisted tree roots and outcroppings of rocks. Navek was about to follow and could hear his father urgently pressing them on. Turning to look back, he saw unfamiliar panic and desperation on his father's face and he knew they were in trouble.

Amid the turmoil, their eyes met momentarily, and then Hatchiman ran straight toward him. Navek was astonished when his father brutally shoved him out of the way, sending him head-on into rocks. Men screamed, shouted and called out. Navek was briefly aware of the smell of sulphur.

Weapons were drawn and heavy footsteps pounded through water. Frantically, he tried to find his father. He searched and searched through bloodied bodies in freezing snow, then discovered him further up the gully where Hatchiman had tried to lead the attacker away from the others. But it was too late. Navek groaned with despair at his sudden uselessness to help his father and his clan after a lifetime of training.

The vague call of a startled bird in the distance was all Navek could grasp before his body flopped back down in the water unconscious. Eventually, his body jerked up as though waking from a nightmare, and he remembered the urgency of the situation. He could not understand why his back felt so hot, or how he had become so weak. His mind spun, he gasped at the pain in his head and fell back down, unable to forget feelings of shame and bewilderment – or why he was shoved away at such a crucial time.

Unsure how much time had passed, Navek was woken by the sensation of water lapping against his body. The river bed felt soft and sandy and Navek could taste salt!

Slowly he lifted his head and saw he was not in the riverbed at all. He was lying on sand with warm sun on his back. He was on an unfamiliar beach, washed up like a piece of seaweed. How did he get there?

Vague recollections came of lightning strikes, big

rolling waves and torrential rain, rasping sounds of the underbelly of a ship scraping along rocks then splitting apart. Memories of gripping onto a piece of splintered wood, as waves crashed over him for hours and hours came to mind. He was trying to find someone in the water – Jake.

Dry and thirsty, he dragged himself up into the shade of unfamiliar tall trees with banded trunks. The sound of waves crashing out from shore and the call of a bird, were his last memories before he flopped back down unconscious. The sun was high overhead when he finally came to, and he managed to pull his body up to sitting position against one of the trees. His eyes and mouth felt gritty; his hands and face were puffed and swollen from sunburn. Opening and closing his stiff hands, he tried to get the swollen stiffness out of them. *"Where am I?"* he wondered. *"Where are my father and the others? Water, I must find water."*

The day was quite hot and Navek knew he must find the water that his body craved so badly, or he would die on this unknown shore. Through blurred vision he tried to discern the strange and unfamiliar jungle behind him, and shook his head trying to get his thoughts straight. The ridiculous notion that he may die of thirst here while surrounded by water made him laugh out loud. His mind was becoming delirious. He rolled over and slowly crawled into the green blur of trees and undergrowth, vaguely grateful for the cool shade they offered.

On and on he struggled for what seemed like hours.

Skin was scratched and scraped off his hands and knees as he went. It must have been late afternoon when a flock of colourful green birds flew through the trees and perched above him. They had red chests and red markings across their wings and sang a noisy song, making a ruckus to warn of the intruder in their territory. A slight breeze from the sea fanned his sweating skin, but he had swallowed a lot of saltwater; it was fresh water he needed or he would not last.

In his delirium, visions of his father and the warriors' blood-soaked corpses flashed through his mind. To a background of eerie, screeching noise, the faceless attacker reared up and laughed at him. Once in shocked disbelief, he caught a glimpse of his father's dead eyes looking at him. This was followed by the lovely calm face of his mother, before her eyes widened in terror and blood spilled from her throat.

In fits of futile rage and despair he called out, knowing after all his training he had not helped them. *"Senseless. No justice. All gone now,"* were words that ran through his mind. *"The river of hope has run dry, dry … just let me die."*

He fell down in the sand and a voice in him said, *"Give up. Life's not worth the struggle"*.

Doomed to die of thirst in a strange, unknown land, he could go no further. It was here, far from his ancestors in some jungle he would end as a pile of white weathered bones. *"Good,"* he vaguely thought. *"I'm tired of life anyway."*

Navek closed his eyes and felt his head spin. He fell

into a deep, blurry abyss. He felt sick, but he did not care anymore. He wanted to be rid of the nightmare, of the past which haunted him.

Navek twitched and jerked his arm at the sharp object that prodded his ribcage. With a rough shove he was rolled over but he lay there beyond caring about living or dying. In the far recesses of his mind he had the notion that it was raining. Then had the ridiculous thought, *"Good, the farmers need the rain"*.

He went to laugh but instead a dry convulsive cough was all that came. *"Water, oh yes water."*

Water dropped onto his parched lips and he opened his mouth, but coughed and spluttered when he tried to swallow. He desperately tried to gulp some of the water down his swollen throat, which he could not get to cooperate. Something kicked him over onto his stomach again. *"Was he hallucinating?"* He did not know or care.

In the darkness Navek opened his eyes. His body burned hot and ached all over. *"Was he dead and in the warrior's heaven? Would he see his father? Or more likely, in the coward's hell which was burning his body away."* For the remainder of the night, he lapsed in and out of consciousness. He seemed to recall water being poured on his face and into his mouth, and then it ran deliciously down through his hair. *"Had he been dreaming, or had he been dragged along with wrists tied to a wooden rod across his shoulders like some hunted animal?"*

Recollections returned of his head flopping back and forward while his feet dragged painfully along the ground, surrounded by dark men talking in a strange tongue.

As the sun came up over the horizon, Navek was woken by a quantity of water being thrown over him as he lay on the ground. His body jumped in response and he tried to clear his eyes with numb hands that were as puffed up as his face. He blinked several times to clear his blurred vision, till finally things started to come into focus.

Several dark figures stood well back and watched him. Without a word someone came forward, and poured a small trickle of water into his open mouth then across his eyes and temples. He tried to swallow and managed to get some of it down. After a few attempts he sat upright, and saw he was in the midst of some jungle clan, the likes of which he had never seen.

Dark almond-shaped eyes watched him in fascination. These people had never seen a man like Navek, all burnt and red and swollen. He must have looked a strange sight.

As the sun rose behind them, their hair glowed with a chestnut tinge. They were a sleek-looking people with shiny brown skin and dark hair. They wore clothing that wrapped around in varying shades of dark blue. Some of the men held spears and displayed elaborate tattooed patterns over much of their bodies.

When Navek looked among the now curious people, he noticed one man who stood back from the others and watched him. Around his neck hung a necklace of white shells and bones that had carved markings on them. Judging by his proud stance and demeanour, he was the village leader. The dark eyes seemed to look deeply into

Navek, who bowed his head and lowered his eyes as a mark of respect, as best he could in his current condition.

A woman placed a wooden bowl containing dark green liquid near Navek. Someone else pushed it closer using the end of the spear. With great difficulty, Navek picked up the bowl with swollen hands that had no peripheral feeling in them. With everyone watching he managed to get the bowl to his mouth and drink a couple of sips. It tasted of soup made from grass or leaves, but Navek did not care about the flavour, spilling much of it down his chest while attempting another couple of mouthfuls. He flopped back onto the ground with no strength to sit up again.

The people went about their daily routines, chattering away to each other in their strange fluid dialect. Occasionally they would come over in small groups to look at the stranger who had washed onto their shores in the night. Children would poke at him with a stick till he moved in discomfort, or till the women called them away in rapid high pitched tones.

He slid in and out of sleep, having dreams and nightmares of his dead parents and blood splattered snow, then of ships going down. He woke fitfully in a sweat with heart racing, startling the villagers with his delirious calls. During the day, one of the women placed another bowl of liquid near Navek, who managed prop himself up and get some of it down, though he felt quite nauseous.

By evening, Navek was a little better as the swelling and dizziness started to subside. He dragged himself over to a tree and propped himself against it. He even felt a little hungry. The smell of cooking on the evening fires wafted by, but they continued giving him the green liquid, though the added flavour of fish was accepted gratefully and he drank as much as he could get down.

The people were naturally friendly and trusted he was not a threat. They left him at the base of the tree where he slept the night in the mild temperatures. Next morning he made a shaky attempt to stand and clutched at the tree with both hands to steady himself. Dizzy and weak, he had to take in large breaths of air so as not to faint. After some moments he attempted to walk and released his grip on the tree, staggering well away from the village to relieve himself. Then he staggered back in the same way.

The jungle people looked over often to the unexpected visitor with light brown skin and strange clothing. Some of the men remained at a distance from the main activities and were deep in discussion, at times pointing out to sea or drawing diagrams on the ground. No doubt wondering where Navek came from.

Too weak to walk, Navek sat up against the tree. He was given a small bowl of some kind of cooked gruel, and nothing more to eat till later in the day. Having his feet on solid ground seemed an extraordinary contrast to the hours and hours he had spent in the water, when rescue did not seem possible. Navek reflected on the miracle that he was alive, but allowed himself little joy in it, as he had put himself on that ship. Running from loss and not facing up to life on his own had put him on this distant shore; not going back to find the killer; not knowing how or where to look for him; not righting the wrong. These were the reasons he was here. To avoid his own thoughts, he listened to the sing-song chatter of the women and squealing laughter of the children.

During the afternoon the temperature became humid and hot. The chief walked over to Navek and squatted down on his heels, resting on his long spear with one hand. The deep blue of the king's clothing contrasted against his smooth, dark skin, and reflected the depth of vision and wisdom in his eyes. It enhanced his proud demeanour and made him appear majestic. The word 'King' came into Navek's mind and he acknowledged in himself it would be a suitable title for this man.

With a steady gaze, the chief looked into Navek's eyes and into his mind. Navek felt in awe of him, though he was not perturbed or intimidated because his own father had been a village leader. Without words, they both held the gaze. The chief's dark, calm eyes seemed to read him through and through till a shiver ran up through Navek. Fleeting and momentary images of his past started to flash past in his mind, and somehow the intuitive king was also seeing these images. He could see large waves breaking over a tiny ship, Navek being pushed onto rocks in a creek bed, much death and bloodshed, a boy learning fighting skills, harsh freezing winters in high country and ruddy faces of a tribe tending woolly animals.

The eyes of the chief widened at the visions of Navek's shattered past.

Then they all disappeared like wisps of smoke on the

wind, and both men were back on the island.

Unused to such unusual and violent sights, the chief made a geometric pattern in the air with his left hand as if to protect himself, then remained squatted there.

Finally Navek blinked away tears which seemed to break the hold between them. Tears rolled down his cheeks and onto his chest, as he heaved a great sigh and tried to wipe them away with the back of his hand. He did not know why the tears came. It was as though there was a great release of emotions. The chief reached across and placed his open hand about an inch from the centre of Navek's chest, holding it there a few moments. Navek felt heat coming into him from the king's open hand which seemed to help heal his damaged mind and body.

The chief took his hand away and flicked it toward the trees as though flicking off a bug, then stood and gestured for Navek to follow him.

Still holding onto trees for support, Navek walked unsteadily to a clearing, where the men sat gathered under a large, spreading tree. Behind the group a slope lead down to a running creek and some of the men gestured for him to go and swim. The water looked cool and inviting as temperatures were much hotter than the mountain country where he had grown up. The men did not watch, but allowed him in his broken condition to swim and be left alone. Perhaps it was out of decency or perhaps they did not care. With weak legs he reached the creek, and then stumbled straight out into the water without removing his clothes. It was not deep, and he lay in it for some time, washing away the weariness of his mind and body. The fresh water rinsed away the salt and cooled his burnt skin. He drank the water, and for the first time started to feel revived.

"I'm not ready to die yet. I will endure," he thought.

Navek hung his dripping shirt over a branch, pushed his wet hair back from his face and sat nearby while the islanders chattered among themselves. He noticed some of the men looking at him now, with a mixture of awe and compassion in their eyes. He guessed their chief had told them what he had seen in Navek's mind, and felt a pang of shame they knew something of his tangled past. He did not want them knowing of his guilt and his failure at helping his clan. He found no pride in these memories which would forever haunt him.

The chief, looking regal with spear in hand, oversaw the others like a lead male animal protecting his herd. He looked out toward the sea at times, as though listening to a message on the breeze, or seeing if any danger followed the castaway to their shores.

Chapter 7.
Alone. But Not Lonely

"For a man who faces his own extinction
Live every day to the fullest."

A whole moon's cycle passed. Navek's black hair grew longer and his skin darkened from the sun. He discovered they were on a small, unevenly shaped island with mountain peaks at the centre. He hunted with the young men. They taught him to swim and spearfish in the shallows, and dive to collect molluscs.

Without speaking their language, Navek managed to communicate using primitive sign language. Daily tasks and simple village life, in some ways, was no different to life in his own village. They lived day-to-day; food was shared, and Navek was grateful the islanders accepted him into their world.

The men invited him to a sacred ceremony where he witnessed a young man being tattooed as a rite of passage into manhood. The tattooist spent hours tapping a dark ink into the man's skin, using a short spiked implement made from bone. The young man silently endured the pain of the age-old tradition. His hosts were not a warfaring tribe; they had no enemies in the far reaches of the Eastern Sea. Their eyes reflected a life of harmony, as it should be. This made for a pleasant change to Navek, who knew only warfare and defence when he was younger. Much time had been spent training in fighting skills for battles, or strategies for survival. Ancestors and history determined this for him, but that was before his father brought peace between many of the mountain tribes.

Island life was peaceful, and sometimes it was as though Navek had never lived anywhere else. He came to almost forget his past, and any plans for the future. In quiet moments however, a restlessness pulled at him, a feeling of something not being quite right. Perhaps it was the call of a path not yet walked or completed, or an unpaid debt of duty, or guilt to assuage. It became apparent that there would be nowhere he could rest. Serenity and contentment would not be his to attain.

One night a wild storm passed overhead. Navek was startled awake from a vivid dream, with heart racing and mind in a panic. In the dream he was running from an unknown assassin, but could only move in slow motion. Futility was heightened when the assailant easily immobilised him. Jake was in the dream calling out his name from a great height, as though he were a seagull gliding on the wind. He was waiting for Navek to continue the journey and somehow, Navek knew Jake was alive. The journey was not to end on this island; he could not spend his time here, however idyllic. Navek did not know what it was, but something was about to change. He had seen no evidence that ships stopped at the island, but he would be leaving soon.

The next morning, Navek went with some of the younger men to gather seaweed after the storm. They reached the beach to find wreckage from the *Sea Snake* strewn along the beach and up onto rocks. Others were excited at the rare find, but Navek was reminded of the terror when so many men drowned, and he lost Jake in the turmoil.

The islanders gathered in fascination around the different objects from another culture, and chatted about each one. Flotsam included wooden planks, a barrel, two splintered masts held together by pieces of rope and frayed cloth, a large woven basket, empty glass bottles and a sealed wooden chest – padlocked – with no signs of real damage. Of Jake or the crew, there was no trace.

They returned to the village carrying their finds. The islanders gathered in wonderment and discussed the ship's debris in their rapid sing-song way. Navek sat down with the sealed chest in front of him, attracting most of the clan who were keen to see inside. Using a hardwood spear as a lever, he prised the lock off easily enough, and then slowly opened the lid. Navek half expected to find something useful, but inside were some of the captain's clothing, a rolled map, the ship's logbook, several gold and silver coins in a leather drawstring bag and an ornate knife housed in a decorative leather sheath. He drew the steel bladed knife and turned it over in his hands, marvelling at the elaborate, oriental patterning on the hilt. Small turquoise stones were inlaid in the dark wooden handle; it was a beautiful and ancient thing. Navek admired the skill and workmanship gone into making the knife. He would have liked to keep it, but handed it to the island king, bowing his head out of respect as he did so. The gesture came automatically to Navek from a time when his own father was revered this way in the village. This is how it was between good and worthy men, or rather, how he remembered it had been once.

Turning the knife over and over in his hands, the chief looked at the intricate detail and delighted in its beauty. The skilled craftsmanship must have been a wondrous sight to these islanders, whose own knives and spears were much more primitive in nature and design.

Navek opened the logbook but made no sense of the writings, then unrolled the map and placed a small stone in each corner to hold it open. Chatter continued as they squatted around to touch the thin sheet of paper. Navek studied the colours and shapes, and eventually figured out they depicted land and sea, and dotted lines were the courses followed by the ship. He could not read or write, but knew the *Sea Snake* had only one scheduled stop planned at the port of Mazzara on the Parrot Islands.

He tracked the dots from the mainland near the top of the map down to a group of three small islands. The dots continued on to meet the mainland near the bottom of the map. For the first time, Navek had an idea of where he may be in relation to the rest of the world, as the map showed dotted lines going to the largest of the three islands, which he assumed would be where the port of Mazzara would be located.

He deduced the ship must have completely missed the large island and was blown further south-east, where she scraped along rocks during the storm. He must be on one of the smaller islands shown on the map. To the east, was no other land for many leagues.

He showed the map to the islanders and tried with gestures to find out if they knew of the surrounding islands, but to no avail. He took some of the clothes and about half of the bag of gold and silver coins, thinking they may be useful to him yet. The rest he left for the entertainment of the islanders, who were particularly fascinated by the wooden chest. Long discussions and debates went on about the glass bottles, the woven basket and ropes, and the cuts in the timber.

Navek felt strangely at odds with himself after finding the items on the beach. It pulled him back and reminded him of a world left behind. He went down to the creek and sat awhile to muse over his situation. The dream had also sown a seed of restlessness that sprouted to disturb his peaceful lifestyle. He thought of Jake and felt responsible for his demise, and wished the boy was here with him. He had had enough of death.

Navek woke before dawn and made up his mind to explore the island further. He wanted to find out if he could see the next island, if there was any chance of reaching it, and if getting to Mazarra to continue the journey was a possibility.

He packed his few possessions in a rough sack made from his old shirt, with sleeves used as straps tied across his shoulders. When the elders saw he was going, they insisted two younger men go with him, and some of the women busied themselves packing food. Though Navek would have been happy to go alone, he accepted their company.

The chief sat back from the others and watched with dark, perceptive eyes, knowing before Navek knew himself, he would leave them and not come back.

Navek approached the proud man and knelt before him. The chief did not want Navek to leave, but finally crossed his fist over his chest and nodded in resignation. He reached out and put a hand on Navek's head as though giving him blessings for the journey ahead.

After the trio departed to the east, the king stood looking off into the distance long afterward with a furrowed brow, as though divining the future or seeing the battles that lay ahead for Navek.

The two men, named Guyra and Jurien, walked carrying long pointed sticks and woven bags across their backs, happy for the outing though they had travelled to every part of the island many times. After a few hours of walking along the beach they came to the east side of the island, which was a long stretch of white beach with high rocky points jutting out at the far end. This side seemed more protected from the wind, and the waves were much flatter away from the open sea. After they had walked awhile, the men indicated for Navek to follow them up into the treed area, where they drank from a freshwater stream, still running from yesterday's rain across the sand and into the sea.

The beach ended up being much longer than it looked, and by the time they reached the rocky point, the midday sun was overhead. Guyra and Jurien stopped near the rocks and stripped off before walking into the sea for a swim. Soon after, they came back out to get the spears.

They were experienced divers, diving down around the rocks and staying under for long periods of time, coming back up with shellfish.

In the shade they sat and ate the food packed by the women, and the raw shellfish which the men broke open with a stone. Navek felt good in the warm climate, living a natural life in the sunshine, and he envied the two companions who lived without a care. "Come on," he said finally, tipping his head in the direction around the point.

They got up to continue, copying the foreign words a few times to their own great amusement.

Once around the point, another island came into view across the water. The tide had started to go out, and Navek could see with the dropping sea level, that the white sand went out a long way.

By communicating with gestures, Navek asked the

others if they had swum across to the other island, and both shook their heads. Guyra made a snaking movement with his hand to indicate a swimming shark, letting Navek know why they did not make the crossing. They continued all the way to the northern side of the island, where intermittent rocky outcrops extended down into the water and clumps of seaweed lay washed up along the sand.

The tide was well out as they walked further from the shoreline on wet sand that would soon be covered again by water. The tide was starting to turn and come in again.

Between the two islands a deep channel flowed where the current looked quite strong as it rushed by. When they came across a weathered round tree trunk washed up on the sand, it occurred to Navek he could get to that other island today by floating with the log on the running tide.

During the time spent with the islanders, he had become fairly adept at holding his breath underwater. However this plan would require strength and timing to get free of the running channel. He would risk being carried out to sea if he miscalculated the ride, and the sharks he did not want to think about.

The channel was only a hundred or so paces wide. Navek looked back and forth from the moving channel to the other island, gauging where he should put the log into the water so it would pass close to the southern tip of the other island.

Guyra and Jurien looked at each other and shook their heads from side to side, at the same time breathing in air through their teeth to show their disapproval.

Navek started to feel an excited urgency to get into the water. It was a crazy idea and he had not planned it this way, but he had to move on and would take his chance today. Why wait for another low tide? Even the log seemed to be in the right place for the job. Reluctantly, his companions helped carry the slippery log further upstream, and rolled it to the sea's edge. Navek fixed his makeshift bag across his shoulders, ensuring both ends were tied.

Finally, Navek faced the direction of the village which was across the other side of the island from where they stood. He understood now, the island king had known he was not coming back before he had even left the village. For a long moment he sent a message of respect invisibly across the island, to thank the leader and the villagers, and he knew Guyra and Jurien would tell them every detail of the day's events.

Navek faced the young men and bowed as a mark of respect and in his own language he thanked them for everything. Jurien gave Navek his spear insisting he take it with him, and secured it quickly to Navek's bag so it lay horizontally across his shoulders. Navek was grateful to have the spear as he did not know what lay ahead.

Out into the running channel he pushed the log and swam rapidly with it toward the centre of the fast moving water. The current was surprisingly strong. Navek jumped up to lie on top of the bobbing log as best he could, kicking and paddling to try to steer. Several times he was tossed around and went under when the slippery log rolled. He was carried along where the tide took him, and it soon picked up speed. He looked back and gave the men a quick wave. They waved back to him, then started to head back to the village, but followed and watched him all the way.

A swift flowing current transported him further along and he looked over to the other island to get his bearings. It was time to move to the other side of the channel; he did not want to be held in the middle and swept out to the open sea. By swimming sideways and kicking his feet as hard as he could, he managed to get near the other side of the torrent. He kept turning the log to the left to get it through, so that when near the island he could disengage from the tidal river. When the channel snaked in toward the other island like a giant serpent, Navek made a concerted effort, fighting and swimming hard with the log still under him. He managed to free the log from the channel and move into calmer water near the island, eventually letting go of the log to swim to the shore.

He pulled himself out of the water, and leaned over with hands on his knees for a few moments after the exertion. He stood up to see Guyra and Jurien standing on top of the rocky point where they had eaten lunch. He could make out their dark bodies in the distance and waved to signal them. They immediately responded, then turned and disappeared around the point, out of sight.

Navek took the spear and wet bag off his back, and then hung the dripping clothes over a low branch to dry.

He went up to the trees and sat in the shade to collect himself. He realised this was the first time for many weeks he had been alone. A spontaneous leap of adventure rose in him, being on his own in a warm tropical place.

Sharian's words 'Alone. But not lonely,' came to mind, and brought a smile to his face as he leaned back against a tree. *"What is next,"* he asked himself, enjoying the moment and in no hurry to go anywhere.

Chapter 8.
Black Bamboo

"Wipe the autumnal rind from your sword oh warrior
And seek a formidable master
- Whose hegemony it is worthwhile fighting."

Four years later …

Khelvan journeyed on through the Everest Forest, where trees were so dense he had to dismount and walk hunched over in front of the horse. Little sunlight penetrated the high canopy, as mist rose from the forest floor like steam, and rich earthy smells brought back memories of his youth. Though access was easier from the east, he approached via the shorter northern route, where few ventured this deeply into the woods; even the animal tracks petered out. In this forest, a person could easily become disorientated as there was no way to gauge direction.

An array of sounds filled the forest, but eventually he heard the sound of running water, the sign Khelvan listened for. He was going in the right direction, and had reached creek.

Steady rain fell and though he wore an oilskin coat, cold, dripping branches brushed against him and he was wet through. Daylight faded, and still another hour's journey lay ahead. For the last part of the journey he would have continued through the forest to reach his destination, but decided to travel along the creek. With little warning, the creek could swell into a flash flood, and wash him and his horse away. In his mind's eye he saw his teacher shake his head at the risky choice.

Khelvan quickened his pace, pulling and hurrying the reluctant horse behind him as it skidded and slipped down the muddy slope. With boots and socks already saturated, he stepped straight out into the running stream, onto slippery rocks that lined its bed. He muttered grimly, "Don't choose today to sweep me away". The shallow creek had deep pools to watch for, and the going was slow. Steam rose from the horse's flanks as it snorted in disapproval, but both horse and man continued on, shivering with cold and stumbling often.

In the evening light, Khelvan stepped out from the forest and onto the edge of a familiar manicured lawn. He straightened his aching body to take in the oriental scene before him. With hands and feet numb from cold, he felt a warm glow, an unexpected anticipation and a sense of belonging. Even a few tears tried to well up, but were quickly quelled.

The old wooden house with its weathered veranda and dragon carvings above the door were as he remembered. Smoke billowed from its stone chimney and then hung low in the damp air, adding a misty and ancient atmosphere. Next to groupings of large rocks, stands of black bamboo stood gracefully bent over from the weight of the rain. The tranquil scene was a stark contrast to the dark and unruly forest left behind.

From his seat on the veranda his teacher, Lamaar, watched the traveller through the rainfall. Lamaar had sensed Khelvan's presence in the forest long before his arrival and waited for him. Somehow he knew exactly where the young man would emerge from the forest. A slow nod was the only greeting, and without words Lamaar saw the unfulfillment in his former student.

Relieved to be back, Khelvan stood in the rain looking at his teacher and friend, who appeared youthful with his short cropped hair and strong body, though he was probably well into his sixties. Khelvan felt he may as well be standing naked before those all-seeing eyes. Those eyes could look upon him and uncover his soul in a glance.

There were stirrings in the forest all around, as the evening orchestra of insects seemed to amplify. He bowed slightly to the teacher, and turned to take the horse around the perimeter of the lawn, as he did not want to leave a trail of hoof prints across the grass. Lamaar stood and beckoned Khelvan to walk straight across. "Don't worry. Come across. Come," he said, but Khelvan politely took the horse around the lawn to the barn where he found dry straw and water already prepared. The teacher stayed on the veranda with both hands joined behind him, watching Khelvan with a pleased look on his face before going into the house.

Khelvan took off the saddle and rubbed down the weary horse, smiling to himself that his old teacher's psychic abilities had not waned. In fact Lamaar had anticipated his visit that very day. Getting out of the rain, he appreciated the roof over him and the familiar smell of the barn where he once slept. After a few big breaths he headed toward the house. On the veranda, he took off his soaked coat, wet boots and socks before entering the welcome warmth of the familiar old house.

Flames leaped and danced from big logs in the fireplace. The fire had been stoked up well, with more wood stacked to the side of the hearth. A delicious aroma of cooking food wafted throughout the house, and soon they were sitting around the open fire, eating while they talked.

Khelvan was a strong, young man, who had lived much of his life here in relative isolation. About three years ago he grew restless and impatient with this existence. Lamaar sent him away so he could experience 'normal' life with other people out in the world. At first it was hard for Khelvan. He felt more lost and more alone surrounded by people than when he lived his solitary existence in the forest.

Eventually, he found temporary work cleaning the floor of a flour mill in a large town. He would work all night for a few coins, barely enough to even buy a meal. He soon learnt to gather some of the sweepings to take with him to make into a porridge or unleavened bread.

When that work ended he found seasonal work helping farmers who gave him a roof over his head and food in exchange for his labour. He worked the soil and experienced the taste of hard work, salt and sweat. He broke the clods of his pride in the hot sun, and worked the barren soil of life, cultivating the land over and over and getting to know its nature during the turning over of the seasons. He learnt to improve and prepare the earth that nurtured the seeds of life's harvest, losing himself in work with the good of the people in mind, he thought.

He was a hard worker and the farmers and their families treated him well enough. However, though he came to enjoy some of the work, no one talked about wisdom or a deeper purpose to life like he was used to during his growing years. Others seemed content with their lot, and he struggled to find anything that kept him interested for long. When the work ran out, he could not see what to do next or where to go in his life. He felt alone, walking the face of the earth with no roots, thirsty for a worthwhile purpose for his energy, a cause worth fighting for.

In sincerity, he called out to the power that breathed him, to show the way and give him an answer.

Of course he saw goodness and kindness, but he also

saw cruelty, waste and the devastation humans are capable of. Khelvan witnessed a few incidents that shook the foundations of his ideals and his very faith in basic human goodness. He came back humbled and empty, full of ignorance and failings, but with more respect and recognition for all Lamaar's efforts and wisdom, which he had sometimes taken for granted.

Khelvan knew now, real strength came from inner commitment, and the everyday practice of accepting and feeling his own existence. Contentment lay within himself. This is what supported Lamaar, who had found his peace, and lived happily.

The purpose of returning to the forest retreat was to find himself again, as the world held no attraction for him anymore. Attaining peace and contentment was not a priority anywhere else. People were busy surviving and feeding their families. No one addressed, or even knew about, the significance of life. Lamaar had taught him that every person is valid, and should know how to stand on the face of the earth and feel at home. Khelvan had learnt since, that fear and self doubt are like thieves in the night that robbed him of his own joy. He suspected Lamaar knew all along what the result of his journey would be before he had even left, but he had to find out for himself.

To a backdrop of the forest sounds and rain, Lamaar listened in silence to the unspoken words of his student's heart, sensing the depth of sincerity as he looked into the flames. Moments passed before Lamaar enquired about small matters, extracting deeper meanings from Khelvan's simple answers, till eventually he said: "You must be tired, we can talk tomorrow," indicating with a nod toward the bed already made for him.

For the next few days intermittent rain fell, and in the late afternoons they moved outside to the veranda. Lamaar sat on his usual chair and Khelvan sat nearby leaning up against the wall. Sometimes they would talk, and other times nothing was said as they looked out enjoying the tranquillity. They never tired of viewing the ambient and oriental scene which constantly changed and was enhanced by the mist and the evening hues. They only moved back inside if it became too cold or dark.

A few weeks went by. Khelvan and Lamaar spent time repairing the barn roof and doing other jobs around the house. They collected a large stockpile of firewood from the forest, and walked together into the forest collecting herbs and plants for cooking. Other times, Khelvan went off on his own, happy to re-explore some of his favourite places. Life in the forest sanctuary replenished and refocused him. He belonged here and felt whole again. Life was good.

One evening as they sat out on the veranda, Khelvan looked across at Lamaar and felt for a moment he was in the company of a divine presence. Lamaar sat in an aura of stillness and peace. Only a lit candle could light unlit candles, which was why Khelvan was drawn to learn from him. Khelvan reached this experience at times, and strove for it the rest of the time. Serenity washed over Khelvan, and when he looked out again at the grounds, the whole scene became more enchanting. The design of the landscape enhanced the surrounding forest with its minimalistic effect. It was a natural scene but the balance of components was constructed with much artistry. Khelvan remembered spending days defining and shaping the gentle contours of the lawn, then manoeuvring the large rocks into position. One group of rocks had taken three days of moving and changing before the teacher was satisfied with the positioning, as seen from every angle. The stands of black bamboo had grown tall, enhancing and framing the whole scene to add to the ambience.

Against the sound of gentle rain, the teacher's words sounded clearly, "What does it matter if you lose or you gain Khelvan? A life does not balance on only one end of the scale, but the whole. If a man finds peace throughout his short temporary existence, if he finds the root of all union, then surely that is the measure of a life well spent. Finding peace within your own self denotes a worthwhile life my friend. A man who achieves this has not thrown his time away." He turned to Khelvan before continuing on. "Yours is not an easy road to travel, and I know the way has been lonely, but don't let despair be your companion. Instead, choose the joy that springs from life itself, and always filter out what goodness there is. It is as simple as appreciating the colour green in the trees, or the blue of the sky. Feel the breeze against your skin, or feel a breath coming in and out. Accept your breath gratefully. It's not an entitlement that will last forever. It is a mere wisp of a thing that can be snuffed out without warning."

Lamaar paused and leaned toward Khelvan, "Do you know that a breath is the only thing that stops you from turning back into dirt!" Lamaar laughed at this and then became more serious. "Life is fragile and precarious. We don't know its deep value till death knocks at our door and threatens to take it. Come back to *you*. Accept simply you exist, and start there. Feel the moment called now, and you will be at home wherever you are. Ah, sometimes the answer is too simple for the mind to grasp, but that is the challenge my friend. Hold peace in your heart, and do not listen to doubts. Clarity requires that kind of effort."

The fresh smell of pine drifted from the forest as they sat awhile in silence enjoying the tranquility.

"Thank you Lamaar," was all Khelvan said, grateful because the teacher's words had again set him free and dispelled his ignorance. Khelvan knew well that it was rare to find anyone so truly free and at one with his own purpose. Unlike many others, Khelvan had always appreciated having a teacher who imparted the true depth and meaning of life, as he had always been keen to learn such a subject.

Lamaar stood from the chair and squatted low on one leg with the other leg out straight. He changed position and squatted on the other leg, doing the same, stretching his muscles and balancing with ease. "Let's eat. Tomorrow I will tell you of a new adventure I must ask of you."

Khelvan wanted to stay in the sanctuary away from the world, but knew then it was not to be. Not yet anyway.

The following evening, Khelvan carried cups of tea out

to the veranda, and placed one on the floorboards next to his teacher.

Lamaar sat looking out through the rainfall, past the black bamboo and the forest, as though he looked beyond them to something in the distance. He had travelled far on journeys a man does not tread by foot or by road alone, and learned much in his lifetime. His heart had mellowed and become pure from following the path of truth.

Lamaar had not always lived in the forest like a hermit. Khelvan was a boy of twelve when he first met him in Alizach, a settlement on the east coast. In those days, Lamaar owned his own blacksmith workshop on the edge of town. He worked hard forging steel by day, but in the evenings he taught the fighting arts to any who came to learn. Payment for the lessons often went in accordance to a person's ability to pay, but Khelvan came from a poor family who could barely afford to feed themselves, so he would not approach the group. He would hide behind a ramshackle building to watch in fascination, as he had never seen such techniques and was drawn to learn the skills. He would never forget the day Lamaar left the group of trainees practising in the yard, walked over to where he was hiding, and asked if he wanted to join them. Khelvan had looked up to the kind smiling face, embarrassed at being found out. He politely turned down the offer before running off.

Lamaar had known about the hiding boy for some time and knew where he lived. Later, Lamaar went to the boy's parents to ask if he could help out at the forge a few times a week in return for lessons, and that was how it started.

During their time together, Lamaar would toss Khelvan a coin or give him a bag of millet or a cut of lamb to take home, as his family, like many others, struggled to survive.

Over the years Lamaar became renowned as a master at the various fighting techniques. Sometimes he would watch and absorb the merits of other groups, or travel to do demonstrations, always adding and incorporating new styles to his current methods. He taught his students to excel in both the theoretical and tactical components of the art. The focus was on training for skill, as well as keeping a quiet and peaceful mind. Techniques were practised to gain focus and strength, or as a sport for good health, and were never to be used against others unless life was threatened.

Khelvan had come to learn it was a privilege to be Lamaar's student, and he trusted the man with his life.

When Lamaar shifted, the profile of his face in the evening light was like granite coming to life. "I once knew a man named Hatchiman," he said. "He was a great warrior king, who led the Videha clan in the northwest. The man was a friend of mine. He was born in the high country, at a time when war, ruin and senseless killing were a way of survival. In his lifetime he managed to unite and lead many of the warring clans under one banner. Through much determination and relentless effort, he got the clan leaders to communicate and go beyond their historical rivalries and differences. He spent years travelling to meetings and talking to people to achieve his quest of living in peace. He appealed to the elders to ask the people of their villages whether *they* wanted war or peace. In the end, simple wisdom and practical commonsense steered them to see peace is a far better outcome for everyone than war.

"I was there the day his deep, booming voice resounded out to a gathering of leaders. He said: 'For centuries we have all warred against each other, and for what gain? Instead of working our fields to feed our families, we are busy killing others who are in the same situation! So let's live in peace.'" Lamaar smiled to himself at the memory of the wise and well revered leader, who had brought a hush over the arena, before all the leaders stood and cheered him in agreement.

"He started the trading of food and goods between clans, and even initiated the concept of having sporting competitions each year on the autumn solstice. No injury or killing was allowed, and an event schedule was developed, so participants knew what to train for. Much effort went into athleticism and training before an event. I went along a couple of times to absorb new techniques and skills. Some were fairly primitive, and others stemmed from skilful ancient styles, and since then I have not seen such an array of abilities.

"I remember well the son of Hatchiman, who demonstrated an outstanding display of new fighting techniques which he developed himself. It was like watching a dance of kinds. The attack and defence were performed in spherical motions using the momentum of the attacker against himself. The son's name was Navek. He became known as 'Sidewinder' after that day because of his unique fighting style, and was cheered by everyone watching. It reinforced to me, fighting could be polished as an art form and practised even for good health. Anyway, the clans continued to train their sons in the techniques of fighting as a sport. Each year, they would come together in competition and celebration, not war. Those days are over now," Lamaar said with a sigh. "Since then, most of those clans have been wiped out and killed. The only survivor of the Videha clan is Navek, the son of Hatchiman. He alone escaped."

Khelvan detected a slight shaking and a tinge of anger in Lamaar's voice. Such emotion was rare in his teacher's words, but when Lamaar continued the tremor was gone, and his voice took on a more solemn tone.

"Unfortunately, another man works to bring back the warring and unrest between the people. There is an outlaw sorcerer named Jackyl Nazarak, who uses dark spells and mind control to manipulate humanity. He is the one who cast a binding spell over Hatchiman and his clan and then killed them. He has killed many of the surrounding clans and villagers as well."

As Lamaar spoke the sorcerer's name, a chilly breeze rustled through the bamboo and brushed passed them, before disappearing into the forest. Lamaar frowned when he felt its cold touch, and cast his eyes over the forest, scanning the perimeter for the unexpected.

He paused awhile to sip tea, and then his words took on a quieter tone, "Now here is the mission I am asking of you. It will be up to you if you choose to accept, but hear me out first. I would want you to find this sorcerer and put an end to his powers". The teacher turned to look directly at Khelvan, "The mission would be highly dangerous and fraught with challenges and difficulties. It involves going far to the north to confront and defeat this sorcerer named Jackyl, and remove his ability to use his powers. That is the main task, but first, there is someone who would travel with you, a man you would find after you leave here. He is the same son of Hatchiman who survived the killings. I would want you to find Navek, or Sidewinder as his friends called him. Not because his fighting abilities would be useful on this mission, but because of his inherent intentions and his need to fight a worthwhile cause". Lamaar paused a few moments before adding, "And his father would have wanted this".

Khelvan turned with a questioning look, but Lamaar continued on talking. "Also Navek was born in the icy high country and knows how to survive in those northern mountains," he went on. "You would both travel together on this journey. Each of you has different strengths, and by working together you can defeat this rogue who hides out in a remote region."

Khelvan drew a breath to say something as he had always travelled alone before, but Lamaar's hand went up to silence him, and he went on.

"For years now he has used his self-taught powers to

wreak havoc and evil on others like the Videha clan. The destruction to mankind spreads further and further to the south with every passing season. On the unseen scale of good and bad in the world, he alone is responsible for tipping the balance toward darkness, but the time has come to correct the damage before it's too late to repair. Ultimately, it is only one man you would seek, but he has many eyes that report back to him, and he even draws on the afterlife which he manipulates to do his bidding. He is as dangerous as they come.

"Jackyl now operates from a remote icy dungeon under a mountain, from where he sends out his vengeful powers against mankind. He was actually born in the north-west high country, but moved to his distant lair in the north-east. He is past the furthermost reaches where no man cares to roam.

"Think well before deciding Khelvan, as this is an enemy who will use dark powers and forces against you in ways you have not come across. He may even try to kill you from afar with his dark intentions and invisible spells. If he finds out you are coming for him, he would not want you approaching his domain, and may pit forces against you to prevent an approach. To defeat him would require not strength and weapons, but surrender to a greater power. The most important shield in this battle would be the ability to trust the power which exists behind all life. It breathes us, weaves our destiny and turns the great wheel of time, and would provide the help needed to diminish him."

Lamaar leaned back to let him absorb the information.

"No need to answer now Khelvan, think about it overnight. This is a serious matter, harder than any task you have done before, and such a journey would involve grave risk."

"I'll do it," Khelvan said evenly, not managing to hide the disappointment of being sent away from the forest shelter so soon. He agreed because his teacher would not be asking this of him if it were not important.

Lamaar already knew Khelvan wanted to remain in the forest, and did not miss the disappointed tone in his voice. Several long moments passed in silence, till Lamaar went inside to make tea. He brought out a full cup for Khelvan, before going back inside to start cooking dinner.

Khelvan sat on the old wooden veranda beneath the dragon carvings. Talk of leaving again sent a flutter of panic through him. He regretted agreeing to the mission so quickly as he had only just returned.

At first the request had sounded gloomy and extreme and his mind had been closed to the task. It would take him out into the world again where survival is difficult. Besides, a rogue sorcerer living under a mountain, what does it have to do with him! He thought about the venture he had committed to, and then something shifted in his subconscious. An unexpected spark ignited. Doubts were removed and a small excitement grew, like the excitement he felt as a young boy waking up in the mornings to the possibilities of a new day. He would brace himself for this venture. He would do what was asked of him, what was needed. It was a worthwhile cause.

Chapter 9.
The Lone Wolf

After dinner, Khelvan stoked the fire with the metal poker, his mind occupied by the previous conversation.

Lamaar had more to say, but waited awhile to start. "To defeat the sorcerer it is best you know a few things about his history."

Khelvan sat back against the chair, sighing in resignation at the task that lay ahead. "Ok, tell me what I will need," he said.

"When Jackyl Nazarak was a young boy his parents treated him dreadfully, and often kicked him out on the street to fend for himself. He endured years of brutality, and became an outcast. Jackyl was actually very intelligent, and would have made a promising apprentice shaman in his village, but no one gave him a chance or helped him. Children in the town shunned and bullied him, making his life even more miserable. They nicknamed him the Lone Wolf.

"Revenge and hatred built inside him, till one night, using his amateur powers, he killed the village shaman. He stole a book of spells and fled, never to be seen again. Over the years he taught himself sinister magic and dark spells from the book, twisting and contriving the meanings to wreak his vengeance on the world. Nevertheless, he's had a hard life and did not deserve the brutality.

"Now, this Jackyl the Lone Wolf lives as a recluse down in the tunnels of an abandoned mine shaft. He is under Mount Perilous. The mountain stands in the glacial north-east amid a vast mountain range, and is hard to reach. They say Mount Perilous is a sacred place, where a grid of energy lines meets right under the mountain. Only a few such locations exist to stabilise the vibrations of the planet.

"There are tales the mountain itself did not tolerate the mining that went on beneath it years ago. Dangerous tremors and quakes caused the mines to close down. The mountain wants to spit the wolf out of its lair because now, it is a blemished place from which much wrong has been initiated. That runs contrary to the mountain's nature. The sorcerer living in its depths must be stopped, never to operate again. He causes adversity and strife to the world.

"An angry man is an afraid man Khelvan, and what is he afraid of?" Lamaar paused before adding, "a life without meaning and purpose. Out of vengeance he created his own misdirected purpose. It's not his fault he knew nothing but anger and hatred, and never had a good man to mould himself on, but he has gone too far and must be stopped".

Lamaar paused so Khelvan could digest the information, and they both sat awhile, looking into the fire.

"Now I will tell you a little of how he can be defeated. Certain things will bring him down and end his control over others. Firstly, be sure to take stone and flint with you, as fire can help defeat him. He hides himself away with remoteness and extreme cold as his allies, but if you can create heat in his domain, then his spells will be ineffective against you. Secondly, it will not be skill or your weapons that will bring him undone, but your inner strength. On such a journey, knowing what to do will not always be obvious, so at those times remember to be still. Listen to your inner voice, and then the path will become clear."

Lamaar paused again for the information to be absorbed.

"Thirdly, get rid of his eyes so he cannot see. He sends out supernatural spies that report back to him, so cut off his information channel to guard your safety. Even tonight his sendings try to breach my domain. And fourthly, he is not as powerful as he thinks he is. He is just an unloved and unhappy little boy lashing out on others with weapons that have devastating consequences. You must give him a chance to redeem himself before his soul flies back to its source. This is most important Khelvan. Don't forget this. *The sorcerer must be given a choice before his ending.* A clear choice, to see if he will recognise that all the killing and destruction he has hurled against humanity, is the result of his own vengeance. If he is willing to accept he has become the very thing he hated so much in others, he may be redeemable, as he does deserve a better chance. Otherwise all the efforts and the whole journey you make could be in vain, and he will be reborn into the world again to continue his destruction."

Unexpectedly, a small explosion of sparks spluttered upward from a log in front of them. Though it was warm in the room, another chill passed over them both. Lamaar looked around quickly, as though expecting to see someone. He waited several moments before continuing.

"Find Navek and when the time is right, go together to Mount Perilous. Seek out the Lone Wolf. You will only defeat him where he lives, and the confrontation will happen there. Go into the sorcerer's world where he will likely be waiting. This is where you will defeat him, man-to-man. Be aware his dark force will try to trick you and destroy you, and like a thief he will try to rob you of your certitude and strength.

"Once you leave and start this mission he may recognise your intentions, and even from afar can direct his dangerous crafts against you. Remember he collaborates with the afterlife and has eyes everywhere, but if the darkness from the north is not pushed back, it will take over life as we know it; only greed and cruelty will remain. Mankind will become his minions who will strip the earth bare and turn it into a desert wasteland. This wheel of destruction is already underway and gains momentum even as we sit here.

"This is a lot to ask of any man Khelvan and great risk is involved. You can change your mind of course." Lamaar paused before asking, "After hearing all this, do you still accept the quest?"

"Yes I'll go," Khelvan replied reticently. He did not entirely grasp what he was agreeing to, but sensed the gravity and the importance of the request, and Lamaar had never asked anything like this before. Nevertheless, he did not know if he would be able to achieve such an immense undertaking. Did he really have the abilities his teacher gave him credit for? He ignored the fleeting doubts.

Lamaar knew Khelvan would not speak of his reservations about the strange appeal, but he also knew Khelvan was the best man for the job. The journey would take him beyond limits never travelled and would uncover his true potential. The teacher walked over to a small wooden table near the kitchen, and sat down to face it. He reached under to release a hidden catch, causing the surface panel to lift slightly. He lifted the panel to reveal a hidden compartment full of gold, silver and copper coins. With indifference, Lamaar filled a drawstring bag with a large handful of coins, and then tossed it through the air to Khelvan.

"You will find Navek in the port of Welpecca in the shadow section of town. These days, he wanders hopeless and lost and has forgotten the ancient ways that were once his birthright. Find him and take him with you to face this enemy. Help each other. Hear me Khelvan. The task will be too much for one man alone.

"Navek knew the way of truth once, but his blade grows rusty in its scabbard. You will need much patience to help him polish it again and get him back. However, when you find him, judge him not. Under the surface he suffers greatly because he has lost his valour and his purpose. He runs from the guilt of surviving without his family and clan. Navek is a solitary soul, not so unlike you really. He has his own extraordinary strengths, but he must be found soon or it will be too late for him."

With a furrowed brow Khelvan poked around in the fire, pushing the unburned ends of logs toward the centre, while he thought over the new prospects.

"To reach the port of Welpecca from here, the most direct route is south through the desert, and then east to the coast. On the way, you will encounter others who will help you, though some may seem unlikely companions. Recognise them by their light and wisdom which cannot be fabricated by pretence. Acknowledge the ones that will call from the sky, and remember to ask of the spirit world to light your path."

Lamaar leaned his head back against the chair adding: "I would not ask this of you lightly my friend. Few even know of this blight on humanity, but it is imperative the source is removed. If not, the well of joy will run dry and a millennium of darkness will ensue. I thank Life for knowing you Khelvan, and giving me the privilege to teach you a few small tricks and skills".

A small reverent smile came to Khelvan's lips at hearing the depth of his old teacher's humility.

"You are the best I have ever taught, and I have been most fortunate to play a small role in your life. You can always talk to me and talk to your guides, as we will be with you on the journey. Even from the afterlife my job would not be done until you succeed against the one who unravels righteousness. Remember the peace you feel here is always with you – deathless and imperishable. Trust and hold fast to your faith, and you will join me here soon enough."

The next morning Khelvan walked back to the fast flowing creek, while more rain started to fall. Conditions were cold, but he was happy and enjoyed the sensation of simply being alive, currently free of worldly cares. He breathed in the fresh smell of the forest where cypress pines released their refreshing aroma in the rain. The forest was full of pleasant sounds, and when the rain came down harder, Khelvan smiled at the pleasure of it all.

In his heart he sent silent gratitude to Lamaar, who helped make this freedom possible, and gave him the strength to do what had to be done next. As he walked along with his horse beside him, tears of happiness flowed and mixed with the rain to be absorbed into the dense forest floor. He rejoiced in life, and smiled at the thought of his teacher's liberating wisdom.

At the time of departure, Lamaar had stood on the

veranda watching with arms folded over his chest. In that dawn light, a grey hue was cast over the forest, giving the garden an ancient quality which appeared to be an extension of the teacher himself. Upon reaching the edge of the forest, Khelvan had turned and their eyes met. An eternity seemed to pass, and a tremor fluttered up through Khelvan as he bowed out of respect. He had looked up once more to the man who taught him much, and did not know if it would be the last time he would see him. Gracefully framed by black bamboo, Lamaar had emanated a great and solemn presence, and this parting image was imprinted onto Khelvan's heart, to be recalled many times again.

Several hours later, Khelvan reached his former camp, where a few weeks ago he had slept a night. After a brief rest he slipped into the saddle, and set off at a rapid pace as the horse was eager to be away. "To the south my friend," he said to the horse. With an open desert to cross before reaching the coast, he had plenty to contend with. He had heard reports of the port town, none of them very good.

Chapter 10.
Crossing the Desert

The Devil's Gate. That is what the camel herders had called the region when they dropped Khelvan off. He had sold his horse in the town before they had given him passage across the desert, pointing him in the direction of the oasis.

Three days earlier he had farewelled them, as they continued on their journey south-west, but his food and water were almost finished.

Under a blistering sun with cracked lips and parched throat, he pushed on across the barren, shell of a place. Winds blew sand off the top of the dunes, dancing along like sea spray off the top of waves. Hot sand cut into him, blurring his vision. He could barely put one foot in front of the other at times. The surroundings were a complete contrast to the cold, wet forest around Lamaar's hut only weeks ago.

A bird circled high overhead, calling out as it veered toward the mountains. The call was not missed by Khelvan, and it reinforced he was going the right way. He re-secured the white scarf around his head, and the bird called out again in the distance.

"Alright alright. I heard you," he muttered.

He trudged on toward his destination – the white mountain range in the distance. All day he walked toward it, and never seemed to get any closer. In the afternoon heat, a mirage appeared and shimmered like a lake of water at the foot of the mountains, and the mountains became like a hovering spacecraft. Winds blew stronger and Khelvan adjusted the headscarf to cover his face, so only his eyes showed. He quickened his pace – he wanted to reach the mountains before another dust storm obscured all vision.

Unexpectedly, a strange sight caught Khelvan's eye. A small, dark shape appeared and then disappeared near the mountain. It may be an animal, but he saw no other signs of life in the arid location. Remembering Lamaar's warning about the sorcerer, he was alert to danger, and travelled a longer route behind the cover of low dunes. He went crouched over, stopping occasionally and straining to see who or what lay ahead. The shape reappeared and a gold gleam flashed beyond the shimmering mirage.

When he reached the foot of the mountains, an unexpected sight stood just thirty paces away. A confident, young woman peered out through swirling dust toward the north. She seemed to be waiting for someone. The woman belonged to a desert tribe and Khelvan looked around for others, but the woman was alone. She stood braced on the valley floor proud and defiant, feet apart, hands on hips, her long, black hair blowing wildly around in the wind. She wore a knee-length light blue tunic with elaborate embroidery around the neckline and sleeves, worn over black pants drawn at the ankle. The fabric flapped around her strong body while gold chains around her neck flashed in the sunlight. This must have been the gleam he had seen earlier.

Though Khelvan was quite near the woman, she was either unaware of him or was ignoring him. With squinted eyes she looked into the sun toward the north, scanning the horizon with a sense of urgency. Extreme heat rose off the sand, the mirage shifted and moved, and at times the woman seemed to disappear.

"Was his mind playing tricks? Was he seeing things?"

Shifting sands blew erratically from various directions at once, pushed along by increasing wind speeds. An ominous feeling pervaded the atmosphere when the sky darkened over, as though a fierce storm approached, but there were no clouds in the sky. Unsure if he should advance from his crouched position, Khelvan looked out through the sandstorm for any danger, but saw nothing.

Suddenly, the woman hurried several paces in his direction, with knees bent as though ready to run. She looked directly at him and called out over the roar of the wind. "Come on!" she called, gesturing to him. "Hurry!

Run toward the mountain. Move now!" she yelled. Without flinching, the desert woman held his surprised look, then glanced back once more to the north, before running toward the illusory mirage. She ran bent over, as if to avoid some invisible danger. Her pace slowed and strain showed on her tanned face, as though she fought against a strong head wind or an invisible barrier. No danger was visible, but the woman struggled on, and then disappeared from view.

Khelvan could not make out what it was, but something other than a sand storm threatened. A voice in him told him to go and move quickly. He had been wandering through an endless desert with no supplies, and would not survive on his own. He must trust this woman. He stood up and ran toward the glaring mirage, feeling the same dense force that prevented the woman's progress toward the mountains beyond.

"Was the sorcerer already conjuring the forces of nature against him, trying to prevent his progress?" Khelvan had been warned by Lamaar, but was surprised the dark one was onto him so quickly. Never had he come across such a phenomenon.

After a long day of trekking through the desert, he fought the storm being pitted against him, pushing against its force with waning strength. Something from his training resurfaced. "Relax," he heard Lamaar say. "Let go of that which you can no longer control." As soon as he stopped pushing, exerting and spending energy, the force against him disappeared. He came up near the woman and got close enough to touch her elbow. She turned in surprise at Khelvan's unexpected touch, and then looked up to read the message in his eyes. After seeing his relaxed bearing, she knew what to do. She completely relaxed and drew a big breath, and then exhaled before standing upright. She stepped into the shimmering haze, which evaporated from around them as though it never existed.

Khelvan turned to the desert woman, and saw she had a beautiful face. Light brown eyes, the colour of a young camel's coat, shone like the gold she wore. With high cheekbones and a confident, proud stance she looked like a descendant from royal lineage, and he wondered what she was doing out here unaccompanied. They walked on together toward the mountains, almost as though nothing had happened, and soon the green of an oasis appeared ahead. "What is this place? What happened back there?" Khelvan asked.

"This is the place you seek," she said. "Our shaman told us you were coming, and I was waiting for your arrival, but it is as though the desert fought against you, and did not want you to reach us. I have lived at this oasis all my life and have never seen such a bizarre storm, though we have noticed other strange occurrences of late," she said. "I think I know who is behind this, but I must speak to my father."

They neared the oasis and it was like stepping into another world. The stormy desert seemed far away from the calm green paradise they now walked into. Wind did not blow wildly, nor did the heat of the sun beat down. It was a normal day; they were soon walking under the shade of palm trees. The mountain range he sought to reach now loomed up all around him, no longer dry and barren but lush and green with the sound of running water nearby.

They followed a narrow track till they reached an open area. Various tents were arranged in semicircular groupings, all near to a small creek that ran downhill from one deep well. All of the tents were the colour of the sand on the outside, but if a breeze blew or the tent flaps were tied back, variations of vivid azure, indigo, purple and green lined the insides. The colours were dazzling to behold after days of seeing desert sand. People squatted in the shade of palm trees and chatted, others tended camels and women cooked over open fires. Many looked up to watch the stranger go by, as not often would a man come alone on foot through the desert to their camp.

"I am Jamilla. I will show you where you will stay, and then I must talk to my father – the tribe's leader." She took him to a smaller tent at the far end of the camp, and then pointed to a place where the creek flowed away from the camp. "You can wash in the spring down there, and then go back to your tent. I don't want you wandering around by yourself right now. I will send someone with water and food then I'll come back soon to get you."

Khelvan went down to the water's edge and washed the sweat and dust of the desert from his hands and face. The water was so refreshing he splashed his whole head, took off his boots and bathed his feet before walking barefoot back to the tent. On a beautifully carved table, a covered jug of water and a bowl of fresh dates awaited him. An elaborate carpet covered the floor and embroidered cushions lay scattered around. The tent was surprisingly cool inside. After drinking, he ate all the dates which were delicious and what he needed. He sat against the centre pole and waited for the woman's return. He needed time to collect himself and think about what happened in the desert.

Lamaar had told him the sorcerer could pit invisible forces against him, but he did not expect this so soon. *"Was this the force that had killed the northern tribes? Surely it hadn't found him out here in the desert."* If the weaver of spells was nearby, he would be more on guard from now on. He realised with some concern, he had now faced the sorcerer's first act against him, sent invisibly from afar in an attempt to prevent his journey. Khelvan sat back to feel a pleasant breeze against his skin. *"What strange mission have I embarked on?"* he wondered.

After the heat of the afternoon passed, Jamilla called by Khelvan's tent to take him to see her father. Near the centre of the camp, they arrived at a large open tent where several men, all wearing coloured turbans, were seated around on a carpet. Jamilla's father sat at the fore position, with two of his main men either side, and the tribe's shaman sitting nearby. They all turned to greet Khelvan with amicable nods, looking with interest at the stranger. Jamilla introduced Khelvan to her father Rashid, and the other men seated around. The leader of the desert tribe was a tall, proud handsome man, dressed in the long flowing style worn by the desert people. As soon as Khelvan's eyes met those of the leader, he knew Rashid was a good man and could be trusted.

"Welcome Khelvan. Jamilla told us of the strange battle in the desert," said Rashid. "What do you know of this, and why does such a peculiar force seek to hinder your travel?"

Khelvan addressed the desert people and told them something of the mission he had just begun. He could only repeat some of Lamaar's words about a lone sorcerer who works against the good of mankind for his own evil purposes. He told them how the sorcerer, by way of magic and spells, is behind many deaths of northern clans and villages, and sends destructive powers further and further southward. Khelvan finished by saying: "So my friends, strength and fighting skills are no match against this sorcerer, but something must be done to stop the spread of his powers, before it is too late for us all. I have been sent on this mission to find him, and end his reign. But first I seek to travel to the port of Welpecca before I go north".

While Khelvan was talking, the shaman became noisy and agitated, and rocked from side to side. He shook the long wooden staff he carried and rattled the bones, feathers and other strange items tied to it. During the discussion Rashid glanced over to him several times, but did not appear concerned. Finally, with one definite gesture, the shaman raised his arm up and brought the wooden staff down hard on the carpet. He then sat motionless, staring ahead.

Khelvan sensed with that final gesture, that the shaman gathered some lurking darkness, and sent it down into the core of the earth to be permanently dissolved in the fires there.

Rashid looked across at Khelvan, and spoke after a long pause. "We know already of this rogue sorcerer who sends his energy against us. Our shaman has told us some of what he sees in the spirit world, and spends much effort warding it off."

Khelvan felt somewhat relieved the desert tribe were already aware of the shadowy force, and knew something was amiss with the world. They had heard rumours of whole tribes wiped out by unexplained phenomena in the northern steppes, and were keen to know how to guard against such peril. So far, no one but his teacher had ever talked about it. Even the townsfolk where he had worked must have heard rumours, but they went about their daily lives not believing a downfall would happen.

"Peace is priceless," said the Bedouin leader. "We live on the border of life, death and survival out here, and can't afford damage from one who would seek to destroy us. We agree to help you however we can. In a couple of days we can give you passage to Tanzahar which is a market town to the south-east. This will take you part of the way to the port of Welpecca."

The short conversation seemed to conclude, and then Rashid added: "Tomorrow is the night of our moon ceremony. We hope you will join us as our honoured guest".

Khelvan felt he had been dismissed and bowed respectfully to Rashid and the others before he left, unsure if he had explained his mission or not, or whether the tribe had really grasped the dire importance of the situation. *"No matter. The task is on my shoulders,"* he thought. *"Me and some fellow I've never met from the alleyways of Welpecca!"*

It was almost evening when they left the central tent and headed back toward Khelvan's assigned tent. Jamilla pointed out various places of interest so he would know his way around the camp. The shaman's tent was slightly apart from the others, facing north. When they passed by, the pungent aroma of some brewing concoction floated out. Inside, his young apprentice tended the fire under a large, charred metal pot, and the shaman scurried past to check on his apprentice. Khelvan would have liked to talk to the shaman to see if he had any useful information about the sorcerer, but he looked busy, so they continued on. Jamilla left Khelvan at his tent and went off to her friends who prepared the evening meal. He stretched out on the carpeted floor and dozed off with the peaceful image of Lamaar standing on his veranda imprinted in his thoughts.

The next evening, Rashid and a few men stood gazing out at a spectacular desert sunset. The sun slowly turned hot pink before it dropped down behind the horizon, sending orange and yellow beams across the sky overhead. At the same time, a large golden full moon hovered above the other horizon casting shadows onto the moonlit evening, while people went about their evening routines. Next to the ceremonial area, tribesmen arranged drums and other musical instruments while others groomed and fed camels and started preparations for the forthcoming journey to the market town. After two nights Khelvan would depart on a camel train to Tanzahar, from where he would continue on to Welpecca on the east coast to search for Navek.

He sat at the door of his tent, enjoying the slow transformation of day into night, taking in the magnificent display of changing colours and the alluring atmosphere of the desert evening. Such a display would not be seen in the north and he understood why these desert people lived out here, surrounded by such ever changing beauty. As daylight faded the men dispersed back to their tents to get ready for the night's ceremony.

After dinner the tribe gathered around the fire pit in the central meeting area. Khelvan sat on the carpet near Rashid and the other men, while the women gathered and chattered nearby. He listened in fascination to the deep base sound of drums that evoked a connection to an ancient source, like the primordial rhythm of a heart beating.

After awhile the shaman arrived carrying his wooden staff, seating himself across from Khelvan. He looked toward the stars then around at all the men gathered, before closing his eyes and rocking slightly back and forward. Khelvan had tried to talk with him that day, but the shaman had been busy instructing his apprentice on which dried plants to add to the brew he boiled, and had no time for him. "Tonight, tonight," was all he said when Khelvan had approached his tent.

The apprentice arrived at the gathering carrying a large ceramic urn with a narrow neck, which contained the brown liquid they had boiled during the day. The apprentice poured some into a bowl and handed it to the king, who took a few mouthfuls before passing it along to the next man. The bowl was passed to Khelvan, who hesitated, and looked across to see the shaman watching. For confirmation he turned to Rashid, who gestured for him to drink up. The men either side of him told him it was an ancient plant potion, "a way of shedding light" they said. To be a polite guest he took a couple of mouthfuls of the bitter brew, thinking it to be some kind of alcohol, and then passed it along.

The fire was stoked and the music played on. As time went by, Khelvan felt a strange sensation come over him. He wondered at the strength of the drink he had tasted, as the colours around him started to look vividly clear and striking. Some of the tribesmen had their eyes closed, others were staring into the fire, and a few were laughing and chatting with each other beneath the loud drumming. Khelvan watched the flames leap and dance as though they were animated, and started to see patterns and iridescent lights form complicated but perfect geometric designs. Even though the sun had set, when he looked out beyond the camp, vast glittering cities began to appear in the desert.

The bitter potion seemed to be providing a portal to another world, an otherwise unreachable realm. Khelvan sat in one world, but saw another which existed alongside the desert settlement. The situation he found himself in was certainly strange and extraordinary, yet held his fascination. Beneath the canopy of glittering stars, the sights were other worldly, but somehow he felt at home and in no danger.

Under the full moon, the drummers continued into the night. At times Khelvan's body moved spontaneously to the rhythmic sounds, and the hair on his arms stood on end. He came to appreciate that the rhythm offered something familiar and earthly, grounding him amid all that was going on. Time did not exist and dilated to fit a multitude of experiences and revelations at the same time. Khelvan could not tell if he had sat there for a few minutes, or for an eternity. He felt an incredible lightness, a feeling of belonging. His feet did not walk, yet he felt he was travelling. Inner sounds flowed from the source of Life itself, where every sound was born; a feeling of peace permeated his whole body then expanded to fill the universe.

Tall robed beings, perhaps ancestors, now stood around the outside of the group, with indigo coloured robes blowing gracefully in the breeze. He closed his eyes and walked down a tunnel of soft, billowing light, and an endless supreme love enveloped him. Without thoughts, he understood the beginning, the middle and the end of all things. *"Is this what the ancients meant when they talked about Knowing the seed of all eternity?"* he wondered briefly. He witnessed a myriad of perfect patterns and dimensions, and an unending diversity of forms that went far beyond his imagination. Strange, wonderful and rich with association.

An eerie, high pitched wail was heard nearby, or was it far away, Khelvan could not be sure. The sound of others shifting and breathing around him became amplified, and he rubbed his face and eyes with hands that felt foreign. *"This mix of plants brewed together is potent and intense,"* he thought, unsure whether he wanted it to continue.

The experience became telepathic and gave visual and auditory information about remote events. At one point, he was flying north over villages, soaring like an eagle looking down over the earth. He crossed green forests and icy mountains, and then in an instant, zoomed to a dilapidated hut, away from other huts in a village. A small boy was being beaten by his cruel and merciless father. The mother's face was turned away, not protecting or helping the boy, and not caring. Somehow, Khelvan knew the child was Jackyl the sorcerer. This had been his life, just as Lamaar described. Fleeting emotions passed by of the boy's utter isolation and his loneliness. Khelvan saw the bullying by other children who would not include Jackyl, and why the boy felt he never belonged anywhere. He also saw Jackyl was highly gifted, but was never offered any way or opportunity to uncover his gifts. The scene shifted and changed to the image of the young boy Jackyl under the cover of night, peering through windows and watching families as they ate and laughed together. With heaviness in his chest and tears falling down his grubby cheeks, the boy vowed: *"Someday I will be free. Someday I will show you all what I can do"* .

All this and myriads more, Khelvan comprehended in a moment of the world's time. After seeing into the identity of the sorcerer he must find, he felt compassion for Jackyl and his pitiful past.

In another moment, Khelvan was back sitting at the fire, but behind him, a large vine started to move. The vine writhed and wrapped itself around him, quickly turning into a creature like a giant anaconda. It clung to Khelvan's back and then slithered and wrapped itself around his chest, squeezing the air out of him till he could not breathe. Khelvan was nauseous and urgently tried to cry out. His heart raced. He could no longer inhale and started to panic. The drums became louder and the rhythm beat faster. Faces flashed before him, faces of people he had known or seen, and many faces he did not know. Suddenly, one face appeared out of the many, and loomed toward him. It was sinister and evil. The haunted image of the sorcerer himself came at Khelvan, full of anger, and hissing his hatred. Khelvan tasted sulphur in his throat, and felt the evil intention and revenge of a psychopath incapable and devoid of any human mercy. His eyes opened wide in desperation, as the giant snake continued to wrap around his throat and chest, icy and cold as it pressed the air from his lungs.

Someone stood in front of Khelvan and gently tapped

his shoulders. The person chanted in a low voice, and then the snake creature and all the faces disappeared in an instant as though they never existed. Khelvan looked up, grateful to see the shaman standing there with eyes closed, making strange gesticulations above Khelvan's head. When he looked across the fire he was astonished to see that the shaman had not moved at all, and was still seated across from him, looking into the low flames with eyes half closed.

A pair of black butterflies flew up above the group in slow orbital circles, a flickering of iridescent red coming from the oblong eyes on their wings. The shaman turned behind him to meet the eyes of his apprentice, before turning back to gaze into the fire again. Without any words being spoken, the alert apprentice stepped past the others seated around the fire. He picked up the unburnt end of a stick from the fire and shook off the embers, before swiftly aiming it at one of the black butterflies overhead. The creature sizzled and dropped to the fire's edge, and he kicked it into the coals where it burnt, leaving a small trail of black smoke. The apprentice quickly looked up for the other one, but it circled slowly higher and higher, out of reach and out of sight. After this, Khelvan detected a faint frown of disdain on the medicine man's face when his hooded eyes peered across the fire at him. The shaman stood and departed back to his tent with the apprentice following close behind.

Seeing into the life of the sorcerer and glimpsing his menacing powers disturbed Khelvan and he was shaken by the ordeal, but he had accepted the mission and would not veer away from it. He threw off his fears, steeled himself for the quest ahead then turned back to stare into the fire, drawn in again by its beautiful colours and natural dancing movements.

"Staring into the fire the wisdom cometh," whispered a clear voice from nearby, or was it the desert breeze speaking to him. He gazed at the burning coals again, where he found a welcome resting place for his mind. Words continued coming and he leaned back and closed his eyes to listen.

"You will find friends on your journey who are like the pillars of the earth. Fear not. You will not be alone and you will not fail. We will accompany you to his icy domain and help you achieve your purpose. Remove his chilling grip before the wheel of life runs awry, awry, awry ..." spoke the voice. Khelvan opened his eyes to see if someone was speaking to him, but there was no one, yet he still heard the clear message before it trailed off.

Khelvan felt a presence and turned to see a black jaguar sitting regally beside him, with the flickering flames reflected in its yellow eyes. The creature was magnificent but when he turned again the jaguar was gone. Soon after, he was relieved to walk away from the fire and the drumming, and out into the cool bright night. A rush of nausea swept over him and he walked further away before vomiting and retching in the moonlight.

By the time he wandered back toward the camp, his legs were rubbery and he wanted to lie down. He reached his own tent and lay down. As the potion finally started to wear off, he wondered in fascination at all the dimensions that had become accessible that evening. The experience was intense, though he held no regrets about any of it. *"Life is so much bigger than we mortals with our little minds can fathom,"* he thought. *"This is surely a strange journey I am on."*

Now, all he wanted to do was relax and feel serene. He was grateful to his teacher who taught him to meditate, and showed him the sanctuary of the soul within himself where he could always come back and find peace. He thought about Lamaar and wondered what he would say about all this, then centred his mind in meditation and eventually fell asleep.

Chapter 11.
Ships of the Desert

After the moon ceremony Khelvan stayed with the desert tribe for one more day. He was somewhat fragile after the festivities, but spent the next day resting and reflecting on experiences from the night before. The moon ceremony had facilitated a transformation, an enlightenment of sorts. His mind had been opened to another dimension and he understood more about the one he would seek.

The desert tribe decided he was to accompany the camel train leaving at dawn, to reach the trading town of Tanzahar situated on the south-east edge of the desert plains. Traders gathered at the Tanzahar central market, where an array of weird and wonderful merchandise was bought and sold, camels and goats often being the main currency.

On the last night, Khelvan thanked Rashid and Jamilla

for their hospitality, as well as the shaman for an enriching experience he would never forget.

The next morning as Khelvan left the camp, he turned to take in the green oasis and the colourful desert people, who had welcomed him into their remote and rich world.

The journey through the vast desert plains would take four days, so Khelvan adjusted and balanced himself atop a cantankerous camel. He settled into the unhurried, deliberate pace of the animals as they meandered along carrying both man and cargo. During the slow, winding trek through the hills of sand, he asked one of his companions why they remain living in the desert.

The man answered: "Our parents and our ancestors have always lived this way because the desert is beautiful and the air is clean. Also the camels and goats are happy here, so we could never live in the towns".

A little later the man added, "Sometimes we trade for supplies, but if we can't, it doesn't matter. We can survive on very little".

Khelvan pondered the words as they ambled on, marvelling and learning from the desert dwellers' simple appreciation of the world they were born into. The people were earthy and grounded with no wish to change their circumstances.

In the evening they stopped to set up camp. Later, the men and boys gathered around the fire and started telling lively and animated stories, often acting them out in hilarious ways, which caused an uproar of laughter from the onlookers. At nights, storytelling was a tradition with the tribe, and Khelvan became enthralled by the characters around him as he was unused to such entertainment. These desert dwellers really knew how to appreciate and encourage each person's differences and talents. Some were comical, others more serious, and they were not required to all think the same way, as is often the case.

They pushed Khelvan, insisting he join in and tell them a story from his travels. Reticent at first, he struggled to find a worthwhile tale, but to please his companions he recounted his days as a boy working in the blacksmith shop. He began telling how he just did odd jobs around the workshop, and gradually was taught how to heat the steel and beat it into the required shape, such as a gate or a blade or a horseshoe. He told them the owner was a known craftsman in the region, and people would come for miles to buy from him or have items custom made. The account was fairly boring, as he was neither a good story teller nor animated, but he enjoyed sharing a small piece of his life which seemed to fascinate the listeners. They liked to hear anything at all about other places or cultures, and when the story finished they fell silent a few moments, before another man started up with an eventful yarn.

In the desert, temperatures fell during the night and some of the men slept against their camels to keep warm. Khelvan lay awake listening to the strange grunting noises made between the camel and its owner, as they talked back and forth to each other before going off to sleep. He admired how close they were to their animals, often treating them like part of the family, as the goats and camels were a means to survival for them.

The camel train continued on through the desert following an ancient trade route, at times winding across flat sandy plains and other times trekking along the top of high rolling dunes. Out in such an expanse, the desert all looked the same to Khelvan, but the desert dwellers knew the way with no compass to guide them. Sometimes the desert was calm and the heat unbearable; other times wind would pick up speed and develop into a fierce sand storm, which howled and blew against them. The men would have to stop the camels and go through the slow process of getting the animals to sit down till the storm passed. At such times, the tribesmen and their sons sat against their camels, waiting the storm out with scarves pulled up to protect themselves from the stinging sand. The camels would sit patiently with their eyes closed – visibility at these times was nil and shifting sands obscured the way.

The menacing image of the sorcerer had not appeared since the moon ceremony at the oasis, but Khelvan did not forget the disturbing experience or the serious mission he was on. He was still very much committed to the task ahead.

It occurred to him however, that his mind was no longer restless or searching for contentment somewhere else. He was happy right here and right now, ambling through the desert on the back of a camel, enjoying the journey while he could. From Tanzahar he would proceed to the coast as soon as he was able, and responsibilities would become more pressing.

On the third day, they passed by the outline of a dry lake where only white salt lines remained, and bleached bones of animals lay scattered about. Further on, a white glaring sight caused them all to squint as they came nearer. It was a low, flat tract of sand, which the men called the Sea Of Salt. Here, they climbed down from the camels and let them have their own lead. The animals hurried over and began licking at the salt which was sustenance to them. Khelvan stood watching with cracked lips, intrigued at the endurance of man and beast, and their connection to the environment out in these conditions. He thought back again to his recent trek through the wet, green forest, and the extreme contrast brought a smile to his face.

By late afternoon, the surroundings started to change. Rocky outcrops appeared, also tussocks of dry grass and low scrub. In the distance, a young boy surviving the desert wilderness with his herd of goats stared at the camel train as it passed. Eventually the camel train came to an area beside a stony outcrop, where they made camp for the night. The leader of the expedition had lead the party directly to a watering hole, remotely situated in the dry desert.

Had they gone a hundred paces either side, they would have missed the deep hole lined merely by a ring of rocks at the top with no other markers. The opening of the well was about five feet across, and dropped into the ground over fifty feet. Two thousand years ago it had been dug by hand, and tapped into a subterranean water table far below. *"How could anyone walk across the desert to reach this precise location?"* Khelvan wondered, *"and who would know precisely where to dig?"*

He held much regard for these desert dwellers who traversed the desert with no maps, who for generations read their way from the stars or from memory.

Thirsty camels gathered boisterously around the well, and for the next hour or so, Khelvan helped haul water for them. The men drank, then refilled the skins used to carry water, which would last them the rest of the journey. Once again the sunset unfolded into another resplendent exhibition of colours and artistry spread across the sky. Khelvan collected a large pile of dry sticks for the fire, and then leaned back against a rock to enjoy the colours and the peaceful evening atmosphere. He would miss these men and their camels, and the simple desert life and all its beauty. He had even grown fond of the camel he rode which, he discovered, had its own unique personality.

The night was cold in the low area where they camped. Khelvan slept fitfully till the early hours when he woke suddenly from an unsettling dream. He dreamed of the sorcerer and felt his evil power. In the predawn light Khelvan quickly opened his eyes and saw the sorcerer's face materialised over him, before it flew away, disappearing into the desert. He was alarmed by the eerie experience and lay awake watching the stars. He thought about what he had witnessed, what he had been told about the sorcerer, and reminded himself that Jackyl started off as a frightened little boy. He would not let the sendings diminish his resolve.

At first light, the travellers packed up and headed off without breakfast. They soon neared the city of Tanzahar, where they slowed to let the camels eat from the scrub and bushes outside the city.

They reached their destination where busy streets were filled with people bustling around the market place. Khelvan appreciated the assortment of dazzling colours after days in the desert, and the bold clothes worn by both men and women were a kind Khelvan had never seen.

The camels were led to a large open area where many desert tribesmen squatted in groups and chatted together, their animals tethered nearby. Occasionally, friends would call out to greet the weary travellers, or call out a friendly jibe at their expense, drawing an outburst of laughter from some of the crowd. This was one of the few times they would get together and socialise, so they were all happy to see each other.

After tethering the camels, some of Khelvan's party went to a communal well to haul up water for the animals. A few of them set about making camp, while others went off to get breakfast from an array of food in the marketplace. It was a happy occasion for the desert dwellers, and Khelvan was content to squat in the shade with some of his travelling companions and take it all in.

Incredible aromas of cooked food and spices permeated the air, and it was not long before breakfast arrived. They sat gathered around, sharing a meal of fried pastries filled with spinach and white cheese, spicy cooked lamb with chickpeas and vegetables, flatbreads and various sweet cakes and fresh fruit. The men shared everything with Khelvan. Rashid had told the men to take good care of the guest who was on an important mission and carried a lot of responsibility on his shoulders.

A young boy came by, pushing an old three-wheeled trolley. A tray of glasses rattled on top, next to a large silver teapot with an elegant narrow spout. He offered to sell them tea, but they politely declined, and then were entertained while he poured hot tea for others using a well practised method of lifting the teapot from a height well above to fill the glass.

With the day still early, some of the men went off to sell or trade the large dried dates and olives they brought with them from the oasis, for goods and supplies needed back home.

Khelvan wandered about, fascinated by the activity and the range of exotic goods available. Passing by the fish sector he saw boxes of fresh fish layered with rock salt, and nearby stalls selling char-grilled fish. Other stalls displayed meat dishes cooked in clay tangines, honeyed sweets, dried beans of various colours and much more, but he was aware not to become too distracted by all the goings on, as he needed to find his ride to the east. He was also wary of pickpockets and skilful thieves.

Khelvan enquired here and there about getting to Welpecca, but found no one willing to take on a passenger. A few dusty vehicles were parked in the streets with no sign of the drivers. Eventually, he found several inns or taverns which offered accommodation, food and drink.

He asked the owners if they knew of anyone going east to Welpecca, but no one knew of a ride going that way. By mid-afternoon he questioned his chances, sitting down on some steps to rest and collect himself. An old saying he had learnt came to mind:

Sit still and keep God company.
Sit still, sit very, very still
So that the peace can find you ...

"Of course," he thought, "I've forgotten all about letting go, and asking for help".

Khelvan stilled his mind and talked silently to his guides. He remained on the steps for an hour or so with his head leaning back against a post, centred and in the moment, as practised many times before.

To anyone watching, he looked like a traveller from the north, sitting on a step, watching the picturesque world go by. On the inside however, he slowed his mind, attuning to the infinite power which breathed him. He allowed himself to feel peace and accepted the tranquillity. He felt an affinity with the world and looked out through the eyes of a child with no boundaries or judgement, simply seeing life as it is. It did not matter anymore if a ride was there for him or not. In that moment he was content and all was well with the world.

On the street, brightly dressed women carried wares on their head. Some had babies strapped on their backs; some had small children running at their side. Herders drove goats and sheep through the streets to the market. People walked past with roosters and chickens in cages, or baskets of fresh produce or cooked food. Around the corner in a lane way, Khelvan watched three large women clad in vibrant attire, as they joked and gossiped while washing clothes in bowls at their feet. Their faces were full of character, and Khelvan smiled when he heard their outbursts of raucous laughter at the jokes they told. From what he could make out, the jokes were mostly wise cracks about men.

Chapter 12.
Thick as Thieves

An old truck slowly weaved its way through the hustle and bustle of the crowd. The vehicle had a dusty canvas canopy and a heavy steel bull-bar across the front. It pulled up down the street, on the opposite side from where Khelvan sat. He thought about getting up to talk to the driver, but decided to remain awhile longer and observe. A few minutes passed, then an odd character of medium height, stepped down from the truck and went around checking that the canopy was tied down. The driver was plump and wore calf length baggy pants, work boots and a shirt with sleeves rolled up to the elbows, covered by another shirt which was faded and frayed where the sleeves had been cut off.

"Certainly not from around here," Khelvan thought bemusedly. The driver slung a canvas bag over the

shoulder, and walked confidently across the street, up steps and into one of the inns. Khelvan decided to wait on the steps and catch the person if they came back out or walked to the market place.

Evening approached, with no sign of the driver. Khelvan was hungry and thought about heading back to the camp, but first walked toward the inn. As he crossed the road a boy bumped into him from the side. In an instant Khelvan grabbed the boy's wrist and spun toward him. The boy kicked out at him. Khelvan knocked the kick aside and twisted the boy's hand into a painful wrist-lock, forcing the boy's shoulder upward and he stood on his toes to avoid the painful pressure of the grip. He wore no shoes, his clothes were worn and dirty, and he looked to be in his teens.

Still maintaining the wrist-lock, Khelvan looked his captive in the eye and merely held out an open hand. Onlookers stopped and were gathering to watch the incident. With his free hand the boy sheepishly retrieved Khelvan's coin bag from his pocket and returned it to him. The thief's eyes darted around at the spectators' faces showing he was more worried that he had been caught than having any remorse. Khelvan saw there was no use going any further with him, applied more pressure causing the boy to call out, then roughly shoved him to the ground. The thief got up and scurried through the crowd relieved to be away, rubbing his painful shoulder as he went.

Khelvan found the driver leaning casually against the

end of the bar with a drink and rolling a cigarette. For the second time on his desert sojourn, he was surprised to see that the person was a woman.

She had been watching the disturbance in the street through the window and was impressed at what she had just witnessed. When Khelvan walked into the room she turned toward him and nodded a casual greeting.

The girl had light blue eyes, a round face and shoulder length fair hair knotted into dreadlocks. Though she appeared tough and street smart, she seemed young to be on her own.

Some of the few men in the room looked at her in fascination while others looked on with disapproval. A woman alone, drinking in a bar or smoking was not customary in these parts, but her casual appearance and attitude demonstrated she did not care what others thought.

Khelvan walked over and said, "Hello".

She glanced up and down at him with narrowed eyes and took a long draw on her cigarette. "Hello," she replied, leaving the conversation up to Khelvan.

"I saw you pull up in the truck outside," he said awkwardly. "I wanted to enquire if you're heading east from here. I'm looking for a lift."

Another long awkward moment passed and she leaned back and coolly checked him out. He was not one of the locals and she liked what she had seen through the window, but wanted to find out more before answering. She drew on the cigarette with one hand, and turned the glass slowly on the bar with the other.

All the men in the room watched them, and Khelvan knew it did not take much in these parts to become the topic of conversation around the campfire at night. He was unused to such awkwardness, and by the girl's certitude he started to see why she would confidently travel on her own.

Finally, she said: "Pull up a stool and have a drink, and then we can talk".

Turning to the barman she ordered two glasses of raki, a locally brewed drink.

Khelvan grimaced when he tasted the aniseed flavoured brew, as the drink was fiery and would go straight to his head on an empty stomach.

She talked about the dry weather and other small matters, till the others in the room went back to their chattering and left the two at the bar to talk privately.

She enquired after his name before introducing herself. "I'm Lorette, you can call me Lori," she told him. Then lowering her voice so others would not hear she asked: "Which place are you heading?"

"To Welpecca," he answered. Deciding she would trust Khelvan she said: "Yes, I am going east after loading up in the morning. I might take on a passenger, if you are ready when I want to leave." She leaned in a bit closer to ask where he was staying and where she would find him in the morning.

He told her about his friends from the oasis and the camp site.

Lori was impressed the desert dwellers had allowed him to travel with them. This reinforced he was unlikely to be a danger to her.

Before parting, she warned him not to mention the departure details to anyone; she did not want the risk of being ambushed and robbed by thieves on the road. She also warned him that the walls have ears.

Khelvan thanked her for the drink and left to go back to his friends. He meandered through the dark streets, warm and relaxed from the heady drink.

Seated at the bar, Lori ordered dinner of slow cooked lamb with preserved lemons and potatoes. After the meal, she picked up her bag and walked out of the bar to the front counter, as if to organise accommodation for the night.

Once out of sight from the watchful eyes in the bar, she slipped through the side door and into the night.

Sneaking down the back street a short distance, she turned into a narrow alleyway, glancing backwards occasionally to check she was not being followed. When Lori reached a faded blue doorway, she looked around again and furtively knocked on the door. A friendly voice greeted her before ushering her inside.

Shortly afterwards, she crept back to the main street, quietly got into her truck and drove to the market place on the outskirts of town, where she parked among some other trucks. In the back of the truck she slept to the sound of drums playing into the night.

At daybreak Lori bought supplies of food for the trip,

including several flatbreads, koftas cooked on a stick, a container of spiced chicken cooked with vegetables and rice, a large hessian bag of almonds, three containers of preserved lemons and several sweet pastries. She found Khelvan in the trader's camp, drinking tea with the men who were aware he had found a ride and would leave this morning. "Are you ready?" she said to him. "I'll meet you over there," indicating with her chin toward the parked vehicle. "Don't be long."

The traders looked over at her unusual appearance and the oddity of having a foreigner in the camp, especially a woman with knotty hair who wore strange clothes and boots. She started to walk back to the truck, aware all eyes were on her, then as an afterthought, turned back and walked up to the head trader. She asked him the price of four boxes of the large dates stacked nearby, as well as four large containers of black olives.

The eyes of the men widened at the possible sale before they gathered around to discuss the important topic of price. A decision made, they turned to Lori and gave her a figure. Lori haggled for several minutes till they agreed on a final price, with the added condition the men would carry the goods to her truck. She handed over the money and left them happily standing around after the easy sale, nodding and counting, then recounting the money.

Meanwhile, Khelvan said goodbye to his new-found friends. He had enjoyed their company on his otherwise solitary journey. He almost envied their routine lifestyle in the desert, and felt some reluctance to leave and move on to his own uncertain future. But he had accepted the assignment from his teacher and would remain committed until it was achieved.

The engine was running and Lori was ready to leave when he opened the door and climbed into the passenger seat. He had seen vehicles like this, but this was the first time he had ridden inside one. It was a strange sensation to be carried along by a machine, and a little frightening, yet the acceleration was empowering after the camel speed he had become used to while crossing the desert plains.

The sun had not long risen as they headed eastwards out of town. They journeyed across rough and dusty desert roads, making infrequent small talk but saying little, with neither asking for details of the other. Occasionally Lori rolled a cigarette, using a well-practised technique of simultaneously holding the steering wheel with one knee, before sending the rather pleasant aroma of tobacco through the cabin.

From time-to-time she checked behind for vehicles following, but the only traffic they encountered was one vehicle and two camel trains that were headed toward Tanzahar. They drove through two small settlements and stopped at the second. Lori had bought plenty of food and shared lunch of koftas, chicken and rice with Khelvan. She filled canvas water bags with water, as well as filling the truck and two jerry cans with diesel.

By mid-afternoon the temperature soared. As they continued on, it was a relief to see the surrounding landscape change from vast desert dunes to scrubby low bushes, then green mountains appeared in the distance. Occasionally, they passed a herder minding his goats, or a woman and child carrying heavy bundles of sticks on their backs.

"I've heard of a short cut over those mountains, though it could be treacherous," said Lori. "I haven't been that way before but it would cut several hours off the trip." Then as an afterthought she added dryly, "If all goes well that is. After that, there'll still be another day's travel before we reach Welpecca". She glanced across at the mountains and raised her eyebrows, before getting the tobacco from her pocket to roll another cigarette.

Khelvan observed the approaching cliffs with an uneasy feeling about going that way, but said nothing. He hoped she knew what she was doing.

They reached the mountains and started to climb upward along a winding road. The higher they drove, the more treacherous the road became. Hours later, the track was so dangerous Khelvan could see the sheer drop straight down to the bottom. The narrow ledge seemed precarious; he expected it to give at any time and send them free falling over the edge to a rocky grave. Tense and uneasy, he required no encouragement to get out of the truck to guide Lori through particularly narrow spots, or move fallen rocks from the road. Under one overhang they just managed to fit the vehicle with only inches to spare.

The mountains that had appeared green from a distance were stony and arid up close, scattered with scrub and low bushes. Now and then they passed people walking in single file and saw the upturned remains of a vehicle wrecked at the bottom of the ravine. Fortunately they met no oncoming vehicles, though Khelvan was nervous at the approach of each blind corner as the road was only wide enough for one vehicle.

"Russian roulette eh?" said Lori with a wry smirk. Her eyes never left the road as she concentrated in earnest, shifting gears to slow the vehicle down a slope or get it up a steep incline.

Khelvan exhaled loudly trying to relieve the tension and replied: "It's a risky business alright".

Once they made it over the first mountain, Khelvan was discouraged to see there were several more yet to cross. He tried to relax as the anxious journey continued. There would be no respite from the hazards; he wished they had taken the slower route.

In the late afternoon long shadows fell over the track as the sun dropped behind the top of the mountains. As they continued, groupings of trees appeared and vegetation become thicker. On a flat area, they passed an old man walking with a stick. He was bent in half, no doubt from a lifetime of hard work and the weight of the firewood he carried on his back. It seemed like an impossibly heavy load for a man his age. Soon after they passed him however, Lori stopped the truck abruptly, then backed up so the tanned and weathered old face of the man was at her window. He straightened up to look at her with twinkling eyes. Their eyes met for a few moments as though summing each other up, before his eyes went to

Khelvan.

Lori indicated with gestures for him to get in, then waited to see if he would accept the lift. The old man decided to accept, gave her a nod and a grateful smile. Lori left the motor running and got out to open the canopy. She helped him take off his load and put the bundle of firewood in the back. After being bent over so long, he had difficulty climbing up onto the front seat. His clear dark eyes went directly to Khelvan as he clambered up, nodding a greeting as he settled himself between the two. He sat forward on the seat, holding the dashboard with strong working hands covered in gnarled veins.

This was his first ride in a vehicle and the dials and levers captured his interest. "Where're ya going?" Lori said in her own language.

The old man waved his hand in a forward direction to indicate up ahead.

Soon they approached a junction where one track sloped down to the left toward a treed area, and the other continued ahead. The old man indicated to stop and let him out.

Lori helped him down from the cabin before opening the canopy. She gave him a large handful of almonds to eat on the way.

He looked at the almonds, then looked up at her. His lined old face lit up with genuine gratitude. He nodded and smiled at her generosity as she helped heave the heavy bundle onto his back, before he headed off down the narrow track to the left, while they continued ahead.

Not long after, they approached another bend where they heard deep rumbling, then tremors and reverberations come up through the truck. An eerie foreboding passed over Khelvan like a chilling breeze. Echoing laughter resounded through the mountains and hair stood up on the back of his neck. He gripped the door handle with one hand and the dashboard with the other as they came around the next bend, not knowing what to expect. Dust swirled in the air. Lori hit the brakes hard, narrowly missing an avalanche of rocks and dirt that now covered the road. They could go no further.

A large cleft had opened up in the mountainside and muddy purple-coloured fog streamed out from the cavity, mixing with the swirling dust above them. In the turmoil the sinister laughter trailed off. The sight was strange and unnatural but Lori seemed not to hear what Khelvan heard, or notice the opening in the mountainside. Khelvan's eyes darted around expecting to see more danger.

"Oh shite," said Lori, "that's all we need."

Unable to turn the vehicle on the narrow road, she backed slowly away.

A shower of small rocks and stones started to buffet the truck from above. Khelvan had a strong sense something more serious was about to happen. "Drive faster. Hurry!" he shouted. Without questioning, Lori accelerated in reverse, employing all her competence to control the vehicle and not veer over the edge. Above them a large boulder came hurtling through the air. Just inches from the bull-bar it hit the track with a heavy thud, bounced up, and continued toward the edge then into the ravine. The vehicle shuddered from the impact. They glanced at each other in relief, both knowing if they had not sped up, the rock could have killed them.

Feeling vulnerable Khelvan said nothing, but knew the menacing sorcerer was behind the threat. He exhaled deeply and sat back in the seat. He was tired of these treacherous mountains and the tension; he wanted to be away from here. However he firmed his resolve and focused on Lamaar's wise words and the purpose of this mission; he would not be intimidated and bullied by this sorcerer and his spells.

They continued in reverse all the way to where they had dropped off the old man. They would have to take the low road and look for another way through the mountains. A short distance along the low road, they found the old man who would have heard and felt the tremors.

Lori wound down the window to talk to him. "Where does road come out? Welpecca? Welpecca city?" she repeated using simple sign language, hoping he would recognise the name of the nearby city.

The old man indicated with wiggling hand motions accompanied by sounds, that the track went down and around the mountain and then went up, reaching a rugged area before coming out on the other side.

"Will I get across with this truck," she gestured pointing to the vehicle as she spoke. He replied with a side-to-side head movement that meant maybe. With two hands he described a narrow track, adding the side-to-side head movements again. After a few moments of deliberation, he pointed to himself then to the passenger seat, to communicate he will travel with them and show the way.

Lori looked across at Khelvan who seemed resigned to the situation. She sighed and put the old man's firewood in the back again, cursing she had not gone via the simpler desert route.

The old man climbed up and motioned to go to where the track became narrow and overgrown in places.

They pressed on slowly down into a valley, the heavy truck pushing through overhanging branches and hostile terrain. Surroundings became more lush and green, before they reached a clear tract where Lori thought she could turn the vehicle, but the old man insisted they go on. Lori was becoming apprehensive; the sky started to turn light orange, and with dusk almost upon them they were now well off the main track and heading further into unknown territory.

Suddenly, the old man became animated, and indicated for Lori to stop and let him out. He jumped out and walked on ahead, pointing and beckoning them while he held back branches for the vehicle to pass. In the middle of a clearing they found an abandoned stone ruin. The old man signalled for them to drive the vehicle right inside the ruins, and to park in an open area where the roof had long since gone. Without the noise of the engine, the tranquility of the area was immediately tangible. A goat bleated nearby. In the twilight they saw a small herd inside a stone wall enclosure.

The old man collected his sticks from the back of the truck and beckoned them to toward the corner of the derelict building. Khelvan smelt smoke from a cooking fire and followed the old man to a room at the back which had been rebuilt from the original stones.

Standing in the doorway was an old lady smiling shyly at the visitors, and waiting to help the old man take off his load.

As darkness blanketed the mountains the old couple welcomed the visitors inside, offering what little food they had for dinner.

Lori brought in the left over flatbread, almonds and some of the sweet pastries to add to the table. It was a small pleasure to see the delight in the eyes of the old couple who were used to eating frugally. Such food was a treat in this remote area.

After dinner, the old couple offered the tired visitors a bed in their hut, but Lori insisted on sleeping in the truck. Khelvan was happy to sleep under the stars, but lay awake thinking about the strange occurrences and the risky drive.

Eventually he closed his eyes and drifted off, but was abruptly woken when tightness gripped his chest and started to squeeze him like the giant anaconda in the desert. In his mind the sinister snigger of the sorcerer laughed at his fear. It sent his heart racing, but this time he made a concerted effort and managed to shrug it off.

Everyone woke early the next morning. When the old man appeared, Lori 'discussed' the route with him again, with driving motions and pointing ahead, saying the name Welpecca. He seemed to understand, nodding that the track would get them there, but it would be a perilous journey.

"Let's do it. We'll take our chances," she said to Khelvan, who nodded in response. Having no choice but to go along with events as they unfolded, he was quietly apprehensive. The possibility of more hazardous, steep ravines and sheer cliffs was ominous.

Before departing, Lori asked Khelvan to give the old couple a box of dates and a jar of olives, while she rustled around to get a bag of almonds and a jar of preserved lemons to give as well. "I always buy more than I need so I can repay the hospitalities of the good people I meet," she said. "The desert people share everything with strangers, and many of them live a hard life, so I don't like going empty handed into their houses. Besides, it is a pleasure to give them back something."

The old couple graciously received the food, happy to receive such rare gifts. Tears rolled down the cheeks of the old woman as they waved the visitors goodbye from the midst of a trail of dust.

Khelvan admired Lori since he first met her. She was indomitable, tough and independent and did not care how others thought she should live.

He realised his own outlook on life was not the only perspective available, and promised himself if he finished his assigned task and came back alive, he would live more freely. She was refreshing company, though too impulsive when it came to taking short cuts. There was a good and decent person behind the tough exterior, and he wondered what she was really doing out here.

The continuing journey over rough and treacherous terrain was fraught with difficulties, and at times Khelvan gripped on with white knuckles, ready to throw the door open and jump if he had to. The risk was harrowing and unrelenting, certainly no easier than the day before. Lori proved to be an experienced driver. She coped relatively well with the conditions as she shifted the gears up and down, smoked cigarettes and cursed often, vowing never to come over these mountains again.

The sun rose higher overhead and the heat of the day set in. They passed no other vehicles or people and eventually started to catch glimpses of the open desert to the east. They descended to a more open expanse where sparse trees and scrub grew and the land began to level out.

Upon reaching a junction, they turned and continued until they were finally down from the mountain range. Once more, they headed across the desert, greatly relieved and more relaxed as they snacked on dates and almonds.

Lori liked Khelvan; he was contained, focused, and did not waste words and energy on superficial or trivial talk. During the difficult drive, she was glad not to be out there alone.

"Easy eh?" she said with a sardonic smile on her face.

"Yeah right," he replied dryly.

"Where are you heading anyway? Why are you going to Welpecca?" she asked, tired of driving along in silence and daring to probe into his private territory.

Khelvan hesitated and weighed his words before answering. "I'm going north to visit a sorcerer," he replied. "But first I have to find someone in Welpecca who will travel with me."

A few moments passed where nothing was said.

Shaking her head, "That's about as dumb as dog shit," Lori said before relighting a cigarette that had gone out.

"It does sound kinda dumb," he said, looking away through the passenger window to avoid any further questions, but unable to keep a smile from his face at her casual remark.

In the early afternoon they stopped at a small town to refuel and stretch their legs. With a row of shops in the main street, the town seemed decadent after the previous settlement towns they had driven through. After refuelling, they crossed the road where Lori bought tea from a nearby vendor.

From the corner of his eye, Khelvan noticed two men acting suspiciously. Sitting at a table under a canvas canopy, the men kept stealing glances of the travellers. Something about the men put Khelvan on alert, and Lori had noticed them too, though she showed no concern.

"Perhaps the men were unused to seeing foreigners out here, especially a woman like Lori," thought Khelvan. Nevertheless, he kept a watchful eye on them while

drinking the tea.

One of the men, a thin, tall man wearing a green turban, leapt on a motor bike and tore off up the road.

Feeling the men may be a threat Lori jumped into the truck, locked the door and wound up the window leaving only an inch for air. She urged Khelvan to do the same.

Eager to be away, they headed east out of the town and across the desert plains. Lori kept a sharp eye on the rear vision mirrors to ensure no one followed.

Once out of town, Khelvan noticed fresh tracks made by the tyres of two motorbikes.

Bumping along the deeply corrugated road, Lori had to slow to a crawl so as not to break an axle. Not far away were the remains of a shabby building with render falling off the walls and no roof. Khelvan was instinctively on guard as they approached the building.

Without warning, four men sprung out from behind the building and quickly surrounded the vehicle. Dressed in typical desert garb with turbans and scarves, their faces were almost hidden. But Khelvan recognised the two men he saw earlier in town. They looked like a dangerous gang of thugs; it was obvious they hung out in town for unwary travellers to ambush.

Aiming a rifle straight at Lori, one of the men peered through slitted eyes while the other three carried swords of different lengths and types. Khelvan felt the cunning in their merciless eyes, which revealed the dark shadow of those who had killed before.

"Get out! Get out!" the men shouted as they tried to

open the doors.

"Don't move," Khelvan said to Lori, opening his door then raising his hands to face the men armed with swords.

With all attention on Khelvan, Lori slowly reached down to grasp the sawn off shotgun under the seat, bringing the gun up onto her lap with the barrel facing the door.

"Open! Open!" yelled the leader who now shook the gun in Khelvan's face. Khelvan jumped down and pointed to the back of the truck.

"Wait, I'll open it. You can have everything," he said.

The leader walked to the back of the truck as two of the men menaced Khelvan, their blades against his shirt, surrounding him as he walked around to open the canopy. As Khelvan started to untie the straps, pain seared through his back as the force of a rifle butt pushed him forward against the truck. Using the momentum of the lunge forward, Khelvan swiftly stepped to the side and spun away from the sword wielders. He now faced the same direction as the gunman.

With the back of a clenched fist Khelvan struck the gunman in the face, stunning him. He grabbed the gun, stepped in behind the man and sent him to the ground with a swift boot to the back of the knees. With the weapon pointed directly at the back of the astonished gang leader's head Khelvan commanded: "Put the weapons on the ground". The men were no match for Khelvan. His skill, alacrity and speed from years spent practising the martial arts, undermined their position.

Seeing their leader was now defenceless, the men reluctantly obeyed, placing the swords on the ground, then stepping back.

"Now lie over there, face down," ordered Khelvan, pointing to a place on the hot sand next to two small trees. He shoved the leader over to join the others, before checking the gun barrel to see the two bullets loaded inside.

From the front seat, Lori watched through the rear view mirror. Khelvan's rapid response and skills impressed her. She unlocked the door and stepped down, sawn off shotgun in hand, but warily kept her distance.

Khelvan's eyebrows went up in surprise when he saw the weapon in her hands. "Any rope?" he asked her.

Grabbing a coil of rope from behind the driver's seat, she tossed it to him, then leaned casually against the truck with the sawn off directed straight at the nervous men.

Khelvan tied the thieves up, but far enough apart that they couldn't help each other escape.

Eyes fixated on the men, Lori rolled a cigarette. She blew the aromatic smoke toward them, knowing, in their nervousness, any smokers among them would want a cigarette by now.

After securing the thieves, Khelvan threw the swords into the back of the truck and picked up the rifle. Behind the building, they discovered two motor bikes. Khelvan emptied the weapon of its bullets and smashed it against a wall before burying it in sand. He kicked over the bikes, unscrewed the petrol caps and drained the fuel. He then picked up a heavy block from the derelict building and smashed it down hard onto the bikes several times. He ensured the bikes were so damaged they would never be ridden again to ambush travellers. This kind of transport was not easily replaced out here and few could afford them. After burying the bullets he said to Lori, "They are amateurs. Dangerous amateurs".

Back at the truck, Lori checked the ties, while the worried men sweated in the open heat of the desert. Lori walked over and kicked the leader in the crotch, then picked up a couple of handfuls of sand and threw it in their faces. They all shook their heads, blinked gritty eyes and tried to spit the sand from their mouths. Their eyes started to clear, so she picked up more sand and repeated the action, making them uncomfortable. "This is your punishment, and it's not much of a punishment," she said. "You'll have plenty of time as you lie here, to think about the thieves you've become. Is this what you teach your sons, that they can just take, take, take from innocent, hard working people without accountability! Life does not work like that boys. You *work* to survive," she said, and kicked another of the thieves hard, causing him to yelp in pain. "You are weak, lazy men who carry weapons to bully your way through life, because you are too lazy to put in real effort," she berated and kicked another man as she walked around them lecturing. She was not finished yet. "You don't take from people who work hard to survive. Do you hear me?" and kicked the leader so hard he howled in misery, nodding desperately in agreement. She kicked another as the reprimand went on. "Thievery is the weak man's way out," she said loudly, kicking the last of them as she spoke. Not happy at his half-hearted response, she kicked him again till he acquiesced in sufferance. "Any questions?" she said in a sardonic tone before returning to the truck.

Meanwhile, Khelvan leaned against the truck, observing as Lori dealt out the penalties, though they both knew it would do no good once the men were free of the ropes.

Once again they headed off, and Khelvan wore a wry smile on his face from the memory of the way Lori lectured and kicked the men.

Soon after, they approached a family with two young boys, walking with their goats toward the town. Khelvan asked Lori to stop the family; he wound down the window to speak to them. Using gestures and very basic language, he let them know four thieves were tied up ahead. He urged the family not to untie the men as they were desperate and dangerous, then asked if they could alert the authorities in the town. The father understood and agreed, and thanked Khelvan for his warning.

Lori looked across at Khelvan with renewed respect and admiration. She was impressed how he had swiftly saved the situation and protected her as well. Not for the first time, she was glad of his company and was grateful to have him on board. She decided there was a lot more to him than he had let on.

They accelerated away with only four or five hours to

go before reaching their destination, and Lori decided to tell Khelvan more about herself.

"This is the last trip I'll be makin' out here," she said. "I've done it a couple of times, but it ain't worth the risk anymore."

"Why do you do it?" Khelvan asked.

"For the money," she replied simply. "I don't usually tell anyone this, but I'm pretty sure I can trust you. I pick up diamonds for a buyer from Kashmera who pays highly for them. I only do one trip a year and I can live off the money for a long time, but it has become too risky. I am lucky you were on board this time, but it'll be the last trip. She added dryly, "No use bein' the richest person in the grave yard".

Late in the afternoon they drove into the large coastal city of Welpecca. Crowds and colours again became a vivid contrast for both of the travellers after being so long in the desert. People rode camels and horses, but also cars and other vehicles drove on the streets, sometimes honking their horns to move others out of the way. Near the central market place, Lori pulled over and parked the truck. The noisy engine shuddered to a halt and she exhaled in relief after the long ordeal.

From here she would go further north to the city of Kashmera, and Khelvan would stay and look for a man named Sidewinder who was somewhere in this bustling city. However, the time had come for them to part ways after an eventful couple of days together. Lori opened the side canopy, and put together a big bag of dates and almonds for Khelvan as a parting gift for his travels. "I'm sorry to see you go Khelvan. It's been good travellin' with ya," she said, handing him the bag.

"Oh, thank you," he said for the heartfelt gift. He looked at her in earnest, "and thanks for the ride Lori. It's been an adventure that's for sure," he added with some irony. "Thanks for everything. Take care," he repeated, feeling a bit awkward as to what else to say.

"Maybe we'll meet again somewhere," she said hopefully, then impulsively stepped forward and gave him a quick hug. Feeling a bit emotional at the parting – she had become used to the stoic man – she did not really want to travel on alone. She turned to refasten the canopy, and by the time she turned around Khelvan was gone. Lori climbed back into the front seat, pulled out into the street and disappeared along the busy road. She would miss his silent company.

Chapter 13.
Finding Sidewinder

"Lie down with dogs
You get up with fleas."

In the city of Welpecca, Khelvan looked around for somewhere to stay. He would need a base to prepare and plan his trip before going north, and somewhere to come back to.

He heard about an old, abandoned beach house in fair condition, though it was remotely situated out of town to the south. He decided to go and talk to the owners.

A friendly, elderly couple invited him into their small house, serving him tea as they chatted about the vacant house by the sea, where they had lived most of their lives. Over a year ago they moved into town because of their age and to be nearer to relatives. Khelvan told them he did not mind the isolation and needed a base, as he worked seasonally and would be coming and going. The white haired couple liked his solid character and good manners, and asked about his carpentry skills. The house was deteriorating and needed repairs. They told Khelvan they would be glad for someone to live there as caretaker if he would repair and maintain the house as payment.

They gave him directions and the key, requesting he call by from time-to-time.

Leaning forward Khelvan shook the old man's hand in agreement and promised he would keep them informed.

A few days later, Khelvan was out on the streets again, wandering around asking questions of the locals. He told them he was searching for his brother who was known to be in the old quarter. They observed his upright demeanour and warned him not to go to such a lawless part of town alone. Dangerous gangs roamed about and some did not return from there. Eventually he found the building he was looking for.

Khelvan opened the door slowly and stood for a moment in the haze. Late afternoon sunlight streamed in on an angle, highlighting tendrils of smoke that hung on the air and barely moved. The room was stuffy, and the sickly, acrid smell of the delirium drug 'ambrosia' was almost overwhelming.

As Khelvan's eyes adjusted, he perceived at least seven people sitting slouched against the walls. He stepped tentatively inside not knowing what he might encounter.

A warning signal resounded inside him. At once his

right hand went to the blade concealed under his jacket, and his knees bent imperceptibly in readiness to defend himself if needed. Hair stood up on the back of his neck, yet there was no visible threat. He could sense, rather than see, that the man he sought was right here in this room – the man who would travel with him on the journey north.

The eyes of the addicts were half-shut or closed, and they seemed unaware of Khelvan's presence as he quietly moved around the room. Khelvan noticed a few lines scrawled across one wall which read: "HOPE = Hold On while Pain Ends".

"Hmph, yeah right," he thought dryly. He focused and listened to intuition that years of training had taught him, and came to stand before one man. The man sat slouched in the shadows like the others, but something drew Khelvan to him.

Slowly, as though the man realised someone was there, he lifted his dark, matted head and looked up at Khelvan through narrowed eyes. The dark, almond shaped eyes seemed not to focus, while black ooze dribbled from one corner of his mouth down to the already stained shirt. Unwashed and unshaven he looked to be about thirty-five, but was probably ten years younger. His once handsome features appeared prematurely aged by the addiction and squalor that had become his life.

The sight disgusted Khelvan who smelt the odour coming off him like that of a wild animal living trapped in a cage. He knew instinctively this was the one he searched for, and pursed his lips while considering how this wretch could have once been a skilled fighter. "*Hmm*" he thought, "*Surely Lamaar is mistaken*".

But the words of his teacher came to mind: "*Remember Khelvan, when you find him judge him not, as under the surface he suffers greatly. You must go on this mission together*".

"*Yeah right, we're all suffering greatly,*" Khelvan thought cynically. He stood a moment longer, as a sense of despair at the task ahead weighed heavily on him. The decrepit sight of someone who was once one of the best added to the weight he carried.

Without warning a foot kicked out toward Khelvan, as if the man was finally startled by his presence and sensed alarm. More likely, it was an involuntary and dulled response from the dishevelled body, though the inherent instinct to fight was still in him.

Khelvan responded with lightning speed and struck the wasted body in the solar plexus, stunning him easily as the emaciated body had long since lost its former strength. Khelvan knew nothing could be gained right now; the man was sprawled on the floor in no condition to reason with. With disdain, he grabbed a handful of the man's grimy shirt, roughly jerked him to his feet and pulled him out through the door away from the den of addicts. He dragged the half-dazed body down dusty steps and out into the street, not caring about the questioning looks from the few townspeople who passed.

Outside the building, Khelvan became aware of a group of disreputable looking characters who started to circle the pair. The group had seen Khelvan enter the building, and had milled around, waiting to rob the stranger who entered their territory alone and with no protection.

It was a dangerous area of town where winding back streets were full of hovels for addicts, street workers and the homeless. Street laws applied here and attacks without mercy were common.

Khelvan dragged the drugged and wasted man behind him, keeping to a high brick wall on his left. In his mind's eye he knew at least five of the street gang were closing in behind him. He tightened his grip on Navek, and then abruptly stepped out to the right. At the same time, he swung Navek's limp body around in a full circle, using it to hit four of the gang members in the face. While he still had the element of surprise to his advantage, he let Navek's body drop to the ground, and in the same motion his sharpened blade was at the throat of the one perceived to be the leader. Khelvan held his ground, staring into the man's eyes with confidence and certainty, saying nothing. The gang leader glared back in anger and shock at the stranger's swift action.

No words were needed. The gang leader knew this was a fighting man who, though outnumbered, could kill him in an instant. A long moment passed. Finally the leader stepped back a pace to demonstrate his yielding and conceded his loss.

"It'll wait till another time," he thought bitterly. Some of the gang looked at each other with rebellious glances,

not used to seeing their leader back down. "Back off," he scowled at them. "Let him pass."

Another uncertain moment went by, till the gang retreated a few steps. Khelvan's eyes never left the gang leader's eyes, though in his peripheral vision he was aware of the others. Unflinchingly, he held the blade at the leader's throat, until the gang leader stepped back another pace. Khelvan picked up the body of Navek with one hand and dragged him out of the alley, still holding his blade up ready for an attack as he continued to watch the group.

Once out in the traffic, he opened the door of a passing taxi and threw Navek's dazed and smelling body into the back seat, then slid in himself. The driver swore vehemently and started to refuse the ride. But once he saw the glistening blade, he drove off into the traffic, cursing at his bad luck.

Back at the remote beach house, Khelvan pushed Navek down the steps into an empty basement. In one dimly lit corner was a mattress with sheets and a blanket, and in another corner was a bucket with a lid in an otherwise unfurnished room. Khelvan locked the door from the outside and went to shower before finally lying down to sleep. The unfamiliar sound of waves pounding the beach woke him well after dark.

The next morning, Khelvan unlocked the door and quickly placed some fruit and water inside, hardly looking at the groaning body of his captive. For the next three days he continued to put water inside the room, cursing as he emptied and replaced the putrid smelling bucket. On the fourth day he opened the door, and Navek sat hunched over in the corner, shaking and sweating. Some of the water was gone, but the food had hardly been touched. The smell in the basement was repulsive. Khelvan grabbed the resisting man and dragged him up the steps, pulled off his clothes and threw him into the bath tub. He poured buckets of cold water over the shaking and foul smelling body for about ten minutes.

Not for the first time did he doubt Lamaar's directive to help this wreck of a man who would travel with him to the north. Khelvan struggled in himself to follow the direction to "judge him not". From past experience however, Khelvan had learnt Lamaar's instructions could be trusted, and even if he did not understand at the time, in retrospect his teacher would usually be right. Looking at this shadow of a man in the shower though, he wondered again whether the teacher had got it wrong this time. Khelvan dried him roughly and then took him back downstairs naked. Back in the basement, he gave Navek water to drink, though most of it spilled down his chest. Khelvan shoved him onto the mattress, covered him with a blanket, then locked the door and went outside to burn the putrid clothes.

For another two days Khelvan continued to put food and water inside the door. Incoherent babbling and sometimes yelling and banging sounded up through the house from the basement. Khelvan went fishing to be away from him. On the sixth day, Khelvan again went to enter the room, but before he unlocked the door an inner voice warned him to be on guard.

He pushed open the heavy door then stepped back a pace and remained standing outside. The offensive odour wafted out through the doorway, but Navek was nowhere to be seen. Khelvan knew he was waiting behind the door to attack. Deftly stepping through the doorway, Khelvan grabbed and immobilised the unsuspecting Navek, repulsed by the rancid odour still coming from the addicts' skin and hair. He dragged the naked and protesting body from the house and down to the sea, where he threw Navek into the cold water again and again and again, till Navek fell in an emaciated shivering heap on the sand.

Khelvan noted the calloused hands of one who had trained long in the fighting arts, but the body which had been strong and muscular was now like a hollow shell. He threw Navek into the cold sea once more to rinse off the sand, then took him back to the basement and tossed him some old clothes, telling him to dress.

Khelvan gathered up the sheets and replaced them with fresh ones, aware his captive watched through angry slitted eyes the whole time. The door was locked again, but later he placed fish and vegetable broth inside. A faint smile crossed Khelvan's face when he heard Navek struggle across the room to get the food.

Two more days passed. Khelvan unlocked the door and pushed a tray inside with herb tea and fish broth, and then stood back outside the door with his arms folded. Navek sat on the edge of the bed still looking frail, but with his hair pushed back and more alert. His head came up to see his captor standing in the doorway.

Navek noted the strong and well trained physique that stood before him and spoke his first words with difficulty. "Who are you?" he asked in a rasping voice.

Khelvan remained silent and watched him.

"What do you want?" Navek continued.

Khelvan took a step forward, squatted down and leaned casually against the door frame. "My name is Khelvan. You don't know me, but I have been sent to find you by my mentor who is a martial arts teacher. Years ago he visited your village and was a friend of your father Hatchiman."

At hearing these words, Navek's head shot up. He rubbed his face and tried to focus, as he had not heard the name of his father for many years. He had a vague recollection of the visiting martial artist coming to his village.

Khelvan continued, "I know only a few things about your past. I know you are named Navek, but they called you Sidewinder because of your fighting style, and that you were born to the legendary Videha clan in the northern Alps". Navek turned away, and then shrugged as though it was trifling and incidental information.

Khelvan knew he had the man's attention and continued on. "You are the son of Hatchiman who was a wise leader, one of their best I'm told."

Several tense moments went by in silence while Navek struggled to take in the words he had avoided facing for years.

Khelvan continued, "I know you remember your roots and the warrior you once were. It is all still in you, just forgotten and covered over".

Navek's eyes widened slightly before he looked away anxiously then shook his head and squeezed his eyes shut.

"My teacher Lamaar has sent me to find you, to join me on an important journey to the north. It would be a dangerous mission which involves seeking out a lawless sorcerer and destroying his powers. This sorcerer has grown out of control and causes much destruction." Khelvan waited for the words to sink in, and then added matter-of-factly: "It is a mission from which there is no guarantee of returning".

This was not the first time Navek had heard about this sorcerer, and distant memories of Sharian's words on the mountain years ago came back to him. He shook his head again, winced and clasped his arms about himself, rocking back and forward. Navek did not want to remember these thoughts that haunted him, and glanced furtively to the open door beside Khelvan with desperate thoughts of fleeing.

"You've wasted your time finding me. I know nothing of all that now … forgotten … lost," Navek stammered. "I've deadened myself to life for a long time now … far away … not what you think I am," he said shakily.

More moments passed, then Khelvan said quietly, "This sorcerer I seek is the same one who ambushed and killed your entire clan with his dark treachery. Many other clans in the north have been killed too".

Navek's pained eyes came up and looked searchingly at Khelvan. Navek had heard once before about how his people were killed, and he had been running from the shame and guilt of being the only survivor ever since."Maybe it was no accident you escaped death that day, and were forced to leave all that you knew," said Khelvan.

Navek started to rock back and forward again with head bent down, but Khelvan knew he had listened.

Navek continued to rock back and forward, "Can't help you … body's ruined …" he stammered defensively. "Don't have old skills," he mumbled.

"Your mind will become clearer, then we will talk more," said Khelvan, as he stood effortlessly from his squatting position. "You will come clear in time, but only if you *want* to. It's your choice. You can go back to Welpecca and become that weak corpse of a man I found, or choose to do something useful with your life. Something connected to your family roots that could right the wrong. It's your choice."

Navek's eyes came up to meet Khelvan's and, for the first time, Khelvan detected a faint glimmer or spark in them.

"*The first sign,*" he thought. "Here drink the tea and eat some food, it will help you heal." Then Khelvan left him sitting on the bed, closed the door quietly and locked it.

The next morning Khelvan unlocked the door and left it wide open. A fragile and weak man tentatively came up the steps and sat down in the living room, squinting against the glare from the sun and the sea view. Finally he had to turn away from the window, till his eyes adjusted after being in the dim basement so long. Several minutes passed then Navek asked in a shaky voice. "What is it you want from me?"

Khelvan came over and sat opposite, handing him a mug of coffee.

"In a few months I am going north to seek out this sorcerer, as he must be stopped. He will not cease with his destruction till the world lives in his dark shadow. He is named Jackyl Nazarak and he was born in the north, not far from your birthplace. I was told he is as lawless as they come and his powers are far reaching. He crosses boundaries between the worlds which he has no place crossing, and has learned to conjure his own brand of evil which is not designed for the good of the people. He now only knows killing and destruction, that's why he has to be stopped before the old ways are obscured and forgotten.

"Here's my offer," continued Khelvan. "If you live and train here with me for a few months, your skills and fitness will return to a degree. If not, you can go back to that black hole in Welpecca, where you will surely die an unworthy death, unnoticed and unfulfilled."

At hearing this Navek grimaced at the reminder of how he had squandered away his life and his money, and forgotten his roots at the ill-reputed old quarter of town. Words of his father he had not thought of for years came to mind, "Lie down with dogs and you get up with fleas".

Khelvan went on, "My teacher, Lamaar placed this

load on my shoulders and I have chosen to accept. Unless this sorcerer is stopped the world as we know it will be demolished and replaced by a shadow-life of ignorance and greed. The destruction is already afoot and comes this way, and as long as he weaves his spells over humanity there will be no peace for anyone".

Navek was stunned. "You still have a teacher?" he stammered in astonishment. "Still practise the fighting arts? No one does that any more. There's no justice and integrity and ... none left ... none left now," he mumbled, "goodness gone ... all killed ... killed".

At these last words, Navek started to weep and his body shook, before he managed to pull himself together, sipping at the coffee to help calm himself.

All the while Khelvan sat opposite and watched Navek with a steady gaze, but his attention was focused inside where all mysteries unravelled, where he had a direct audience with Life itself. From inside, words sprung to mind and he spoke them out loud, "Your mind is a wasteland now, because the drug you are addicted to serves to anaesthetise you to life itself. It is a shadow world, an escape which promises freedom but never takes you there. It never takes you back to the path your soul thirsts after. It wastes your body, your time and your life. If you want to go back to your chosen birthright, choose now to do so, for you will never have the choice again, I guarantee it. I know you are a better man than this, and your true potential awaits you. It will take much time and effort to get you in condition and the path will not be easy, but I am not your enemy here".

Words from Navek's past drifted across his mind, "If you are facing the shadow, you have your back to the sun. Turn around and face the sun". Regretful lines appeared across his forehead when he remembered the old healer who had said those words to him, and helped him years earlier on the mountainside. Shamefully, he had been running toward the shadow ever since.

"Choose the light," said a faint voice in him.

Navek looked up at Khelvan and saw the calm and self-contained bearing of a man with purpose. It was confronting. He once had that self-assuredness and had drifted far from it. He grieved his lost potential. "I don't know if I can get back," he said shakily.

On a kinder note Khelvan added, "It was not your fault they all died and you lived. Maybe it was designed that way long before you were even born. No need to cover the guilt anymore".

Tears ran down Navek's face and he asked roughly, "Why are you doing this? I've squandered my existence. Why bother with such a wretch as me?"

Khelvan answered, "First of all, I have always walked alone and initially didn't want any part of this crazy mission. It is *only* at the request of my teacher Lamaar that I am here and offering you this choice. He lives alone now, enclosed within a dense forest where no one can reach him easily, but he is deeply connected to life, and has the vision to see far without leaving his home. He told me of a dark age which spreads from the north to the south, and he was deadly serious when he asked me to help remove the source of this darkness, this sorcerer Jackyl Nazarak.

"At first I didn't realise the seriousness of his request, and certainly didn't want the job, but I have since seen ominous signs of this forecast for myself. I have decided to put my own goals aside and am prepared to be a servant for the higher good. Also, Lamaar trained me and was my mentor as a young boy, so I owe him that much," he said with finality.

Navek was at least listening to Khelvan, as he reached out for the coffee with shaking hands while Khelvan continued. "Look at it how you will, but because of this one rogue sorcerer, all of us will be doomed. Mankind will become like an unhinged wheel coming off a cart; it rolls helter skelter downhill before it crashes and is destroyed. Think about it and choose," said Khelvan. "The choice is yours. Don't give an answer now but in the morning. Just know that the matter is most urgent." In a quieter tone he added, "Besides I will need your help doing this".

Khelvan got up to cook breakfast, while Navek stood unsteadily and went outside onto the veranda. He looked around at the ocean view with squinted eyes, and then sat down to muse over the information. Soon after a bird squawked loudly as it flew overhead, and Khelvan tilted his head to listen to the call. Unbeknown to him at the time, it heralded an important occasion. A life changing decision had been made.

Chapter 14.
Training Begins

Navek was free to come and go. Khelvan kept an eye on him and purposefully did not tell Navek their location in relation to Welpecca, lest he chose to go back to the ambrosia dens. Many times Navek was restless with tremors running through his wasted and sweating body. Through days and nights that followed he ate little and slept fitfully, often getting up and going to the sea where a cool breeze blew off the water. Watching through the front window, Kelvhan could perceive the turbulence in Navek's mind. With the effects of the long addiction still evident, Khelvan wondered if it was too late to be requiring such a task from him.

Navek waded out into the cold water and kept walking till his shoulders disappeared under the water and then nothing could be seen of him.

Startled, Khelvan ran barefoot toward the door, his usual calm manner now gone. He needed this unlikely wreck of a man to repair his damaged mind and body, and join him on a difficult journey he would not have otherwise chosen for himself. The urgency had become more acute when Navek's black hair disappeared beneath the water, as if the sea swallowed him up left no trace. "*What was Navek doing?*"

Khelvan was apprehensive and raced toward the water; Navek had already been under far too long. Khelvan was about to dive in to find him, when a dark shape moved steadily toward the shore.

Khelvan dived in and swam underwater, steadying himself to calm his heartbeat, so as not to emit the vibration of fear in case the dark shape had been a shark. Memories of his boyhood training came back when he would swim in the forest creeks and waterfalls with Lamaar. He had hidden and waited underwater for minutes on end, conserving energy and oxygen. Lamaar would find him, then they would engage in one of the many underwater training battles that often forced Khelvan to the surface gasping for air.

Visibility underwater was not good. There was no sign of Navek, till the dark shape came into view and Khelvan was astonished to see Navek swimming with the movements of a dolphin toward the shore.

Navek swam frantically; his eyes bulged, desperate to take in the oxygen his body craved. In his urgency to reach the sand, he was unaware of Khelvan.

Khelvan let himself rise to the surface, swimming till his feet touched the seabed. He pushed back his dripping hair, and then slipped unseen behind rocks and back to the house, preferring not to be seen.

At the same time, Navek appeared at the water's edge, heaving in great lungfulls of air before flopping on the sand like a piece of seaweed. He rolled onto his back and lay in the sun with sand sticking to his wet skin.

Khelvan changed into dry clothes and came out to sit on the veranda. He did not look at Navek, but faced the trees to the north and focused on his meditation. He sent a silent message to Lamaar, *"Teacher, he trains"*.

From that day forth, Navek rose early and swam slow laps in the cold water, staying close to the shoreline. He tired easily and collapsed on the sand exhausted, then later washed off the sand and went to the house to rest. He had not eaten well since Khelvan brought him to the secluded beach house. His body ached, and felt weak and heavy, but before the end of the day he dragged himself outside and swam again.

One morning Navek plodded back toward the house after a swim, as Khelvan walked straight toward him carrying two wooden practice sticks. When Navek looked up, Khelvan released one of the sticks in an underarm gesture to send the stick flying at him. The action was abrupt, Navek was slow to react, but a past instinct sent his hand up to deflect the stick, stopping it from hitting him hard in the face.

Before the stick landed on the sand, Khelvan moved to

assume a fighting stance – stick held out in front like a sword – facing Navek, waiting for a response. A moment passed as Navek weighed and assessed the situation. He knew what was required, but doubted he would be able to measure up to the task. Slowly he straightened and, with a quick jerk of his head, flicked the wet hair back from his face. His eyes did not move from Khelvan as he stepped toward the fallen stick, and then rolled it toward himself with his toes. After another deft movement the stick was in the air and Navek caught it in front of him.

They bowed respectfully to each other, stepped back and circled slowly with knees bent in a fighting stance, sticks held out in front.

Khelvan moved in first to hit, but Navek parried the basic strike before darting back out of range. Khelvan moved swiftly forward again, and with little effort struck Navek's wrist then his knuckles, not with great force but hard enough to cause Navek pain and surprise. Khelvan moved in close, then out and away from Navek in spherical motions. Khelvan landed different strikes from various directions, and though Navek parried and managed to deflect a few of them, he felt like a beginner again. Navek stumbled often trying to defend himself against a relentless bombardment. Occasional yells of pain mixed with heavy breathing, and the clacking of wooden sticks striking against each other was heard up and down the isolated beach.

After the impromptu training, Khelvan said, "Let's run," then nodded toward the rocks at the far end of the beach. He knew Navek was exhausted but time was pressing to begin the journey north, so without waiting for an answer Khelvan put the sticks on the veranda and started running.

Navek ran along behind with no chance of catching up. Halfway to the rocks, he stopped and bent over with hands on knees, gasping in big heaves of air as he tried to get enough oxygen into his lungs.

Khelvan passed him on his way back and shouted at Navek: "Come on. Let's go," to get him moving again.

Navek stumbled off again, but struggled all the way. When Navek reached the rocks he stopped again, gasping for air. He looked down at his hands, swollen from the strikes. Callouses were still built up across his knuckles and palms even after years of not training. They served to remind him of the daily fighting and weapons training he once excelled at and thrived on.

He would have bruises on his body later, but it was not the physical pain that bothered him. He had endured far more intense trainings in his younger days, and would have welcomed the challenge in the past. It was the feeling of weakness, nausea and the craving for the drug that promised to dull the pain, but really just dulled his determination. The loss of his own potential and the utter waste of life spent day after day with no purpose, these were the things that irked him most.

He exhaled and shook his head as though not wanting to face such thoughts. *"I must get strength back into this puny frame,"* he thought. *"I'm dragging my body like a weighted sack."* Slowly he ran back along the beach with head down looking at the sand in front of him, dragging himself along he stopped twice more to gulp in air.

He became overcome with nausea, and then anger rose in his chest. Anger at being pushed too far, anger at his own wretched and weak state, anger at Khelvan for finding him then expecting more than he had to give, anger at the futility of it all. He wished he could sneak back to Welpecca and disappear into the anonymity of the smoky shadows again, where nothing was required of him. He thought again about Khelvan forcing him here, and his eyes glazed over with a dark smouldering look.

Navek cursed the man again, and a determination to leave reared up. It was all too far beyond his current capabilities, too far removed from his world, and too great a mission to accomplish. Self-righteously he proclaimed to himself he would give up just as soon as he felt better. He had changed his mind. He would find a way to escape in the next couple of days.

Navek flopped down belligerently on the beach, laying half in the water till his breathing slowed and his angry mind quietened. Eventually he became aware of surrounding sounds; the breeze rustling the trees, birds calling in the distance, small waves rolling in to gently lap against him. The sun became too hot, so he moved up into the shade and stayed there for the rest of the day, dozing off and on, not feeling well since the morning workout.

After the heat of the day passed, he went in for an

afternoon swim to wash the sweat from his skin. Still nauseous and shaky, he rushed over to rocks where he threw up.

In the kitchen, Khelvan looked up from his cooking to see Navek heaving and retching, and shook his head at the sorry sight.

For two nights Navek did not come back to the house. Khelvan started to think he had gone back to the old quarter, back to his addiction. He checked the rocks where he last saw Navek, and was relieved to find footprints headed south along the sandy beach, not north toward town. He followed the prints a short distance then turned and headed back to the house. He did not want to find Navek and knew to give him this space.

The following day, Khelvan rose early to train on the beach as he often did. The morning was quite chilly but he wore only long black cotton pants. Muscles rippled under smooth tanned skin and his body looked almost godly in the morning light. The ends of his shoulder-length blonde hair were bleached almost silver from an outdoor life and swimming in the sea, but the hue of the sunrise gave it a gold tinge.

Khelvan became aware of someone watching him but did not turn around. He continued on with the various kick fighting techniques which had long since become a fluid arrangement of movements to him. Then he ran through several stick, blade and hidden weapon movements, practising both the blocking and attacking aspects of each. He performed acrobatic feats as though he were agile as a monkey in the forest trees.

Navek stood on the veranda, clean shaven, leaning casually against a post. He watched the poetic and artful movements in fascination, arms folded over his chest and goosebumps on his skin at seeing such skill. New tactics with moves that were fast and strong encouraged and inspired him, and a spark shone in the onlooker's eyes. Navek felt a certain loss of something he once had himself, but also felt a renewed respect for Khelvan whose skills were polished and precise. He saw aspects of techniques he had known himself and had practised since childhood; techniques his ancestors had passed down.

Khelvan continued with the spherical movements with knees slightly bent and weight concentrated in his hips to give an agile spring off his feet. He picked up two practice sticks and spun them both around at high speed over his head, then out to the sides, in front and with a quick jump, under him. The sticks became a blur like a wheel spinning. Unexpectedly he tossed a wooden stick from his left hand to Navek, who caught it in mid-air this time, with a fast reflex action.

In one step Khelvan advanced and would have attacked had Navek not defended himself.

The sticks made of white oak, sounded and clashed loudly against each other as Khelvan, who was not using his full capacity, parried with the other man, taking him to his limits and then further, testing his boundaries, sensing his unpolished capabilities. Several times he struck Navek with painful blows to the wrists and hands and other areas left too wide open by his defence. He left Navek dripping with sweat and out of breath trying to keep up. Eventually, they stopped and bowed respectively to each other in the old way of the warrior which they had both been taught.

"A long way to go yet," said Navek doubtfully as he bent over out of breath.

"Halfway there," Khelvan reassured. He turned away to return the practice weapons, before they both went down for a cold swim. Khelvan swam up and down the length of the beach numerous times, while Navek body-surfed, catching the waves and gliding down in a fluid motion that reminded him of his days with the islanders who had taught him to swim.

That night Navek's appetite started to come back and he felt the wonderful sensation of hunger again. Aromas of food he had not cared for or thought about for years now smelt good.

After a couple of days of more swimming and training he started to eat whole meals; strength and alacrity finally started to return to his body.

One morning Khelvan came in from swimming and was surprised to see Navek already showered and in the kitchen cooking breakfast. Navek had tied his long dark hair straight back and his once handsome features were starting to return. "I must say you're a different person now than when I first met you," Khelvan commented as he went off to change smiling to himself.

After breakfast, Kelvhan handed Navek a home-made

fishing rod with only a hook and sinker attached, and they both went off along the beach to find some sandworms and small crabs to use for bait.

Khelvan showed Navek how to thread the worm onto the hook, and they enjoyed the simple act of throwing a line in the water and waiting for a fish to bite. They sat apart from each other on rocks and looked out over the sea, each thinking his own thoughts.

"Life is simple. Life is good," Navek thought as a faint smile crossed his lips for the first time in years. He thought back fondly to his time with the islanders who had taught him how to swim and dive for crustaceans in the deeper pools, and also where to fish when the tide was running.

After they caught three good-sized fish, Navek left his line in the water and went over into the trees with the fishing knife, soon to return carrying a thin spear he made from a sapling. He asked Khelvan to watch his line and slipped into the deep water near the rocks where he knew the lobsters and crabs would feed. He returned with a huge lobster in each hand, then Khelvan wound in both lines and packed up the gear. They now had plenty of food and the late morning sun was becoming too hot overhead.

Khelvan praised Navek on his spear fishing skills and asked him where he had learnt them. He realised after hearing the answer there was much more to Navek than he had given him credit for, and the man had more worldly experience than he had himself. Khelvan felt a regard growing for Navek and even started to be grateful they would travel together on the journey north. *"Who would have ever thought it would be up to the two of us to restore the balance of the world!"* he thought with irony.

Several moon cycles passed, and the weather became cooler as they headed into the autumn months. Khelvan and Navek trained almost every day, sometimes twice a day for a few hours at a time, to build up their stamina and endurance levels. The training was exacting and thorough. Navek had recovered somewhat, and welcomed the discipline and the distraction from the pain of his memories. Running and swimming had become part of the regime, till eventually they could both swim underwater all the way to the rocks in one breath. Khelvan pushed Navek past his boundaries and limitations, and Navek would get up again and again from the sand after being beaten. His body became stronger and he put on condition, while his mind regained some confidence and certitude it once had. Certain techniques used by Navek were new to Khelvan and would catch him off guard. He would have to adapt quickly to defend himself or be brought undone.

At times raw, hostile anger surfaced in Navek when he had flashbacks and recollections of the death of his father and his clan. In frustration he would attack Khelvan with ferocity and release a frenzy of strikes with such hatred that if Khelvan had not been an expert fighter, Navek may have killed him right there on the beach. At such times Khelvan saw the blind fury and wrath in Navek. It ran through him with white hot intensity that Khelvan had never seen before, except perhaps in the sorcerer's face that night in the desert. After a session like this, when Navek had finally burnt the fury from his mind, they would still face each other and bow calmly and respectfully, as the old martial code required. Afterwards Navek would run along the beach for miles and sometimes be gone for hours. Occasionally he was not there for the next training session.

Once Navek did not come home all day or the following night, and Khelvan worried he had gone back to Welpecca town and may not come back at all. But the next morning, Navek was on the beach warming up at daybreak and ready to train. The wild anger and fury was gone from his eyes, replaced by a resignation and renewed determination to go on. Khelvan knew not to question him about where he had been, as it was part of the process Navek had to go through to face life again. At times Khelvan even felt humbled by the man's integrity of character.

For Navek however, many times he wanted to quit and walk away. He would ask himself what he was doing here training with some stranger on the beach, to go on a journey to do with darkness and light and wizards! He thought often of going back to Welpecca to escape into the drugs, but primarily he knew he was doing this for himself now, and the chance would not come again. If he had to face the indignity and humiliation of the raw anger that would surface, and most of all the shame, then he would face his demons. They might even be partially released by the new sense of purpose he was starting to feel.

Sometimes they would both go into town for supplies, running three miles along the beach to get there, and occasionally calling in to see the elderly landlords with gifts of fish and other seafood caught around the rocks.

The old couple missed living in their former beach home and were always very appreciative of these gifts. They usually insisted both men sit for a rest while the woman served them tea with biscuits and homemade jam. The four would chat for awhile and discuss such things as the best fishing spots, where the biggest crays could be caught and how they were going in the house. Khelvan enjoyed the brief visits and felt for the old couple. He sensed they did not get many visitors, and that perhaps the couple's own children did not often visit.

Days passed living simply at the seaside dwelling where they practised their routine trainings. Khelvan had seen no signs of the sorcerer since he had moved here but was planning to head north soon.

One day, Khelvan sent Navek into town with two large lobsters for the old couple, while he cleaned and sharpened some of his weapons, and later fished off the rocks for the evening meal. As he cleaned the fish, he looked up the beach for Navek's return with an uneasy feeling. Evening started to fall by the time a figure trudged along the sand in the distance toward him carrying bags of food and essentials. Khelvan saw a worried look on Navek's face and stood facing him as he approached. Without words, Khelvan lifted his chin in a slight backward motion for Navek to tell him the news.

"There's been trouble in the north. They're talking of whole families found dead on their farms with no signs of any cause," he said in a sombre tone. A grave feeling passed over Khelvan like a shadow, and both men stood there saying nothing as the impact of it set in, aware the cause of these fatalities came from the one they would face.

That night Khelvan decided, "Get ready and pack, for tomorrow we go north". He opened the weapons cupboard and bade Navek to choose weapons of his own liking, to be used more as a practicality rather than for fighting. Being a descendant from the northern Videha warriors, he immediately chose the hatchet and also two knives. The hatchet had its own leather satchel so that the axe could be carried across his back with the handle upright for easy reach.

Khelvan chose a stick made from white oak which could be carried as a walking stick in the hand or worn across the back if required in a sling of black leather. He also selected the large blade which he had carried the day he found Navek, and added a smaller switchblade knife to put in his inside coat pocket. He picked up the bag of coins Lamaar had given him and emptied about one third of them into an old tin which he hid on a ledge under the house while Navek watched on.

They each made up a swag with blankets, including warm clothing rolled in a sheet of oilskin and tied with ropes. They filled water flasks and tied long straps onto them so that they could be easily carried across the shoulder. For the first time in years, Navek felt trepidation and a tinge of excitement about going into the unknown, though he also sensed a new danger he could not quite fathom, but strangely welcomed. It was not the same as the uneasiness experienced before boarding the doomed ship the *Sea Snake*. This time there was a plan and a purpose to the venture.

Khelvan said: "If anyone asks, we go north to do some hunting".

Navek nodded in response as he had learnt not to ask questions or overindulge in conversation with Khelvan, who, being a man of few words, disliked unnecessary chatter.

That night Khelvan slept badly; weird dreams disturbed his sleep throughout the night. He dreamed of travelling into dark tunnels where he could not remember how to get back out. Jackyl's eerie laugh cackled in the background before his face loomed up and spat his hatred and revenge at Khelvan, as it had during the moon ceremony in the desert. In the morning Khelvan threw off the dreams and focused on the trip ahead.

Before first break of day, both men ate a large breakfast and packed food to take. They pulled the storm shutters across the windows and locked the house securely. Khelvan hid the key in the tin of coins, making sure Navek saw where it was hidden. Neither man knew if they would return.

They strode up the beach to the north as the sun broke out in brilliant orange and purple streaks above the horizon out to sea.

Chapter 15.
Kashmera Town

Khelvan and Navek passed the town of Welpecca in the early morning. They continued along the coast toward the fishing port of Kashmera, where they would enquire about passage on a ship to take them north. They hiked along white beaches, climbing hills to avoid the rocky cliffs. Ominous dark clouds gathered overhead as a storm rolled in swiftly from the east. Once around the next rocky point, Kashmera came into view in the distance. A few fishing boats were anchored out to sea, while several others hurried back toward the port trying to beat the approaching storm.

They saw only a few others who lived in isolated huts in the sand dunes, though most of them scuttled away when they saw the strangers. In one place, they passed an old bearded man fishing off the rocks, oblivious to the waves crashing around him. Higher up sat his wife, who was old and weathered from many years of life by the sea. She looked out with calmness and watched the clouds darken on the horizon.

The couple became wary of the two upright men, both of strong physique, carrying weapons. Rarely did anyone pass this way on foot.

Khelvan waved; they relaxed a little and waved back. After the two men passed, Khelvan glanced back to see the old man pulling in a marvellous silver and blue fish, which danced and fought across the top of the waves. The old man took the fish to his wife, then they both disappeared over the top of the rocks, just as gusty onshore winds blew harder and brought darkening clouds in over the land.

After a long day the two travellers reached the edge of Kashmera when heavy rain began to fall. Set back from the sea, the town was constructed on the side of a hill with steep, winding streets and stone steps. They ducked in and out under the eaves of old shops and tried to avoid the downpour, while the few others in the street hurried on their way. Torrential rain came down harder, hitting the overhanging tin canopies outside the shops to make a cacophonous noise. Before long, they were the only ones left on the street. Evening fell and a few dull street lights glowed through the sleeting rain, otherwise vision was minimal.

They stopped outside a rickety, old timber shop, the last shop with an overhanging roof, and waited for the rain to ease.

A small, wooden sign blowing wildly in the wind hung at the front of the shop. The sign was the colour of bleached driftwood. An image, like a family crest and consisting of three overlapping circles, was branded into the wood. Years of salty wind blowing off the sea had clouded the windows. When they looked closer, a small notice was pasted to the inside of the glass. Khelvan leaned down to read the barely discernible sign which read 'Tea House'. They looked at each other then went in, quickly shutting the door and the storm behind them.

The shop was dimly lit and smelt musty and unused. A wooden counter ran along the right side of the room, while three small tables with chairs were arranged on the left. Behind the counter were many dust covered jars filled with all kinds of dried herbs, weird animal parts and sea creatures. A coating of dust lay on the windows and ledges as though no one had entered for years, and even in such foul weather there were no other customers.

"Was something amiss?" Both men began to feel claustrophobic after being outside in the open air all day. They were about to leave when a small oriental looking man appeared. He stood at the back of the shop, with his hands joined inside his sleeves in front of him. His stance suggested he had been there all along waiting for the pair to notice him. His shiny black hair was pulled back into a long plait down his back, and he wore a light grey jacket buttoned to the top over baggy grey pants. He seemed camouflaged in the dim light which gave him an ancient and timeless appearance. Only the blackness of his hair

and eyes helped distinguish him from his surrounds, but at closer inspection, they could see his dark eyes were clear and perceptive.

"Ah you come in stormy times my friends," he said in an oriental accent, his dark eyes not leaving Khelvan's. "For what do you seek here?"

"We come for shelter from the storm and perhaps a warm drink if you have it," said Khelvan.

The two made simple conversation, but another form of communication went on beneath the surface. Eye-to-eye, there was a measuring of each other like two animals meeting in the forest, measuring and sensing the strength and valour of each other. Moments went by before the oriental man finally nodded to himself, "Hmm, strange times". He seemed satisfied there was no threat from the two strangers, who had come to his shop during a wild storm, carrying weapons and only the basic essentials. He was also aware they carried other weapons hidden from sight.

"Sit down, no go out in storm, sit down, sit down, take off bags. I make tea," said the shopkeeper, nodding often while he pulled out chairs for Khelvan and Navek.

He disappeared to the back of the shop where Khelvan and Navek heard water running and the clinking of china. The little man quickly shuffled back carrying a tray with tea cups and a steaming pot of tea, which he proceeded to pour for them. They sipped the hot green coloured tea, which had a refreshing but bitter taste to it, and felt a warmth that relaxed them from the inside. Khelvan sensed the man was no ordinary shopkeeper, and tried to read the man's intentions, but said nothing. For now he was glad of the hot tea to warm him.

The oriental man chatted away, making small talk about the weather as he topped up their cups. He did not fail to notice the physiques of the two men who were toned and fit, or the strong calloused hands with veins that stood out, consistent with hands that had done much recent work or training.

It was getting late, outside the storm continued. Rain came down heavier and torrents flowed down the sloping streets. Navek thought it strange the shop had no customers and enquired: "How do you make business here? It seems no one comes in".

"Oh, only few people want life giving medicine I sell. It very lost science nowaday. No one believe in cures anymore."

While Navek and the shopkeeper talked, Khelvan felt vibrations in the timber flooring beneath his feet and knew someone was moving around in the back room. Then he saw a slight movement near the doorway behind the chattering shopkeeper. From the back room came two small tapping noises, barely audible over the din of the rain, and the shopkeeper turned and left the two sitting alone.

It was an odd situation; Khelvan could perceive no danger. Somehow it seemed natural and right to be here sipping the pleasant tea, yet they both felt some wariness.

Suddenly, Navek stood and darted toward the doorway

where the shopkeeper had disappeared. Khelvan remained seated and waited, but his hand went to the hilt of the blade in his jacket.

Navek entered the back room and found himself inside a tiny kitchen. Three steps led down into a larger living area where there was a low wooden table with four cushions surrounding it on the floor. On one side were antique timber cabinets carved with intricate designs, and a cosy fire burned on the other. Through glass sliding doors that led outside, Navek could just make out a garden, wet branches blowing wildly about in the storm and large rocks that dimly reflected the light coming from the kitchen.

Standing on the steps between the two rooms stood the small man with arms calmly folded across his chest, looking out at the rain pelting down on his garden.

Navek startled a young woman in the tiny kitchen, though he had made no noise.

Without turning around, the oriental man uttered a few words to her in their own tongue, and she went on preparing food. Without turning he said: "We not your enemy. Don't worry," then he turned to face Navek. "Bring friend in here. We eat here," he said resolutely, and stepped down to sit at the far end of the table. "Come come. Sit. Bring friend."

A smell of cooking permeated the room and Navek stepped back a pace to where he could see Khelvan, no longer with his hand on the hilt. With a slight shrug, he motioned to Khelvan, who had heard everything, to follow.

Khelvan brought the two packs and stepped down into the living room, bowing slightly to the young woman as he passed. He put the packs in a corner then both sat at the side positions of the table, feeling slightly awkward but hungry after walking for miles.

"Be guests here. Guests very rare for us. Good joss you trapped by storm, good we have company. Sit, sit. We eat together." The shopkeeper was happy they had come, and his sharp black eyes shone brightly against the dimly lit room. "No ship sail tonight in storm."

"How do you know we want a ship?" asked Navek in surprise.

"I see many things about you," he replied, staring directly at Khelvan as though looking right through him to some point of infinity behind. "If you want I tell you."

A few moments went by then Khelvan tilted his head slightly to indicate assent, and the shopkeeper went on.

"I see journey, hard journey with great big peril. Big waves and island sand. Jungle and jungle people. Oh that already past," he corrected himself looking toward Navek before continuing. "I see you in deep hole in ground with falling rocks. There is wise man around you, will help you. Both have big portant job ahead. These things I tell. Very noble path given to both you." Still gazing toward Khelvan, the man paused for a long moment and Khelvan looked back to him waiting to hear the ending.

But then, as if coming back from some far off place, the shopkeeper shrugged, "Hmm funny but can't see end

… Ah here comes delicious food my daughter cook. Always very yum yum".

All heads turned toward the daughter as she glided down the steps effortlessly with eyes downcast, carrying a tray with four bowls. She seemed too shy to look directly at the guests and set the tray on the table near her father. "My name Linchee and this my daughter Lulu, she no speak much Englis." Both father and daughter bowed slightly out of politeness.

Khelvan looked toward Navek indicating he should introduce them to their hosts. "This here is Khelvan and I am named Navek."

"Please to meet you," replied the shopkeeper.

Lulu gave her father the first bowl then served the two guests before placing her own bowl at the other end of the table. She went back to the kitchen and brought more plates and bowls of food which she set in the middle of the table for them to serve themselves. It was a tasty soup made from fermented bean paste with white squares of bean curd, seaweed and mushrooms added. It was followed by small, charcoaled grilled fish, rice and various vegetables. "Eat up. Eat up. Plenty more. Have more," insisted the shopkeeper. The combinations of food blended perfectly together and they ate till full, grateful for such a nourishing meal. The travellers complimented Lulu several times for her fine cooking, and then thanked Linchee for his kind hospitality.

After the meal, against the polite protests of Lulu, Khelvan helped clear the table while Linchee poured them hot wine from a ceramic bottle that had been heating in a pot of water near the fire. They all lifted their cups, "May light shine on your journey," toasted Linchee, and they all sipped on the wine which had an earthy aftertaste. They felt its warmth radiate from their stomachs, and as soon as the small cups were emptied, Linchee filled them again.

It was a strange contrast after travelling all day along the coast, buffeted by sea spray and salty wind to reach the port of Kashmera, and now be sitting in the living room of two perfect strangers sipping hot wine.

"Why are you being so polite to us, when we are mere strangers?" asked Khelvan.

"Ah, everybody strange nowaday" replied the shopkeeper. "But you two noble guests in humble house of Linchee. Not everybody noble nowaday. I knew I have visitors soon but not know when you come. You both come with angry storm set against you and Linchee been waiting. You see, I not really shopkeeper, that just dusty shop-front out there. I have something to give you, it help defeat naughty sorcerer you seek, l help you fix him for good."

Khelvan stared in surprise at the little man who talked about the sorcerer as though it was common knowledge. Until recently, only his teacher and some in the desert talked about this.

"I give you shield to help you. Linchee been waiting long time to give you. This sorcerer witch been trying to hurt everyone too long now. Soon be too late if you don't stop him. See, I glimpse bit this, bit that. He hide you know, in dark underground hole. I see you are man of strong controlled mind," he said to Khelvan. "I got simple weapon for you to take."

Linchee stood and disappeared up a narrow winding stairway that the guests only noticed now for the first time. Khelvan and Navek looked at each other and said nothing, while Lulu who had been busy in the kitchen, came over and sat with them.

"Don't worry," she spoke quietly in perfect English, "my father has something that you will need for your journey. He wanted to return to our home country long before now, but has waited years for you to come".

They both looked up in response to what sounded like furniture being moved upstairs, and although calmed by Lulu's soothing voice, they were still alert for any trickery. Unrelenting rain fell in torrents outside, as if holding them here. Khelvan leaned back and tried to unwind. He had a sense of his teacher's face laughing and nodding at him, to indicate the situation was meant to be and he could relax.

After a short time, Linchee came down the stairs carrying a small package wrapped in old brown leather and bound with a leather boot lace. "Here what you need," he said, brushing the dust off into the fireplace before laying the object on the table. He carefully opened out the stiff leather wrapping, lined with orange silk. Inside was a flat round disk of silver with a knot pattern etched around the edge. It was about four or five inches in diameter and had a dull silver chain attached. In the middle a triangular shaped mirror was set. It looked old, like a relic from antiquity.

"This very magic mirror. Make sure you don't lose or break. This veeery old, and has power to proteck you from his bad spells. Just face this toward bad sorcerer and he can't get you. It send spell back on sender. Don't forget use this at final showdown. You need this."

Khelvan felt a strange feeling stir within him when he heard these words, and looked up at the man not knowing what to believe.

Lulu reached forward to pick up the item and polished the dull mirror with a napkin till it shone clearly, then replaced it on the table again.

Khelvan still had a sense of Lamaar's face nearby, not serious but pleased, saying, "Take it. Take it. It won't bite!" Khelvan picked up the object and turned it over in his hands. It certainly looked to be an authentic relic to be valued, but he wondered about any magical powers. He carefully wrapped the mirror and thanked them both.

"Don't forget to use. This help you, very magic mirror," repeated Linchee in earnest.

It was getting late, and although the rain had eased it was still teeming outside. The shopkeeper insisted they stay the night and even before waiting for them to accept, he and Lulu brought bedding into the lounge where they would sleep.

Khelvan and Navek both bowed to their hosts in sincere gratitude for all the comforts and generosity given to the now weary travellers.

Linchee stoked the fire, and Lulu came from the

kitchen to Navek. She handed him a small cotton bag tied with a drawstring at the top. "Take this on your journey. When there is no food to be found, you can boil these ingredients in water to make a nutritious meal. It contains the dried ingredients for soup and is light to carry."

She felt the roughness of his hands brush hers as he took the small bag from her. Once again they thanked their hosts, bowing and nodding politely before the father and daughter went upstairs.

Strong gusts of wind blew rain against the glass doors during the night, and the flames of the fire flickered and crackled while the two travellers slept soundly. Early the next morning, the shopkeeper and his daughter came downstairs to find an empty room with mattresses rolled up and blankets folded neatly, and two silver coins placed on top.

"Come Lulu, we eat breakfast then pack up house. Now we go back to mother country," he said happily.

Chapter 16.
Tradewinds

The long journey followed the eastern seaboard to the port of Jenolan, where Khelvan and Navek stood with their luggage on the deck of the carrier ship named *Tradewinds*. It was the only ship that ventured north to the arctic mining settlements. A cold day greeted them to the industrial city, and they looked out at the bleak sight, wrapped up with scarves and hats pulled down over their ears. A tugboat hauled the heavy steel ship and slowly weaved its way around fishing boats to reach the wharf. Ropes were thrown out and caught by local dock workers, whose sharp eyes had seen their approach as soon as the ship had come around the headland. The workers cursed their luck as more icy rain started to fall while they moored the ship securely to old wooden pillars, then prepared to unload her.

For Navek the port city was a poignant reminder of memories he would rather forget. He thought back distastefully to the day, at this same wharf, he had stepped aboard the ill-fated ship that now lay at the bottom of the Eastern Sea. On that journey his impulsiveness had almost cost him his life, and he lost a young friend who had followed him onto the ship. He could not forget or escape his past here; reminders of times he walked the same streets with his father and memories of Sharian and the monks surfaced.

He had changed as a person since then, but had paid a heavy price for his ignorance. The only consolation was the purpose of his current mission, which would at least contribute to appeasing the loss of his family, and perhaps do some good for others. He steeled himself against disturbing thoughts of his past, resolving to focus on the task ahead.

From the other side of the harbour, a dark haired young man sat casually watching the comings and goings. He often came just for something to do, idly observing the few passengers disembarking from carrier ships, walking down the gangplank with their luggage.

Something about one of the passengers made him sit up and squint his eyes to look more closely, checking to make sure. He had not seen Navek since the ship went down near the islands years before. If it really was Navek, he looked different, perhaps more aged and weathered. He wondered at the blonde man who went ahead of Navek, who had a well-trained, fit body. The man walked with purpose and importance. He had a certainty that made him stand out from others. Jake noted the packs on their backs, their weapons, and then smiled. He knew he was about to set out on a venture.

He meandered along, following the men toward the marketplace, watching from a distance. The two travellers seemed alert and aware of their surroundings as they bought food and supplies from various vendors.

At one point, Jake's eyes widened in surprise when Khelvan turned and looked directly at him, letting Jake know he was aware he was being followed. Khelvan's dark eyes briefly assessed the young man before he turned and continued on, satisfied there was no threat.

Finally Jake walked up beside Navek and nudged him with his elbow. "Oi. What are you doin' here?" he asked casually. Navek took a cautious step to the side and then turned to face the young man.

After a few searching moments, Navek recognised the youth. His face lit up with a big smile, a sight which both Jake and Khelvan had never seen before. "Jake! You're alive! I thought you went down with that ship!" he exclaimed incredulously. Happy to see each other, they spontaneously stepped forward and touched knuckle-to-knuckle, fist-to-fist, then fist-to-chest in the traditional greeting of the highland clans, though neither had greeted each other this way before.

Navek stepped back to appraise the boy who was now a young man with scruffy shoulder length dark hair. His cheeks were rosy against the tan coloured skin characteristic of the northern clans. It reminded Navek of his own people.

Navek was greatly relieved the lad had survived the shipwreck. He was amazed to see the familiar face after thinking him drowned. "How did you get back here?" Navek asked in a bewildered tone.

"Oh I get around," Jake answered, shrugging and not offering any further information. Meanwhile, his eyes checked out Khelvan who stood apart, leaning against the wooden stick he carried with a bemused smile on his face. "I thought you went down with the ship! I searched for you ..." said Navek trailing off. "Anyway, anyway this is Khelvan," he said remembering to introduce the two.

Jake felt something jump in his chest when his eyes met Khelvan's; he saw wisdom and valour in those eyes, qualities he had found in his association with Sharian and the monks, but had not come across anywhere else.

They stood in the marketplace assessing each other. Jake wanted to know more about their journey – an involuntarily sense of adventure ignited in him. "And this is Jake," Navek continued on with the introduction.

Khelvan nodded slightly in response to the youth, aware that a lone bird squawked in the distance. He took the call as an auspicious sign that boded well for this chance meeting – which was not by chance.

"You can stay at the monk's house if you want," offered Jake. "Most of them are away right now so there's room."

Navek turned to Khelvan who still seemed bemused,

and he shrugged, leaving the decision with Navek. "Sure that'd be great. First we'll get a few more things here, because we're heading out in the morning," Navek said. Astonished at the chance meeting after all these years, the coincidence unexpectedly lifted Navek's spirits.

After the monks had gone to bed, the three sat up late into the night around the fire, talking in low voices so as not to disturb the others. Khelvan listened to the conversation with some fascination, as Navek did not usually share his past and had revealed little of his previous ventures.

Navek learned that Jake had been washed up on the larger island, along with two of the ship's crew. The three had found their way along the beach till they reached Mazzara, which was the island port where their ship, the *Sea Snake*, had been headed. Navek had boarded another ship to Welpecca from Mazzara. It was incredible to him that Jake was on the island at that same time. The crew left the island on the next ship back to Jenolan, but Jake decided to stay and ended up befriending some islanders. They welcomed him as one of their sons and taught him various new skills.

"I loved those islands an' their people. I stayed there for three years, because all I'd ever known was ice and snow before. That tropical climate was heaven. But eventually I came back," he said with a shrug.

Since he had been back, Jake had found work when he could, but still went back to the mountains each year to see Sharian. He would then continue to the west coast to train and hang out with the monks.

"Where are you two goin'?" Jake asked casually.

"We're going north to Frozia by ship in the morning. It's a hunting trip," Navek replied unconvincingly.

A long pause passed by, then Jake said in a matter of fact tone: "I'm comin' with ya. I know that country and I can be useful".

Both men looked at each other and said nothing. But they saw the light in his eyes and the keen offer of a willing spirit, something that cannot be ignored lightly. "Besides I'm doin' nuthin' hangin' around here," he added.

Khelvan did not know what lay ahead and resisted the option of taking another person. The lad would add more risk and responsibility, but there was something about Jake and the chance meeting which could not be dismissed easily. He remembered Lamaar's forecast, "Others, who may seem unlikely companions, will help along the way". Khelvan said nothing but heard his guides say just as matter-of-factly, "Take him. You'll need him". He had the distinct impression of them brushing their hands together as though brushing off crumbs in a gesture that meant "subject closed".

Khelvan explained to Jake as best he could, about the expedition to the remote arctic north to seek out the dangerous renegade sorcerer. The sorcerer was a murderer and they would face great risk in extreme conditions. There was no guarantee of safety or return. More than once, he gave Jake the chance to change his mind, but the lad's enthusiasm did not alter. He remained undeterred.

Khelvan and Navek looked at each other for a long decisive moment before Khelvan sighed in resignation, and shook his head at what he was getting himself in to. Throwing his hands in the air to signal reluctant agreement, Navek submitted, "Go on. Get ready then".

Jake let out a wolf howl that may have woken the sleeping monks, and madly ran upstairs to put his few possessions together. Jake did not really know what he was doing, but was excited at the anticipation of unknown adventure. It was a secret mission with two purposeful warriors, the welcoming of a formidable challenge in his life.

They travelled onward by sea aboard *Tradewinds*.

The ship briefly stopped at the port of Creolleor to pick up and drop off supplies, before reaching the last frozen outpost of Frozia.

At Frozia, the most northern port, the ship loaded up with iron ore to carry back to the steel smelters of Jenolan and Welpecca.

The captain's expression had been friendly, but his eyes reflected the cunning of a fox. The three watched their backs and their possessions through the entire journey. Gut feelings and previous experience had taught them not to trust the captain or his crew.

The vessel itself was made from steel. It had a round bulbous shaped hull because it travelled to places where the sea could freeze over and shrink. This could immobilise and crush a stranded ship, or crack open the hull to send the ship and all on board to a horrible icy death. The ingenious design allowed a trapped ship to pop up out of the ice so it did not become crushed. Those aboard would have some chance of survival, that is, if they could wait out the winter, not starve to death ... or go mad.

The trip was miserable. Bleak, icy sleet blew against the travellers whenever they stepped out on the deck. The ship's crew wore oilskin pants and hooded coats. They cursed the weather as they worked in cold relentless rain.

One miserable day, Khelvan was tired of his cabin and made his way upstairs where he leaned over the handrail and peered out. Through the icy sleet an unsettling vision of the sorcerer's face appeared, lunging at Khelvan, trying to force him overboard. Eerie voices echoed in the wind. He turned to leave and slipped on the wet deck. Struggling to regain his balance, an invisible force pushed him toward the edge. He clung desperately to the railing and contorted his body to gain a foothold, but his grip kept slipping. He shouted for help, then saw the sorcerer's malevolent face leer at him from the masts above before it disappeared into the cold rain.

Another time he woke in panic from a nightmare. Jackyl's cold hands were around his throat and his cackling sinister laugh echoed in the background. The closer they came to the last port, the more on guard Khelvan became. It took a lot for him to remain focused on all that he had learnt, and throw off the fear that sought to weaken him. Invisible forces were being sent against him before even reaching the final shore, but he said nothing about the scares to the others.

Chilly days and a brief stop at the port of Creolleor passed before Frozia finally come into view. They were all glad to be near land again.

After they disembarked, the motion of the waves continued as their sea legs adjusted to walking on solid ground. They found a cheap room at a guest house ironically named *The Last Chance*, then went out to eat and get supplies for the final leg.

There were not many shops, but the store they went into sold clothing, hardware and a limited variety of other practical items – typical of a remote outpost store.

Khelvan insisted Jake choose some extra clothes to take, as well as new waterproof boots with thick soles, a long oilskin coat and a new oilskin cover for his bedroll.

Jake already had adequate belongings, but they were well used and worn and he liked to travel frugally, even through icy mountains. He resisted – he did not want to carry more gear – and was embarrassed at someone else buying things for him.

Both men insisted however, that if he was to travel with them, he must be well prepared for unknown and extreme conditions. "Don't worry about the money, just get what you need," Khelvan said, throwing in a burgundy wool scarf and a good sized folding knife for him as well. "You'll be no use if you freeze to death," he added. Khelvan was amused to see the young man receiving the new items, probably for the first time in his life. Meanwhile he added a tin billy for boiling water, three tin bowls, a flint and stone for fire making, tea and several dried strips of salted beef and some pre-packaged food which was light to carry.

A faded mining map was pinned to the wall. Khelvan called the others over so they could gain some overview of their destination. Jake and Navek could not read the map, so Khelvan explained some of the details. They were fascinated by the perspective it gave, especially when they worked out where their former villages were in relation to the rest of the world. Khelvan showed Jake where he and Navek stayed in the beach house, far to the south past Welpecca, then described how to get to the house, and who the old owners were. He also told him where the key was hidden if he ever wanted to go there himself, or more to the point, in case one or both of them did not make it back. "You'd like the warm weather there," Navek added, pleased that Khelvan had trusted the youth so soon after meeting him.

Khelvan traced the route they would take north along the coast, before turning inland through the alpine mountains where he hoped to reach the destination of Mt Perilous. Khelvan studied the map intently, committing it to memory as best he could, telling the others to do the same. It would help save their lives in the coming days.

Mount Perilous, a former iron ore mine, was marked on the map as Perilous Mine. The map also showed a mining route which ran inland from Frozia and Creolleor, then turned north-east through the mountains to provide access to two other mines.

They left the store and headed off to find dinner, as prepared as they could be for the treacherous journey ahead. Khelvan was anxious to get started and get it over with.

Chapter 17.
To the Icy North

On the frozen tundra, the three figures were utterly alone on the white landscape, as they persevered and endured impossible conditions. For several days they had trudged on from Frozia; there were no more towns, only the birth place of icy winds and freezing blizzards. The end of the earth was a frozen world, where temperatures plummeted below minus fifty degrees. There was nothing but grey and white mountains and cliffs of ice. Bleakness surrounded them as they lumbered on toward the mountain range where the rogue sorcerer lived.

Jake was born in mountains like this and was unwavering in his resolve to come. He shrugged off the dangers as though inconsequential.

For Navek, being back in the northern mountains reminded him of his former highland life with a family, now gone. The reminder enlivened him and helped drive him on to seek out the villain who killed them all, but even his father and his clan had never gone into extremes this far north. It was all the three could do just to survive each day, let alone achieve the quest they were on.

The day before, they saw a herd of bison foraging higher up on a slope. The formidable animals moved slowly as they constantly nudged and dug away at the snow covered ground, desperate to uncover any vegetation at all. Their brown, shaggy coats were coarse and knotted; icicles hung on manes which were bleached blond by the winter extremes. As they trekked on, Navek felt the old bison bull watching them with one eye as he continued to forage in the arctic wilderness. Life was truly precarious out here, but from legends told during his youth, Navek knew these great animals had adapted and survived since the age of ice, making their ancestral lineage over one million years old.

The travellers struggled on with numb feet and hands, and even their eyes seemed frozen as an icy blizzard blew from the south and came at them. The travellers were blinded and the relentless gale made it hard to stand.

"We must find shelter or we're surely doomed," Khelvan thought. The storm changed direction and blew harder, but at least it helped elude the one who pursued them.

Khelvan had not caught sight of anyone trailing them, but he knew they were being followed – he turned often to check behind. It was more a sinister presence than a person; there was something not quite right with the world, which caused him to feel vulnerable, setting him on edge.

Surrounding mountains soon became obscured by snowfall and ice. Khelvan regretted bringing the others with him, but they continued on, bent over and clinging to each other to avoid becoming lost or blown off course. They pressed on in slow motion as though an invisible force pushed against them. At times, Khelvan thought it was the same force he had encountered in the desert many moons ago.

Jake yelled out over the din of the wind to get their attention, and pointed ahead to some dark shapes. It was a large assembly of Polar penguins all gathered and huddled together with their backs to an icy cliff. Somewhere in his numb brain, Khelvan surmised that they must be near the sea, as these creatures would feed on fish and catch seafood for their young.

From here he knew they needed to head inland to the north-west. They soon found themselves surrounded by the penguins, and some of the birds called out in distress at the intrusion.

Feeling disoriented and without any sensation in his feet or hands, Navek wondered how the other two were going. This was the coldest place he had ever been, and the trip was far tougher than ever anticipated. He remembered why he was here – the injustice done to his family, his clan all killed – and was reminded again this was a chance to do something useful in his life and repair the damage. Such thoughts spurred him on despite heavy, plodding legs and aching bones.

Any strength soon left when he stumbled and fell, plunging in among the penguins. At the same time, he pulled at Jake's sleeve, bringing the boy down with him to the ground.

In that moment, he regretted bringing Jake to such an extreme place amid such peril. The squawking and fluttering of birds in the white blizzard was the last thing he remembered. Penguins started back in fright, then soon regathered, oblivious of the two bodies. The birds congregated around and over Navek and Jake, maintaining their body heat in the process.

Khelvan saw the two of them go down. One minute they were there, next they had disappeared as though swallowed up by nature.

The penguins unwittingly hid the weary travellers, keeping them safe – at least for the while – from the one who gained ground and pursued them doggedly.

For the past two days, Khelvan had caught shadowy glimpses of an apparition following behind. The grey figure seemed to shape-shift and change; appear and disappear; dance and shimmer; with no recognisable definition. He did not mention it to the others because they could not go any faster. As yet, there was no substance to it, but he would tell them at the next rest stop.

The follower was not a person, but a force, a sending, which he could sense rather than see, and Khelvan also sensed the chilling gravity of the pursuer's intent. This was life and death. He could perish at any moment if he was not on guard. His thoughts went to Lamaar and then he prayed this was not his last day on earth.

Khelvan had always preferred to live alone, but he did not want his final resting place to be in this utterly desolate frozen wasteland at the world's end.

An unfamiliar cloak of despair and doubt settled over Khelvan, which he could not shake. Thoughts of giving up ran through his mind. The mission now seemed like a foolish death sentence for them all, and the purpose of the trip was becoming remote and vague.

Howling winds took on the threatening sound of the sorcerer's laugh, and resounded all around. Khelvan shook his head to rid himself of the intruding gloom … and then it dawned on him.

This debilitating shadow was being cast by the very one they sought, by something that did not want them approaching.

"So this is your power sorcerer. This is how you work. You'll have to do better than that," he thought dourly. *"At least I know we're on the right track."* Khelvan became annoyed that Jackyl would strike at this level of a person's mind. He started to understand a little of the sorcerer's guise, that he used methods to insert despair and hopelessness in a person. The real battle with this sorcerer would entail remaining clear and free of his crippling dark influence, as well as vigilance against his use of invisible weapons.

Navek and Jake did not get up. Khelvan could only

hope they were alright; he was too cold and weak to help them. He slumped down against an icy wall and uttered a deep sigh, temporarily dispersing the nearby birds and sending them into a flutter. *"Ah give me strength,"* he said dryly, taking the chance to rest after a brief attempt in his frozen mind to communicate and greet the king of the birds. He hugged his arms to his chest and put his head down on his knees. The penguins gathered back around and then leaned up against him, offering a small comfort as he thanked them silently.

Khelvan sat for what seemed like several hours, but it could have been just several minutes, in a place where there was no way of knowing. He heard the call of a bird singing a single note, like the sound of a flute. It seemed both far away and at the same time, very near. He could not tell, but it was a familiar sound, a song without end that filled him with peace and soothed his soul. From somewhere in that inner silence he heard words being clearly spoken. "Come on. Dig deep."

"Was he hallucinating? Was his teacher here or was he in the afterlife?" He recognised the voice of his teacher again, "Get up," he heard. Echoes and snippets of unfinished sentences drifted through his mind as the words of his teacher trailed off, "... can only defeat him on his own ground ... in his own territory ... harder than anything you have done before ... greatest task ever asked ...".

"Get up," he heard again, and when he finally managed to lift his head, it bobbed up and down involuntarily. His body felt stiff and numb. He looked up unsteadily into

227

Jake's squinting eyes just above him, and heard the words: "Common. Get up".

Jake nudged him in the shoulder with his boot, before heaving him up to a standing position. "Common. We can't stay here," Jake urged him. Khelvan shook his arms, rubbed and clapped his hands together trying to get warmth into them while stomping his feet. He looked around for Navek and saw Jake shaking the lifeless body, pulling him up into a sitting position. Jake patted and rubbed him to get some movement, and brushed the powdery snow from Navek's coat.

Jake and Khelvan were both relieved to see Navek's arm finally move, then a shake of his head followed by a snarl: "I'm OK. Get off me". But Jake ignored the protests and hauled him up, telling Navek to get up and move his arms and legs.

The wind died down, visibility returned and the gale cleared as quickly as it started. Penguins dispersed toward the sea which was only fifty paces away, and Khelvan watched some of them glide through aqua blue water then climb onto monumental ice drifts that slowly and majestically floated by.

He knew he must survive, if not for himself but for his teacher who relied on him, and also for the future generations. But right now, his first priority was his two travelling companions.

Jake certainly knew about survival in the glacial mountains. Khelvan now appreciated his company as the lad had handled the extreme conditions better than Navek or himself. They all needed food to fuel them on, and Khelvan fumbled with ties on his pack, eventually using his teeth to open the stiff laces. He looked around as best he could for any sign of the pursuing danger, but they seemed to have lost their pursuer in the storm.

With numb hands he managed to pull out three thick strips of dried meat, rationing it out as the food supply was limited. He tossed two pieces toward Jake who picked them up and put one in Navek's mouth, telling him loudly to chew. "Alright, alright," was the muffled and gruff reply. Glad of the easing conditions, they chewed on the salty strips and moved around stomping their feet. They all knew they must soldier on or they would die out here.

Khelvan suspected that Navek was also affected by the sorcerer's spells, and decided to warn them about the unseen pursuer as they neared the enemy's territory. He gathered Navek and Jake closer and told them the news.

"We must all be vigilant from here on and watch our backs. This sorcerer we seek now follows *us,* and is aware of our approach. We cannot afford to be defeated by unseen weapons and deadly tricks, so keep alert."

Navek, who stared down at the snow while he listened, felt hairs stand on end as dread ran through him. He looked quickly to the south, scanning the craggy cliffs and the horizon for any sign of the enemy, knowing well from experience how quickly the evil could strike.

"And keep a positive mind." Khelvan added, "Don't be weakened by despair or futility. That's what he wants".

Navek glanced at Khelvan, who looked back at him knowingly before Navek turned away. "He can somehow get to your emotions. That's one of the guises he wears, one of his weapons. This gentlemen, is a just a glimpse into the one we seek. He is tricky, he is dangerous, and he knows we're here and will try to prevent our approach."

They became even more vigilant and determined to go on and get the job finished. The protein and salt helped revive them somewhat, so the trio set out again into unchartered territory. They headed inland to the north-west, toward Mount Perilous which stood high above the alpine range.

By afternoon of the next day, the route began to climb steeply and, with grey sleet raining down, they made their way up over the final mountain. Navek missed his footing and slipped. He called out as he fell and slid back down the slope. Breathing hard, he picked himself up and cursed under his breath.

Jake went to his aid as though Navek was an old man who needed help. "Come on grampa," Jake said jokingly, stirring Navek who lashed out with a mock gesture pretending to hit the lad. He wondered at Jake's sense of humour at such a time, as he had never seen it before in the boy.

Navek took in large breaths and pulled himself up to trudge on, encouraged by a small amount of renewed vigour, thanks to Jake's youthful cheek. Both Khelvan and Navek noticed that the further they went, the younger Jake seemed energised and enthusiastic, almost hurrying, and at times they had trouble keeping up with him. By comparison they did not know if they would have the stamina and strength to reach the destination, and then also face what may lie ahead.

Hardly a word was spoken all day, but the two men were acutely aware they neared the sorcerer's domain. They proceeded with caution, and with less oxygen available at the high altitude they felt exhausted and weak. There was no wind but a constant dense pressure pushed against them like a strong head current. They plodded on as though in a slow motion dream. Khelvan and Navek mentally battled dark forces that tried to enfeeble their minds and bodies. Strange echoing voices seemed to laugh at their plight. Increasingly, a sinister undercurrent pervaded the region, which did not bode well for the two weary men who were gradually losing their edge. They felt alone and small on the side of a vast mountain range.

The travellers journeyed through the bleak grey and white landscape. Ice clung to their eyebrows and eyelashes and covered the hooded oilskin coats and packs. Underneath they wore woollen hats with scarves wrapped up around their faces, but throughout the exertion they remained immutably cold. A dense mist settled in the valley and obscured the view, reducing visibility to about six paces ahead.

Jake was in the lead, and stopped often to peer through the mist as though expecting to see something up ahead. He did not seem at all affected by dark forces or lack of oxygen, and several times waited for Khelvan and Navek to catch up. The lad was in his element in the mountains. He had almost taken on the role of carer, looking after the men as if they were elderly.

They reached a jagged ridge, where Jake turned and gestured for the exhausted men to rest under an ice shelf which offered relative shelter from the elements. Khelvan dropped his pack and fell down next to it onto his back, breathing heavily as he tried to get enough oxygen into his lungs. Navek propped himself up against the ice shelf with his head back, grateful for the rest, and then slid down and curled up on his side. Unintentionally, they both drifted in and out of sleep, weird dreams infiltrating their minds. Jake unrolled their bedrolls and covered each man completely over, before lying down between them, arranging his own bedding and oilskin cover to overlap the others.

They survived another night at high altitude. Hostile arctic winds formed into another blizzard during the night and picked up speed before dying down hours later. Moaning gales blew sleet and snow in over the top of them, but they remained huddled together in sub-zero conditions.

Just before dawn, Jake's eyes flew open when he sensed they were not alone. Something or someone moved nearby. He briefly thought of waking Navek and Khelvan but decided against it. Instead, he pulled off his gloves and delved into his jacket for the knife. Without moving the oilskin cover, he reached over the top of Khelvan to grip the wooden stick that lay there. Slowly he sat up feeling the weight of several inches of snow on top of him. Jake peeped out over the cover and saw straight away a pack of five hungry wolves, which had probably trailed them or smelt the dried meat they carried. He liked wolves and knew a lot about their methods and tactics. He had even befriended one once. But he saw desperation in their glowing eyes, almost evil, and knew there would be no reasoning with this lot.

Suddenly, he jumped up and sent snow flying with the oilskin cover. He growled defiantly and fiercely like a wild animal, and banged the stick on the snow to startle the hungry wolves who snarled before they ran off. Khelvan and Navek woke from their frozen sleep, groggy and stiff with cold. They flailed around trying to get out from under the oilskin to get their weapons, at first not knowing what was going on.

With the ice shelf behind him, Jake stepped out and quickly looked around, on alert in case there were scouts or other wolves nearby. He knew they may regroup and try again in their desperation, now that they had smelt food. He hoped they were en route to the coast where they would prey on baby penguins or seal pups. The animals were gone for the time being.

Navek sat rubbing his head, his legs still under the cover, and Khelvan stood with one arm leaning against the wall for balance.

Jake twirled the stick across the back of his hand, spinning it easily around and around as the monks had taught him. "Good thing you brought me along," he said jokingly, then tossed the stick through the air to Khelvan who managed to catch it between two gloved hands.

Khelvan nodded and saw there was far more to their young travelling companion than he knew.

This would be the last day of trekking before they reached Mount Perilous, which loomed ominously above the next ridge. They remained at the icy shelf to eat a frugal breakfast and sort out what food was left. The food was rationed out for each person to carry his own, in case something happened to one of them. The trip was taking longer than planned and rations were dwindling, so they all agreed to eat more sparingly. They still had to get back to the coast.

Before they were about to depart, a strange sight appeared, making Khelvan very uneasy. He had seen such a sight once before in the desert. It was a pair of black butterflies with sinister red eyes on their wings. They fluttered and bobbed about nearby as though it was a pleasant spring day in a garden. The vivid colours of the creatures contrasted against the white snow. Such an unnerving sight did not belong among snow covered mountains.

Khelvan stepped forward swiftly with stick in hand. In quick succession he swiped at the creatures and hit both, smashing them to the ground where he squashed them into the snow with his boot. Navek and Jake both looked at him questioningly. "Spies," was all he commented. "Come on. Let's go," he said, with a renewed focus and determination. Khelvan was encouraged that his reflexes were still reliable, for he knew the sorcerer watched and waited for their meeting. It seemed Jackyl did not resist their approach anymore. He was like a cat waiting for the mice to walk into its trap. They were close now, and on the right track.

Chapter 18.
Mount Perilous

In these chilled arctic mountains of the north, the sorcerer managed to survive and live out his days surrounded by bitter cold. Like Navek and Jake, he was born in the north, where at least the seasons changed and the snow melted before summer. But here was a perpetually frozen world in an isolated wilderness.

On the eastern side of Mount Perilous, the three travellers slowly ascended the steep incline. A cliff edge beside them dropped straight down to an abyss, and the three trudged on in silence, minds numb from the cold and shoulders hunched against a blizzard. Navek focused on Khelvan's footprints in the snow, as it required less effort to use the same footprints.

Bumping into Khelvan's outstretched arm which gestured them to stop, Navek came to an abrupt halt. Just ahead, an abandoned miner's hut stood on the edge of the craggy peak. They almost missed seeing the rock and timber construction, because deep snowfall covered the roof and camouflaged it against the vast white mountain range.

Alert and with eyes not leaving the hut, the three hesitated, breathing heavily from the exertion as large drops of rain fell.

When they reached the building, they peered tentatively through a window which had been blown out by strong winds long before. The hut consisted of one small room with a stone fireplace, empty except for a rough wooden table and a few derelict items strewn about the floor. They kicked the snow away from the door and cautiously entered the cold room, grateful for any small respite from the wind and rain.

Jake took off his pack and assessed the place that would be his base for the next couple of days. He was prepared to survive out in the open, but a roof over his head was luxury. From here Khelvan and Navek would go on together as previously agreed. Jake would wait two days for their return. If they did not show, he was to take some of the money, leave their packs and retrace his tracks back to Frozia via the coast. The old mining route through the mountains would take him further inland and thereby risk his survival.

Khelvan and Navek took off their packs, leaned them against a wall, and checked the contents. They took weapons, food, the stone and flint, and left the rest with

Jake. Khelvan came across the package containing the mirror from Linchee, as well as the dried ingredients from Lulu, which he had forgotten till now. With the image of the couple's friendly faces in his mind, he put the mirror inside his coat pocket and left the dried soup ingredients. He removed his right glove and with difficulty, reached inside another pocket with numb fingers, pulling out the last almonds and dried raisins he had quietly saved. He held them out to the others who took a portion each, leaving him a portion. They chewed slowly and savoured the taste, thankful for the pleasant morsels as the two men prepared themselves for the last leg.

Not knowing what they were about to encounter, Khelvan turned to Navek, their eyes meeting momentarily. Then he turned to Jake. "This is it my friends," he said.

The three gathered around and touched fist-to-fist, knuckle-to-knuckle and then fist-to-chest in the old way; all aware they may never meet again.

"Be vigilant and stay alert. Do not follow us. Remember this sorcerer is a killer far worse than any wolf," were Khelvan's parting words to Jake.

Navek felt regretful at leaving Jake alone. He looked at the young man with the burgundy red scarf wrapped around his neck and the bright eyes which did not appear at all worried. In fact, he still seemed happy to be on the venture. Navek stepped forward and gave him an impulsive hug, then cuffed him lightly on the side of the head before turning to leave with Khelvan.

They set off through the sleet searching for some kind

of entrance or mine opening further up the mountain.

It was not long before they reached the back of another derelict hut, and stood a few moments to catch their breath after the steep climb. Hanging by a solitary hinge, a door jutted out on an angle, fixed in place by thick snow. *"It all seems too easy, something's not right. Jackyl would surely be aware of us on the mountain by now,"* Khelvan thought, uneasy that they may be walking into a trap.

Through howling winds and rain they listened for signs of life inside. Ducking under long icicles, they slipped in through the opening. Inside they found themselves in a gloomy damp room, sparsely furnished with a few broken wooden chairs and a wooden bench under a grimy window. In one corner, timber slabs topped with scatterings of old straw had once been a bed. On the other side was a fire place built from rocks like the walls of the hut. The hut offered little comfort and was just as cold inside as it was outside.

At first it seemed like an abandoned hut, but a sense of foreboding and the stink of the place caused Khelvan to hold out the wooden stick and quickly scan the one-roomed building for any sign of the sorcerer. He crept around the small room with knees slightly bent before coming to a halt in front of the open fire place. He saw no signs of their target.

Meanwhile, Navek was unfazed by the empty room and stood upright and confident by the door with knife drawn at the ready. With his other hand, he reached over to a leather sheath near his right hip, and unfastened the clasp of a longer knife.

Khelvan glanced back at Navek and shrugged at finding no sign of the one they sought. He straightened and began to walk toward the doorway, but after a few paces, spun around and went back to a corner where the floorboards were stained with grime. He moved his hand over the boards, and then put his fingers into a small hole in the wood. A trapdoor! He opened it carefully.

Khelvan stared down into the dark underground cavity. He sent a silent message to Lamaar and braced himself for the task ahead, recollecting the purpose of the mission.

Navek felt a certainty and a gravity emanating from Khelvan, a real focus of mind, something he glimpsed during their trainings on the beach. He wondered briefly how he ever doubted this man all those months ago, when Khelvan had walked into his nightmare and dragged him out through the streets to rescue him. Whatever happened from here on, Navek was proud to be associated with such an intrepid and worthy man.

Without warning, Khelvan stepped down into the small dusty space and disappeared from sight.

Navek knew instinctively to follow and was soon behind him. Peering down through the gloom, they could make out a set of ancient steps made of rough grey rocks, barely visible in the dim light.

As their eyes slowly adjusted, they became aware of small movements on the walls.

About five black butterflies, the same as the ones

encountered earlier, guarded the passageway, leering at them through fiery red eyes on their wings. The creatures positioned themselves on the walls, flapping periodically. Khelvan swiped at them, killing four against the earthen wall, as the fifth one spiralled downward and disappeared into the tunnel. "Hmph. Go and tell your owner we're coming," he said to the escaped butterfly in a dry tone.

The two men proceeded with great caution into the darkness. Descending down slippery, narrow steps, they stooped over as they felt their way through the dank narrow passage that lead down under the old hut and disappeared into the unknown.

The air smelt damp and mouldy in the unused cavity that must have been dug out years ago by the miners. They could feel timber planks lining the walls and ceiling, but further along, only rough faced rock and earthen walls surrounded them. The tunnel became even narrower where the walls were mostly damp dirt.

In eerie silence and pitch black of the underground, they fumbled along, struggling with feelings of panic and claustrophobia which at times were barely controllable.

Sometimes they stumbled or tripped over piles of old diggings or loose piles of dirt eroded from the walls. Other times the passage narrowed to less than shoulder width where they had to squeeze through sideways, adding to the intense feeling of restriction.

There was nothing to stop the old tunnel from collapsing on them. Hidden and cut off from the rest of the world, they would be permanently entombed if that should happen.

Navek felt regard for the miners who once worked down in the appalling conditions to feed their families, and vowed if he ever got out alive, he would never work as a miner.

The winding tunnel seemed to go on endlessly and progress was slow. The men felt around with arms out and gloves off, and then tested the ground before each step. Occasionally they disturbed some bats which made high pitched sounds, then fluttering wings brushed their faces in the narrow space. In the darkness both men ducked and swiped as the creatures tried to exit the tunnel to the outside world.

The underground was freezing and absolutely motionless, except for the sound of their boots on the ground. They ventured on, passing other passageways that branched off from the main drive.

The deeper they went, the more they felt the terrible dark horror of the place, a place where atrocities against humankind were being instigated. The old miner's hut above was a front for the sorcerer's sinister operation; the men were on guard and felt edgy in the confined hell hole. They could be walking into a deadly trap, but had to confront the perpetrator head on, man-to-man, if they were to stop his path of destruction and revenge.

Eventually the ground underfoot levelled out and the tunnel headed inward toward the core of the mountain. Strange sounds emanated from deep below, eerie sounds like steel grating against steel, or the cogs of creaky old machinery grinding. The sounds became like a woman's high pitched rasping scream, followed by the cackling laugh of the one they hunted.

Hair stood up on the back of their necks. Jackyl certainly knew they were here.

Then the sounds would fade away and there would be silence again.

The familiar acrid smell of sulphur and stale smoke put Navek on edge. Memories came back of the day his father and his tribe were hunted down and killed. The unknown assailant had been accompanied by that same foul smell.

As cold as it was inside the core of the mountain, sweat broke out under Navek's shirt and trickled down his back. He struggled to control the panic and slow his breathing.

A small dull light became visible ahead, and as they came closer, it threw shadowy light through the tunnel. They stepped out into a large, barely lit underground cavern, where Khelvan and Navek stood back-to-back in the utter silence. In a crouched position with weapons in hand, they quickly scanned the dark corners for the one they sought.

On one side, a rusty tin cart sat on two metal wheels, an old sweat rag stiffened by time was tied to its handle. Inside the cart were a worn, rusty pick with a wooden handle which had been repaired more than once; a small scutching hammer; and a rusty bucket with a wire handle.

On the opposite side, two rusty shovels leaned up against an earthen wall, but there was no sign of a sorcerer.

Damp and unused, the cavern reeked of sulphur and

mould like the tunnels. White cobwebs hung down from the ceiling and grew in the crevices; they seemed alive – like vines. As their eyes adjusted, they could see some flat rock spiders and moss that amazingly existed at this depth.

Khelvan and Navek both turned when they became aware of movement in the corner. They peered through the haze to see an upright wooden post with a moving mass of black butterflies, clustered together at the top of the post like a hive of bees. The black creatures were a strange sight. Each had four crimson eyes on the back of their wings, all of which turned and leered menacingly at them through the gloom.

Another cackling laugh echoed from far away, and a few of the winged creatures lifted up into flight on their way back through the tunnel to the outside world.

When they flapped past, both men dodged the nasty looking creatures; their sinister appearance irked the men.

Strangely, the hanging cobwebs started to writhe and move, and then they exuded a pearly, phosphorescent glow like hot vapour, keeping the room dimly illuminated. The chamber took on an unearthly atmosphere.

Khelvan straightened from his crouched position and walked around, looking deeper into the shadows for their target. He could sense danger, but could not see its source. His instincts told him they were near.

He searched again for a sign, then stood a few moments to focus. *"Which way now? Which way?"* he silently asked his guides.

He did not want to retrace their path all the way back

without completing the required assignment, nor risk becoming lost by searching the offshoot tunnels. If anything happened to them down here they would never be found.

A butterfly rose up and flew in a slow orbital circle above their heads, before it flapped its way to the far side of the chamber and disappeared into the darkness.

The men thought they had come to a dead end, but Khelvan discovered another narrow tunnel branching off from the chamber, continuing further into the underground labyrinth. He sighed heavily and gestured to Navek to follow, arming himself with his wooden stick held out in front as he trailed the dark creature into the abyss.

Navek grabbed one of the shovels and broke off the old handle with his boot, then coiled it in cobwebs like candy floss on a stick. It seemed to writhe, shrink and expand on the handle, but he ignored its strangeness and stepped into the narrow tunnel, holding the stick up to illuminate the way. With perseverance, they advanced into the unknown realm, both anxious to face the sorcerer and get the job done.

Navek soon became frustrated and impatient. Their confinement, the acrid stench of sulphur, constant fear and trepidation all started to aggravate him. Then a streak of old anger rose up at all the trouble this one man had caused. *"He's only a man, a man who lives like a rat in a dark hole!"* Navek thought bitterly, as he persevered doggedly behind Khelvan.

Khelvan could hear Navek breathing heavily behind him, and wondered briefly whether to send him back to the surface and not risk both their lives. But Lamaar had told him they would both be needed to accomplish the task. They must meet the sorcerer man-to-man, face-to-face; this was the only way he would be defeated. The occasional black butterfly flapped past them, and if Khelvan saw it approaching, he would destroy the creature with one sharp swipe of the stick.

The strange cobweb lamp continued to move and writhe about on the end of the shovel handle, creating strange elongated shadows shifting about the tunnel. It helped their progress in the otherwise pitch black darkness.

The narrow passageway remained fairly horizontal but went on and on, till it seemed they must have surely passed the heart of the mountain. Eventually it curved round to the right, and as they reached the bend, a slight breeze of fresh air came from their left. They paused a moment to breathe the more agreeable air and realised there was more than one entrance to the mine. From here the tunnel travelled gradually downward, passing several other offshoot drives either side of the main tunnel.

Under tonnes of earth and rock, the light from a cobweb lamp waxed and waned, and at times almost died out. As they descended, they both became aware that a strange pressure pushed against them. The atmosphere became thick like cold treacle and felt more dangerous with every step. Neither man spoke. The pace slowed involuntarily, till their actions and efforts became possible only in slow motion.

Suddenly it was too late! They had walked into a dangerous trap; ensnared by a devious captor. Invisible imprisonment pressed in on them and hands and feet were bound.

Navek cursed and growled in a low guttural voice, angry at being immobilised against his will. As they came under the dark spell, Khelvan shook his head in an effort to clear the fog from his mind. He knew they were trapped and the easy capture deeply disturbed him.

The suffocating spell wrapped around their throats and chests like tentacles, and crushed the air from their lungs. The more they struggled, the more their movements were restricted, and they could not retreat now even if they chose to.

The giant anaconda-like creature in the desert flashed through Khelvan's mind and with it a fleeting image of the shaman. "*Had the experience in the desert been a foreboding of this?*" The Bedouin healer had easily dispelled its stranglehold that night by a mere touch. Khelvan needed some kind of intervention and in desperation, called out in his mind for shaman's help.

He was unsure how long they remained immobilised, but somewhere in the distance, he thought he heard the sound of the medicine man's staff with its strange rattling trinkets. He had the faint impression someone tapped his shoulder, just as it happened in the desert that night. He tried to relax and focus. Slowly, he found he could breathe a little easier; his lungs were able to expand when he did so. Finally, he had slight movement again.

Khelvan sent a message of gratitude to the shaman and turned slowly toward Navek who struggled in frustration at the bondage.

Khelvan lifted his arm and placed his open hand on Navek's chest, in an attempt to relay a message to relax.

Navek understood and slowed his panicked breathing as Khelvan's touch released him from the spell. They both regained some control as tentacles loosened their grip and retracted into the gloom.

Affected by the spell, they tried to shake off the ordeal. The cobweb lamp, almost extinguished in the struggle, now faded into a dim flicker before going out altogether. They had never been anywhere so black. Even if you close your eyes on a dark night there is a light that can be seen for those who will watch. But here it was oppressively black.

As if in a dreamlike trance, they carried on – arms out in front, feeling the way, the stink of sulphur burning their nostrils and throats.

Navek scowled in anger at the remnants of the spell which still clung about him. He hated the reminder of the despair and futility he had lived with for years, and fumed at the sorcerer's cowardly tactic – the same tactic used to chase down and bind his tribe before he killed them. The memory of Navek's father Hatchiman firmed his resolve to buck against the spell and not be defeated. There in the freezing underground hell, it all became clear.

This was his destiny. He was in the right place and

there had been no wastage. All the threads in the tapestry of his life were interwoven to reach this point; he was part of a bigger plan. Navek had survived to confront and defeat the rogue sorcerer, not only as retribution against the crimes, but also for the benefit of future generations. Others had suggested this to him before, but now it was clear. He understood. He could not dwell on this new epiphany. He swallowed the bitter sweet information as he hurried on with determination to confront the sorcerer, refusing to accept the invisible prison that worked at slowing him down.

Khelvan struggled on doggedly, still holding the wooden stick out in front. He could hear Navek close behind, walking faster and almost on his heels. Khelvan detected a shift in Navek's demeanour and a new determination in his footsteps. There was a resolution in Navek, a certainty not evident before they entered the tunnels; a certainty which Khelvan did not feel in himself right now. His companion had managed to break free of the shackles, and the warrior Navek now walked behind him. This strengthened Khelvan and gave him a glimmer of hope. More than ever, he was grateful Navek was here, but the biggest challenge still lay ahead.

Khelvan tried to clear the fog from his brain, and could sense the sorcerer not far away. In his vulnerability, he appealed to the spirit guides from the afterlife for help. They needed a miracle; he felt cut off from any help from anywhere, as the screeching sounds restarted underneath them.

The more they journeyed, the more the enormity and magnitude of the sorcerer's dark powers pervaded the atmosphere. Acute peril and cold merciless intentions were palpable throughout the tunnel and out beyond. Khelvan felt small, out of his depth. *"Would they be the next ones to die? Would they be defeated by the very shadow of all he had believed in and lived for?"*

It was too late now, they were here and there was no going back. Khelvan had to find a way to reach the hermit sorcerer who lived unchallenged in his world of spells and trickery.

Jackyl's powers were born from vengeance and fear. No wonder none had found him; he operated from the bowels of the earth, alone and isolated from the world. He unknowingly reflected his own pain on the world, wanting others to feel the same frustration, self-doubt and anger that he endured as a boy.

Jackyl had developed murderous powers. He trusted no one and wanted to destroy man's hope and happiness, just as it had been destroyed in him. He worked spells on people's thoughts; he construed invisibly to replace good with fear and doubt, and eroded away the trust between people. His methods would surely end in warfare and injustice.

Amid the chilling darkness, fleeting doubts gnawed at Khelvan. Foreign thoughts intruded his mind: *"You're not going to make it. Will all your life's effort be a waste? What am I doing here? Surely Lamaar has overestimated me. I can't do this".*

The doubts floated past but he ignored them, as Lamaar had taught him to do. He knew they sought to debilitate his commitment. Khelvan focused, aware on a deeper level, he was *not* his changing thoughts, but more accurately, he was the one, the soul, who *listened* to the thoughts. If he could maintain *that* clarity, he may have a chance.

Chapter 19.
The Spellbinder's Lair

Far away, on a mountain range on the south-west province, Linchee and his daughter sipped green tea from exquisite porcelain cups the colour of light jade. They sat enjoying the late afternoon ambience, dressed in traditional silk attire of the rich. The embroidered fabrics were refined and ornate with exquisite oriental designs.

Outside, black-necked cranes swooped down low over the river. They circled a few times and then squawked as they flew off to the green valley in the distance, calling out again as they disappeared from sight. Linchee heard the birds' calls, looked up from his tea and tilted his head slightly to listen. He placed his cup on the carved teak table beside him, then stood by the window. Lulu also heard the birds and knew by their tone they were calling on her father.

Linchee followed the direction of the birds and acknowledged the message they carried to him, recognising the call for help. He looked over the meticulous gardens with the beautiful moon gate leading down to the river, then sat on a carved wooden chair and closed his eyes. Focusing within himself, he used his psychic abilities to traverse space. He was shocked and disturbed by the state of the two men he saw. Not by chance the same two men had blown into his shop at Kashmera months ago. He saw the dark tomb where they were now trapped and in a dreadful state. He sent them a silent message, "I am with you my friends. Don't forget mirror. Take out mirror," he transmitted.

~

Khelvan and Navek found themselves standing in another chamber which was larger than the previous one. They had no memory of how they had reached it or how long they had been there. Both men were frozen and could hardly move, leaving them vulnerable. Their bodies were immobilised but their eyes darted around the chamber frantically seeking the hermit sorcerer.

Around them were weird, abstract objects on shelves and hanging on walls: spinning physics machines, dusty volumes of books, hanging bunches of dried herbs, strange shaped gourds and onion shaped vessels containing strange concoctions.

The air reeked of death or bodies long dead, mixed

with a sulphuric musty smell. The same opalescent cobwebs glowed dimly, hanging from the walls and ceiling.

Perturbed to find they were now trapped in the underground realm, Khelvan shivered with apprehension. They were in the lair of a dangerous animal that lurked nearby watching its prey.

Khelvan's eyes flashed in the dim light as he tried to see their captor. The wooden stick was gone, so he attempted to reach for a weapon from under his coat. He found that as much as he strained, he could barely move, and dropped his arm back down with a feeling of uselessness.

Beside him to his right, Navek squirmed and wrestled against being immobilised. Khelvan wanted to tell him to stop struggling and save his energy, but he could not speak.

In the distance, a deep booming sound echoed up through the depths of the middle earth. The sound continued on and on, like a long roll of thunder. It was followed by tremors that reverberated from deep below their feet, causing the chamber to shake and stones and dust to fall all around them. They feared the chamber would cave in.

Something smashed to the floor to their left. They both turned their eyes trying desperately to see what caused the noise, then turned back in horror when they heard an eerie voice to their right.

Jackyl was sitting in the shadows. He had been watching them all along with penetrating eyes glowing craftily in the dim light. He was bemused by the two men, looking them up and down with curiosity as though they were an entertainment to him.

The sorcerer's aged face even appeared friendly and easy going. But unknown evils exuded from his darker depths, like morning mist off an icy lake. His head fell back and let out an evil, condescending laugh, which sounded hollow and distant as it echoed throughout the underground. He gloated at their capture.

Behind his robed figure, a mass of red butterfly eyes gleamed eerily in the shadowy light. Each of them was exactly the same, with four vivid red eyes on their black wings. All eyes moved in unison as they observed the two trapped men. A few of the creatures flew around the sorcerer's head in slow elliptical circles like planets orbiting. The flickering of black and red could be seen above him.

A few more hovered over the open pages of a large dusty book which looked to be a relic from ancient times. It confirmed to Khelvan that the sorcerer was connected to the creatures. He was using them as his eyes, they were spy crafts sent out into the world to transmit back to him. This was how he was able to monitor mankind, while remaining cloaked in secrecy. He ran his operations from an underground lair which he never left.

The words of his teacher rang through Khelvan, "Get rid of his eyes so he cannot see".

Now he knew what the words meant. He must destroy the black butterflies, but how? The current circumstances held no relation to the skills he had learnt over the years. Nothing in his training had prepared him for this. Lamaar had told him: "In the end it will not be your weapons that will undo him, but your inner strength".

He could do nothing physically; inner strength was all that remained. *"Would this be enough to save them?"*

In the depths of Navek's being, an old and deep anger welled. A chord was struck and a silent scream rose for all the previous injustices. White hot fury boiled to the surface, and he faced it head on.

His clan had been wiped out for no justifiable reason; the waste of good lives was unacceptable! His life had been shattered because of the conjuring of this treacherous creature that held no accountability for his actions. The futility of having no control or choice to defend himself was being repeated.

But this time, Navek would not accept it. Smouldering anger fumed in him. He realised how all his grown life he had listened and given power to the voices of fear and doubt. These voices had been shadowy thieves that robbed him of his rightful happiness. They always told him he did not deserve to feel good. The thoughts had been like a dog yapping at his heels, never allowing him any peace.

Navek knew then that he *was* valid, and all those destructive thoughts were the very shadows of light itself, shadows of his true potential. A new strength awoke in him at this revelation, and power came from his very existence. A validity which said to him: "I am. I exist. This is *my* lifetime. Mine".

Navek's whole body tingled as the blood flowed and revived him. He became free of the binding spell. He realised he could now move his head, his hands and feet, but he remained motionless to consider his next move.

Within the shadows, the Spellbinder shifted his position. Shuffling past them, he murmured and muttered as though they were not there. He was tall and thin but stooped over, with ghostly white skin and the shrivelled face of an old man. His hair was dishevelled and matted; he wore a ragged grey robe. They smelt the stink of tattered and unwashed clothes as he headed toward a smaller chamber to their right, with three of the butterflies accompanying him overhead.

Khelvan felt a nudge in his ribs, and realised with great relief that Navek was no longer bound by the spell. They still had some chance at achieving the mission!

In the other chamber, they could see the outline of the sorcerer's hunched frame, with the butterflies that had followed still slowly orbiting above.

Jackyl turned and looked back at Khelvan and Navek. He appeared deathly, vacant and empty like inert matter. Then he snarled and disappeared from view.

Khelvan saw that Jackyl's menacing eyes were milky, opaque and colourless. The sorcerer was blind.

The spirits gathered around Khelvan and he heard it said again, "Get rid of his eyes". He knew what needed to be done, but now did not have the capacity to do the task.

Khelvan noticed Navek no longer stood next to him. He felt apprehension in the pit of his stomach when he saw his companion, now crouched, crossing toward the smaller chamber.

Navek did not know what he would do, but peeped around the wall to see the sorcerer standing with his back to him. His hands were clasped casually behind his back and he was looking upward toward the luminous cobwebs that now twisted and writhed above him.

Navek quickly turned back to Khelvan, only to see the desperate look on his face. Khelvan's eyes darted up and down from the butterflies to the sorcerer, then back to Navek. He was trying to tell Navek something with his eyes, and Navek's brow creased in consternation, unsure how to interpret the gestures.

From the next chamber a raspy voice called out in mock bemusement, "I can heeear you," though the men had not spoken.

The sorcerer had not moved, though the sound of his sinister voice stayed suspended in the air long after the words were spoken. Ignoring the sorcerer, Khelvan repeated the eye movements and then looked back to Navek, who finally understood what he was trying to say and knew what to do.

With knees bent and alert for any tricks, Navek fixed his eyes on the sorcerer. Before he could do anything, another laugh echoed out from the chamber. At alarming speed, Jackyl spun around to face Navek, who was only a few paces away. Navek smelt the stink coming from him as he stepped forward to strike the frail looking man, but was abruptly halted and his movements slowed to a standstill. He was frozen in place again. White hanging webs began quickly moving and slithering like snakes from above, entwining themselves around Navek's body. When his body was wrapped completely, he was hoisted up to hang upside down from the ceiling just outside the small chamber. He was left slowly rotating like a wind chime in the breeze, wrapped and imprisoned by white webs. Once again, he was immobilised.

"I told you I could hear you … and see you too," Jackyl sniggered. "You can't fool me with cheap tricks." He let out a loud cackling sound as though amused by his own words, leaving Navek hanging trapped in the malicious webs.

With desperation and urgency, Navek struggled and fought against the entrapment and felt he was falling. He slipped back into a feeling of uselessness before numbness … and then unconsciousness.

Jackyl had known all along that Navek was no longer bound by the spell, and had allowed his captive the few moments of exultation and relative freedom, knowing that binding him again would amplify the old wounds even more. The sorcerer exacted abnormal pleasure from causing pain to others, and had never known the attribute of mercy – he revelled in power gleaned from having such control.

Khelvan sighed and closed his eyes. He briefly reflected on the futility of the venture they had set out on with such little preparation for what they were up against. The situation was precarious; his mind scrambled desperately to find what could be done to regain any freedom or achieve their quest.

He settled his panicked mind and with eyes still closed, focused all his attention within, digging deep for an answer.

He came back to the directive from his teacher, "It will not be your skill or your weapons that will bring about his undoing, but your inner strength. Be still and listen to your inner voice".

Eventually Khelvan almost laughed out loud when he saw the only answer available to him. He resolved himself to relax and focus within himself even more as Lamaar had taught him. He stilled his mind, and surrendered completely to the life force hidden within that breathes all of creation. He connected to the power. From birth till death it exists bigger than us all, even Jackyl Nazarak.

All those years of practising and polishing the techniques in training had prepared him for this, to be moved by his own spirit and not his thoughts. He felt a wave of peace wash over him and welcomed its simple and familiar embrace. In its shelter he prayed earnestly and humbly for help, *"You, who sees everything and is within everything with no separation, please help me"*. He opened his eyes as another tremor reverberated up through the mountain, shaking and rattling the weird collection of items around the cavern.

The sorcerer scrunched his face in bafflement. Tilting his head as though trying to decipher the tremors he called: "Stop complaining!"

"Always nagging like an old woman," he mumbled and then scurried past Navek to the small chamber, muttering as he disappeared.

Khelvan noticed that during the tremors, slight movement returned to his hands and feet, albeit only very slight. It occurred to him that somehow, the tremors in the mountain lessened the sorcerer's powers. But that was the last thing he thought before his body suddenly fell to the floor with a dull thud, laying down in an unconscious heap.

Navek did not know how long he had been hanging there, but it was the stink of the sulphuric gases and the tremors that eventually woke him. He looked around groggily through half opened eyelids, and could just make out the unmoving body of Khelvan lying on his side, slumped on the dirt floor at the opposite side of the cavern.

Navek's head felt heavy and his mind felt dazed and confused. He tried to get his eyes to focus as he hung suspended with arms pinned to his sides by the sticky white webs. In exasperation, he realised that the weaver of spells had managed to cast a binding spell over him again.

Long moments passed by in the timeless underground, and through his foggy mind he recalled the dilemma they were in, despairing at how easily they had been disarmed and captured. He knew the outlaw sorcerer was in the room nearby.

Navek had felt like this before, when he had woken from unconsciousness in that creek bed all those years ago, to find his father and all his tribesmen dead around him. He had never liked dwelling or thinking about that event for too long; it stirred hatred and revenge in him.

Mostly he was angry with himself. He had not fought that day, and had not gone to his ancestors with the others. He would still wake from nightmares with his heart racing and his body covered in sweat. Always in his nightmares, he was never quite able to see the pursuer, or reach the dark figure who laughed eerily at him before it slipped away into the shadows. He had never searched for the murderer as it seemed futile for him on his own, and he did not know where to look.

Since that awful day, he had often felt he had no roots, no purpose, and no lineage to identify with or belong to. He thought back to the old healer Sharian, who found him on the mountain years ago. Sharian had seen right into his soul from the very beginning, seen his pain, his shame and his grief, all in a glance … and also his fear of an unknown future. Though Navek had brushed it aside at the time, Sharian had also foreseen his potential as the warrior who would one day achieve great things to help the earth-journey of mankind. "It takes many blows to the steel to forge a strong sword," Sharian had told him.

Another tremor vibrated up through the mountain. It increased in intensity as it rumbled and shook the cavity around them, causing more stones to fall from walls that threatened to cave in.

Navek remained suspended in the webs, his body rotating slowly. His eyes were open and he could see the sorcerer in the next cavern, bent over one of the books, chortling to himself as three or four butterflies still orbited over his head. Old and familiar frustration welled up in Navek again. He did not need clear thoughts in is head to tell him he must fight the sorcerer. Frustration turned to white hot anger which burned the fog from his brain. Volatile and dangerous after a lifetime of pressure built up, his rage was ready to blow.

Chapter 20.
Messenger Birds

On the Parrot Islands the elders sat gathered under the shade of a spreading tree. A flock of large, black birds with white markings flew in sweeping low arcs, checking out the area before they landed in the trees nearby. It was a large flock of about thirteen birds which the tribe had seen before, but many moons had passed since the last visit.

This time they appeared to have flown in after a long hard flight; some looked thin and out of condition with feathers missing. The chief was concerned about their health and noticed that some birds were missing. Three of the weakest birds sat further away from the others, holding their wings out from their bodies to cool themselves, beaks held open.

With a nod of his head, the chief called two boys over, and asked one to chop some meat for the birds, and the other to get them water. He knew the creatures had been through hard times and would appreciate not having to search for food and water.

In the hot afternoon, the birds looked at the men sideways with their sharp yellow eyes, before they warbled and called out to each other in their pleasant tones, while the elders listened to their sounds with serious faces. From time-to-time, the chief communicated back to the birds, drawing in air as he whistled to the creatures in their varied musical language. To anyone else they were just a flock of birds warbling in the trees, but the elders and their ancestors had always communicated with these messenger birds.

The to-and-fro exchange of sounds between man and birds continued. Something was amiss with the world. The old men listened intently, gleaning information with frowns of consternation and solemn faces as they heard the awful news; the wheel of life was starting to go awry.

The islanders were closely attuned to the seasons and the mother earth. They already knew something was not right with the world. A shadow, a darkness, an ignorance of all that is good had started to spread itself. They listened to the birds and understood the message being sent, available to those who knew how to listen. Even on the remote island, passing birds would give them information of the affairs of mainland life if they needed to know it. In this case, it was their help that was needed.

The men turned to look at each other, while the chief sat among them with eyes closed, waiting to see what help was required of them. Skin tingled on the back of his neck when a vision of Navek appeared in his mind's eye. A premonition passed over him that something was gravely wrong when he saw Navek inside a cold mountain, wrapped in white webs and hanging like spider's prey in the gloom. Another man lay on the dirt floor. The chief glimpsed a fleeting image of their captor who lurked nearby, brooding, sinister and dangerous. The vision was unnerving. He felt the malevolent power of the captor, the intention aimed at usurping and extracting all joy from mankind, the source of the unrest.

The chief's eyes flew open at seeing the chilling sight of two men trapped under a mountain by such a demon. He understood the message carried by the birds, and the source of the world's discord. It originated from the mind of one man, a man who lived under a mountain.

One of the birds glided down to land on a branch near the food. Its yellow eyes did not leave the men as it stood cautiously and waited. After checking for danger, it eventually took some of the meat then flew further away to eat. Witnessing the first bird's venture, other birds from the flock flew down to eat, but remained constantly alert because of the close proximity to the men. Eventually the sick birds followed to take some of the food, but the chief knew they would not live much longer; something was not right with them.

Soon after, the birds all lifted up and then departed to groom themselves and rest higher up on the mountain, seemingly pleased after their interaction with the humans.

The men exchanged glances, not as encouraged by the visit as they usually would be. They were not used to such a request for help.

Regardless of the heat of the day, the chief sent for the women to prepare food and water and help them prepare for a trip. They would leave for the sacred caves high on the mountain and would not be back that night.

The old men told their sons to get ready to travel and soon after were on the trail heading up a well-known path to a rocky outcrop. By late afternoon they entered the caves. The elders gave instructions to prepare a fire with a stockpile of timber that would last through the night. They smoothed an area around the fire for sitting and then organised the food. The sons hurried about their tasks, sensing the elders were impatient to begin.

In the twilight, they looked out over the sea to watch the sun setting on the horizon. Though the temperature was warm, they lit a fire.

A simple glance from the chief was all it took for the younger men to form an outer circle behind the elders as protection. The young men leaned on upright pointed spears as they prepared to go on a journey with an unknown outcome. They had stood guard before when the elders had attended the secret ceremonies. Sworn to secrecy they knew not to ask questions. Sometimes, they witnessed paranormal occurrences where the elders went into a trance-like state.

Two drummers started to play in unison, drumming slowly at first like the constant pulsing rhythm of a heart beating. The old men closed their eyes and chanted in a deep monotone drone which reverberated throughout the caves. The ceremony went on for some time, and then the chief stood and invoked the spirit of the whole volcanic mountain range which surrounded them. This included the archipelago of islands nearby and extended for thousands of miles under the sea to the arctic north of the mainland. He transferred information and implored the spirit of the mountains for help, calling upon its power to intervene.

Navek hung upside down, swaying in slow circles in one direction, then unwinding back the other way, straining and struggling to escape from the bindings.

From somewhere, the unexpected image of the island chief came into his mind. The regal man sat in a cave with his eyes closed, the elders gathered around.

"Yield," the message came through. "Yield."

"Maybe I'm dead," he thought. Almost with disappointment, Navek knew he was not dead, not yet anyway. "Yield," was the clear signal that came again, as though the very mountain had whispered into his soul. Finally he understood, and completely relaxed his angry mind and tense body.

The stranglehold of cords lessened their grip on him ever so slightly. He closed his eyes and let go of all thoughts, as Khelvan had taught him at the beach house.

The great wheel of time stood still.

Navek came into the moment where time did not exist. He was at one with life itself and felt like a grain of sand on the shores of eternity, valid and a particle of everything. A magnificent strength and clarity filled him, fathomless and immeasurable. He felt his consciousness expand to fill the universe, and he finally understood his own purpose.

Somewhere in the distance, he thought he could hear the deep droning sound of monks chanting in unison. He had the distinct impression these vibrations were connected to the mountain range itself and helped soothe the unhappy mountain, as well they held back an imminent collapse.

Another tremor came up through the earth, with booming sounds that rattled and shuddered throughout the underground. When the tremors occurred, Navek found he was able to move his body and the binding webs loosened a little more. He recognised, as Khelvan had, there was a correlation between the strength of the sorcerer's powers and the tremors in the mountain. Perhaps the sorcerer's spells were weakened at these times.

Suddenly, Navek dropped silently from the webs and spilled onto the floor like a newborn animal dropping from its mother.

A renewed power came to life in him. He quickly looked around for the sorcerer who appeared preoccupied and agitated as aftershocks continued. Navek did not know how much time had passed, and was disheartened when he saw Khelvan still lying on the dirt floor, bound by spells and in trouble.

He would have to help him later; right now he had a job to do.

The colony of black butterflies continued to cluster around a wooden pole like a swarm of bees; they flapped and massed together on the pole as though it was a homing device. They were alarmed by the tremors that threatened to extinguish them, and frequently lifted off and landed again, repositioning themselves as an occasional single butterfly fluttered in from the tunnel to join them. Some of the winged creatures continued to fly around the sorcerer's head, circling obediently over him and then over the open book in front of him.

Jackyl uttered an eerie high pitched wailing sound, which became mocking and sardonic as he desperately tried to conjure his dark allies from another world, summoning them to his aid in some kind of a defence. In a panic he flailed his arms at the flapping creatures which he relied on as his eyes. He became angry and impatient with them because his vision was spasmodic and failing amid the increasing turmoil.

Navek knew if it was not already too late, he and Khelvan must get out of there.

He went over to Khelvan and rolled him over onto his back. The eyes of his companion were open and staring directly at him. Navek heard the deep droning sound again in the distance, only this time it was accompanied by slow rhythmic drumming which seemed to repeat the words: "Stone and flint. Stone and flint," over and over in tune with the beat of the drums.

He reached into Khelvan's inside pocket and fumbled around in search of the stone and flint. He found the stiff leather package containing the mirror that the Chinese father and daughter had waited years to give them, which he had forgotten till now. He broke the stiff lace easily, and unwrapped the old leather to reveal the ancient mirror on its bed of orange silk. He took the relic out then placed the silver chain over Khelvan's head, arranging the mirror to face outward on his chest, but not knowing if it would do any good. With no time to spare, his hand dived back into to another pocket and this time, pulled out the stone and flint.

Before they had entered the mine, Khelvan told him that fire would thicken the sorcerer's spells and was one of his weaknesses. If he could create heat in this icy prison, they may still have a chance.

The cavern became darker, and pending catastrophe pervaded throughout. Ironically, Navek felt an unprecedented calmness as he shoved the jabbering sorcerer aside. This was the killer of his people. He would not cower. He grabbed the large book that was open and tore out pages to make a rough pile, then struck flint against stone in an effort to ignite the pages in the icy, dank air. Though sparks flew, they did not take. Navek struck the iron and flint repeatedly in the semi-darkness to no avail.

Jackyl reared up at Navek. Navek felt his menacing and dangerous power, but side-kicked him in the chest and sent him flying across the chamber where he hit the wall and slid down. Jackyl got up and spluttered confused curses and evocations, calling out to evil spirits to kill the intruders. Jackyl scrambled to recite spells to do his work as black butterflies scattered in the chaos.

From another world, the deep droning and the primordial rhythm of drums continued on and on. Navek scrunched up more pages till finally one of the pages caught, then another and another as burning paper lit up in the gloom.

In the rising smoke from the pages, he was sure he felt an evil breeze rush past him, and even saw weird goblin-like figures with panicked and frenzied faces, disintegrating in the rising heat.

Navek ignored the sorcerer's wails and fearful anguish, seizing anything else that would burn. To his right was a well-used metal handle on a timber door, recessed into the wall. With a few quick strides, he put his boot straight through the timber door, exposing a row of ancient, dusty books. He tossed them into the fire, adding the broken timber door and timber benches to fuel the fire which filled the chamber with thick smoke.

Aftershocks continued, each time weakening the previously unchallenged hold of Jackyl Nazarak.

The sorcerer heard the books burn and felt the heat from the fire. His head fell back and he let out another eerie wailing sound, then screeched desperately as the ancient books of spells were destroyed. The means to his dark conjuring and evil magic went up in flames. With failing powers, he frantically floundered around, trying to weave a spell that would stop Navek, barking half-remembered curses directly at him. Navek merely shoved him back down each time he tried to stand up.

On one of the shelves Navek saw an old oil squirter made from tin. Inside, there was a small amount of liquid. He turned it toward the butterflies and rapidly pumped the handle to spray oil over them. Some rose up in fright. He snatched one of the burning books and shoved the fire under the mass of butterflies to set the lower ones aflame, and then watched as the fire ignited the others. They flapped around in a frenzy trying to escape, emitting an evil hissing sound before they were snuffed out and wafted upward in the heat like charred paper.

The sorcerer stumbled to the far corner of the small chamber, ranting and raving desperately. Bent over, he rubbed his eyes in torment while his world burned around him. Screeching metallic sounds boomed beneath them, as seismic movements threatened them like ants in a tunnel. Aware that tonnes of earth could come down on them at any moment, Navek remarkably remained calm amid the chaos.

The cavern shook from side-to-side, unleashing stones from the walls and ceiling.

Throughout all of this, Khelvan lay on the floor unable to move. He drifted in and out of consciousness, but was aware with each passing tremor that the debilitating and numbing spell lessened its grip on him. Nevertheless, it still held him there on the dirt floor, with no protection from the grave peril they were in. Surrounded by turmoil, there was a moment when he glimpsed the face of the Chinaman Linchee. His jovial face hovered just above Khelvan in the haze, and peered down into his face, before the bright eyes went to the mirror hanging on Khelvan's chest.

Linchee nodded happily, and then he was gone.

When the shaking finally subsided, Khelvan felt movement return to his numb hands and feet. He lay there a few moments longer getting his bearings. He had lost all his strength and skills when he needed them most, and was frustrated at his own inability and uselessness. He blinked his eyes, tried to focus and took in a few big breaths of the smoky air. With enormous effort he heaved himself up, and rolled into a half-crouching position toward the tunnel entry. From this position, Khelvan was greatly encouraged to see Navek no longer affected by any spells, busily tearing out pages from books and adding them to a fire.

Navek's eyes gleamed as they reflected the flames; he exuded a conviction and authority Khelvan had never seen in him before. His bearing was intrepid and fearless with a steely resolve to defeat the enemy. Khelvan saw the courage of a true warrior.

Some control was coming back into Khelvan's body, a loosening of the sorcerer's paralysing grip, but he was not his usual self.

Navek continued feeding the fire to keep it alive and warm up the chamber. He looked across and was relieved to see Khelvan crouched low, though his companion was unsteady and not fully functional. They were a long way under the mountain and still had to climb back up through unstable passages that may have already collapsed or been cut off. Both men knew they must leave now.

Khelvan straightened with difficulty, trying to regain balance and clarity. There still one more task to be done if he was to follow the original instructions. It was the most important thing of all and the reason they were down in this death trap. He was to give the sorcerer a choice before his death, a clear choice to redeem himself, otherwise the efforts and the journey to rid the world of the rogue sorcerer would be in vain. If the sorcerer did not learn a lesson from all of this, he would be reborn into a future lifetime to plague humanity all over again, like a blight on the sunrise. As sure as night follows day, he would pursue the same path of destruction, only the next incarnation would come with more powers … and there would be no stopping him. The conjurer of evil would be intent on removing all joy from the world; eons of unmelting snow and endless winters would ensue.

Khelvan teetered with one hand on the wall for support. He knew what was at stake, but his strength had been sapped from him. He no longer had the skills or the capability to do what had to be done. If he ever needed help, it was now.

Khelvan's eyes darted around looking for the sorcerer who had disappeared. The cavern was filled with thick smoke, but some of it was being drawn upward and out through the tunnel, which was a good sign that the tunnel was not blocked off.

With time running out, he staggered across the chamber, managing to stay upright as his head reeled. He placed a hand on Navek's shoulder for support and reassurance, then stood for a moment and watched the flames as some strength came back into him. He recalled the components that would undo their target; get rid of his eyes, create heat and rely on inner strength. He was relieved that Navek was busy achieving all of these. He wondered briefly why he had been picked to go on this journey if he was so useless, but ignored the thoughts when he spotted the sorcerer slumped against the wall in the adjoining cavern.

Jackyl the Lone Wolf looked aged and weakened since they first arrived. His senile jabberings trailed off unfinished into the smoky sulphuric air, as he tried pathetically to get up and drag himself away from the heat which was neutralising his spells.

Khelvan made his way into the other room and his hand went to the mirror hanging on his chest. He had no recollection of how it got there, but it comforted him somewhat to have it. He exhaled deeply and recalled his teacher's words, "To defeat him would require not strength and weapons, but surrender to a greater power for the help you would need".

Khelvan was relieved to remember that the demise of the sorcerer was not completely on his shoulders. He held his mind still and called upon the spirit world, sending a humble and silent prayer for help and protection for what was to come. Khelvan stepped forward and faced the dishevelled sorcerer who, from isolation and solitude of a frozen world, had manipulated life and caused much ruin. Jackyl had carved out a lonely existence. He stood at the cold door of death in a no man's land between the two worlds. He kept his feet in one world and was able to manipulate from another. He had managed to invisibly trespass on the path of the living, and had connived to shift the course toward a joyless world. It was no coincidence each year the winters above were lasting longer.

Khelvan approached carefully, not wanting to underestimate the sorcerer who now cowered against the far wall, uttering small yelping sounds like a lost pup.

Unexpectedly, Jackyl loomed up from the ground with alarming speed and turned on Khelvan like a wild animal. Jackyl shrieked and screamed a tirade of strange jumbled invocations in an attempt to cast another spell. Potent prongs of lightening came forth from his fingers and flew across the room to hit Khelvan in the chest with a sudden jolt.

Khelvan braced himself against the force of it, but the mirror on his chest returned the spell to its sender. Jackyl wailed in despair, before slumping down in defeat.

Lamaar had told him about the brutalised child who had never belonged anywhere, and Khelvan had perceived it for himself in the desert. Behind the dark surface was a little boy living a lonely existence, lost and afraid. The little boy only ever needed love, but never once received it. Khelvan felt pity for the Jackyl in front of him now, but it was too late. The sorcerer could not end the dark path he had perpetuated, nor could he remove himself from it. He would never belong anywhere else and his self-made world offered no escape.

But one act of kindness would be offered to him.

Jackyl did not lift his pale, ashen face and remained hunched over, squirming uncomfortably against the wall of the cave.

Khelvan looked down at the blind man with disdain for the man's mind, but also with understanding and even compassion for his soul. Strength finally flowed back into Khelvan. In a monotone voice, he spoke to the crumpled man: "Jackyl Nazarak, you have put a curse on the heartbeat of man in a selfish and misguided bid for power and revenge. You have failed to abide by the basic rules of humanity, and have lived your life by self-made authority at the ruin of others. You have chosen to live as a scoundrel and have become a burden to all life on this earth, trespassing over the rights of others. You have devised a way past the old Keepers in the afterlife, to access records you had no right to see. Somehow you have manipulated and tampered with the wheel of time to affect the rotations of the seasons. Many of the sacred greats and worthy spirits gone before you have decreed that you have not earned any favour throughout your lifetime, and you will not continue further in your false prestige".

Khelvan paused a moment, in awe of himself at the

words and where they were springing from. He was experiencing a message being delivered through him from the Creator to its creature. "This message is not from me, but from the all-knowing ones who have been with you throughout your lifetime. They know others have wronged you badly, but if you can forgive their great ignorance and cruelty against you … then see this as your single chance to redeem yourself. Admit this now before you are taken to the afterlife, or you will never be recycled back onto this precious earth again. It would have been different if others had not been affected."

In the flickering light the sorcerer's head lifted up, and though he was blind his eyes shone with a disturbing gleam. He spluttered as if trying to spit out the sickness and death in him, and then suddenly lunged toward Khelvan again, flailing his arms about in a desperate last effort to conjure up his spells. When he found he could no longer remember them, he gave up. With most of his books and butterflies gone, he could not access the dark spells which went up in flames.

Loud rumbling sounds echoed up through the mountain, and deep reverberations shook the underground chambers, again causing more stones and dust to fall from the ceiling and walls.

Navek listened to the flow of words coming from Khelvan and admired the depth of understanding and meaning, but felt great urgency to get out of there.

Khelvan glanced at Navek, acknowledging the necessity to leave but continued with the address.

"You will die soon, but if you can learn and admit your errors, you may sprout again with a chance at a new life. Don't worry about the others; they will reap what they've sown."

Khelvan waited a few moments before adding, "Are you willing to face up to your misdirection and errors? How do you plead?"

There followed a long silence, while both Khelvan and Navek impatiently waited.

"How do you plead?" he repeated in a louder tone.

In a small childlike voice, barely audible, Jackyl answered, "Guilty".

Navek and Khelvan looked at each other, and with a nod hurried toward the tunnel from where they had come.

More screeching metallic sounds came up from beneath them; the mountain was under great pressure as reverberations shook the entire region.

The situation was dire and it may be too late to escape. It was imperative they leave now if they stood any chance of survival. With pressing urgency, Navek scouted around the cavern for something to wrap cobwebs around. Next to the defeated sorcerer was a wooden stool. He walked over and put his boot straight through it in mid-stride, splintering it in an instant. He grabbed one of the legs and tossed the remains of the stool onto the fire, causing sparks and cinders to fly up through the cavern. Reaching up, he quickly wrapped cobwebs around to form a dim glow at the top of the stick. He noted the same cobwebs that had bound him earlier now had no power over him.

As Navek turned to go, he glanced down at the sorcerer for a final time. His eyes were drawn to the gold flashes of a stone hanging around the sorcerer's neck. He swiftly reached toward the cringing man to retrieve the amulet, which had once belonged to the father of Sharian, the old healer who had saved him in the forest. He jerked the stone from the sorcerer's neck and stuffed it into his inside pocket before joining Khelvan at the tunnel.

As they left, ghostlike tentacles came down from the roof of the cave and sought to grip on to them.

Navek jumped out of range of the slithering snake-like creatures, but Khelvan stood with feet planted on the cold ground, with a determination he did not feel. The tentacles retracted and disappeared into the smokiness.

Khelvan knew it was Jackyl's feeble attempt at sorcery, the death throes of years of evil magic, the ending of a long used habit. Jackyl no longer held such powers.

Gradually, the tremors and rumblings eased. The two men hurried through the opening and started back along the dark, cold passageway. As they disappeared along the tunnel, they heard mine shafts collapse behind them and heard the sorcerer's final wail trailing off in the darkness. A bitter echo signalled the end to a dark age.

The mountain thundered and rumbled inside. Tremors vibrated again and again, hurling more stones and dirt down on them.

They hurried along climbing gradually uphill, pushed along by urgency to get out of the cramped tunnels alive. Falling rocks grazed their bodies, as the pair scrambled and tripped over piles of rubble.

Navek held up the stick with the dimming cobwebs, throwing light into the black passageway. He vowed to himself he would find something useful to do with his life, if he survived this venture. Several times Navek went back to help Khelvan when he fell. Even though Khelvan had been the stronger of the two in many ways, he was now physically drained and needed help. Navek saw his companion was exhausted, and had not fared well down in the subterranean labyrinth. It was up to him to get them both out, but he could not help wondering if, after all they had been through, they would even make it back.

He thought of Jake outside in the snow, and hoped the boy was surviving. He expected Jake to be on his way back to Frozia, as the agreed rendezvous time was well passed by now. He was glad that the boy was not with them down in the underground rat hole.

For hours they pressed on with difficulty along the shaft filled with fallen rocks and obstacles. Their light source faded to a small faint haze, barely useful. Not far from the first chamber, they passed the bend where they had previously paused to breathe in the fresher air. Navek felt a slight breeze against his right cheek but continued on.

A few paces further, Navek came to a halt, causing Khelvan to bump into the back of him with a jolt and let out a muffled groan. "There's a passageway there. We'll go that way," Navek directed as he doubled back and then fumbled around to find an open space in the wall. He stood before the subsidiary tunnel, sniffing the air. "There's fresh air here," he said following his intuition to go that way, though it was a risk with an unknown destination, in an already precarious situation.

Another tremor rocked the mountain and Khelvan called out in a croaking voice: "Stop!"

This was no time for a dead end route where they could perish under stones and dust that would bury them forever.

"Stop for a moment," he repeated.

Navek turned anxiously to look at him, holding the dull cobweb lamp near their faces. Khelvan was exhausted and leaned against the dirt wall with one arm, bent over gasping in air. He closed his eyes tightly, and struggled to focus his attention to ask of his guides if this was the right way.

"Will this take us there?" he asked them bluntly. *"Is this the way?"* he repeated the request for help in his mind.

He caught the brief image of Lamaar's shaved head with eyes closed, the shaved head nodding once in affirmation.

"Let's do it," Khelvan said, as the impatient Navek physically turned Khelvan toward the unknown escape route and urged him into it.

Rumblings shook them again, and in their desperation there was no time to acknowledge the panic and claustrophobia that drove them on. There still was a long way to go in darkness, amid falling missiles that battered them. The ever real threat of a cave-in was undiminished.

Fumbling along in the freezing cold with grumbling, empty stomachs, they tracked steeply upward through the unknown shaft. At times the way became even narrower and lower than the other one, and they had to crawl or turn side-on to squeeze through. They pushed on, ducking and stumbling as light from the cobweb lamp faded almost into obscurity the further they went.

The air became relatively fresher, and at one point Navek thought he saw a light up ahead, only to learn his eyes were playing tricks on him when he found more damp and mouldy darkness.

Reverberations were occurring more frequently, and with an increasingly unknown outcome they continued on as best they could.

Tremors rattled and shook the cavity around them and then intensified. The men stopped and waited while the mountain groaned and shuddered upward from its depths. They waited for aftershocks to subside and rocks and dust to settle. Eventually, all movement stopped and went eerily quiet.

When they stood to continue, a booming sound like rolling thunder echoed throughout, but this time it came from the direction they were headed.

Suddenly, a huge vacuum of freezing air, mixed with dust and ice, surged Khelvan and Navek. It rushed down into the tunnel, almost blowing them along with it, back the way they had come. They crouched low against the rocky wall to protect themselves from the force of it, with faces turned away and buried into their sleeves to breathe.

Not shifting from their positions, they waited for the movement to abate, and then Navek stood and cautiously looked around.

The ancient mountain uttered a deep murmur from beneath them and then quietened.

Up ahead, now only a short distance away, was bright, glaring daylight. An aperture to the outside world had opened up to expose the craggy mountain peak. A magnificent, glorious golden hue shone like a gateway of light all around the opening, and the tiny cramped tunnel now expanded out into a beautiful, bright world.

"Are you alright?" Navek asked, looking Khelvan over for signs of injury as he helped him stand. "Come on. Let's go." Though impatient to be out of the constricted conditions, Navek was unable to keep a smile from breaking out. Dirty and covered in debris they headed toward the daylight, greatly relieved to be taking in fresh air for the first time since entering the mine. Energy flowed back into them and the weight of Khelvan's lethargy finally started to lift after the long subterranean ordeal.

Khelvan and Navek clambered on a short distance to reach the jagged opening, and then stepped tentatively near the edge. From the side of the mountain, some of the cliff face had sheared off in an avalanche and come away like a piece of slate. They squinted as they looked out over the panorama, and viewed pristine white valleys and mountains stretching to the north-west. They gazed in wonder at the amazing spectacle, and the colours which were magnificent and vivid. They were struck, not only by the sheer beauty of the blue sky and daylight itself, but the magic and sublimity which emanated from all of life in the above ground world. They even welcomed the bite of a cold wind and felt a freedom like never before. In their exuberance they did not care about usual formalities, and turned to embrace each other in happiness at their great fortune of getting out alive. After what seemed like days underground, they laughed joyously, with white teeth contrasting against their grimy, blackened faces.

Khelvan stood filled with an appreciation of his own existence and also gratitude for all the help given to achieve the task. The feeling permeated to the depths of his soul, and then tears ran freely down his blackened cheeks when the completion of a long and weary journey started to sink in. It was as though heaven and earth had shifted on its axis and come right again.

Chapter 21.
The Winding Riverbed

On a distant mountain, new buds were starting to form on the plum trees. Sharian was in his vegetable garden planting corn for the coming summer crop. In the distance, mountain jays greeted him from the sky. He straightened and looked up to see the small flock approach. He had not seen the blue and grey birds since autumn, and watched as they circled the valley a few times before landing in the nearby trees.

One of the more daring ones came down and perched on a wooden fence, eyeing him with its black eyes. Another bird came nearer, and a few others followed. The birds warbled and called out in their pleasant way, weaving and ducking their heads up and down as though dancing. Sharian laughed out loud at their antics. He was happy to see the familiar creatures back in the area, and sat down in the shade to listen as they continued with their song and dance. He acknowledged their happy message which told him that corrections had been made in the north, winters would not last so long, seasons would return to how they used to be and abundance and prosperity would surely follow. Sharian closed his eyes and the image of his father's amulet appeared, flashing exultantly in sunlight, bringing a smile to his face that did not fade for some time.

~

It was late afternoon by the time Khelvan and Navek scrambled down the slippery slopes of Mount Perilous, and started to make their way back to collect their packs from the hut. After their hardships underground, they began to feel oddly enlivened, with plans to continue across the valley to the north-west. They reached a plateau within sight of the hut, but there was still some distance to go, with a steep climb uphill before they would get there.

Hunger and exhaustion were catching up with them, and as temperatures dropped rapidly, there was no choice but to press on toward the hut with weakening legs and grumbling stomachs.

Khelvan and Navek had only gone a short distance past the plateau, when they heard a whistling sound above them. They spun around and quickly looked up. At the same time a snowball flew through the air, hitting Navek with a thud.

The pair was alarmed and instinctively assumed a

defensive position, looking around with worried looks to see where it had come from.

They were surprised, then relieved, to see Jake perched above them under a rocky overhang, watching with a big grin on his face. The youth's eyes were gleaming and clear; both men saw the sparkling spirit reflected in them, which was encouraging and inspiring after their recent tribulations. They were physically too drained to admonish the lad for not following the agreed plan, where he had been instructed to head back alone.

Jake was hunched up and cold, but seemed accepting of the harsh conditions. This may have stemmed from his childhood days when he had been forced to live out in such weather.

Khelvan and Navek looked at each other then burst out laughing, a sight Jake could not remember seeing before. He noted their upright composure and saw the steely gleam in their eyes beneath the grime, as well as a renewed vigour. Jake knew without asking that the mission had been successful, but he would not ask about it now. He also saw how physically drained and gaunt both men were, and knew they would not have eaten since the shared snack of dried fruit and nuts three days before.

Jake had heard the rumblings and tremors coming from the mountain, and had gone up and down, back and forth to the old miners hut. He had worried about them, especially when he peered down into the darkness of the tunnel. He was afraid of what lurked in the underground. There was no way he would enter the black cavity or sleep in that hut. The smell of evil emanated from it and he wondered, not for the first time, about the courage of his two companions. Even after he heard and felt the avalanche that day, he had gone to the hut to look for them, not giving up on the two men coming back out alive. He was a wilful boy who had no intention of following instructions or leaving without them.

Khelvan gazed beyond the youth's head, sweeping the sky with glinting eyes and a smile on the corner of his lips. He was just happy to see colours and be free of the oppressive tunnels.

But daylight closed around them and he knew they should keep moving. Khelvan called up to Jake, "Let's go".

Jake jumped down, then from his pocket took out a small portion of the dried beef he had saved. Jake handed it to the hungry pair who thanked him gratefully, before relishing and savouring the food as long as they could before swallowing it.

Jake took the lead and moved along at a rapid pace to get back up to the hut before dark. They kept up as best they could, sometimes stumbling or sinking into deep snow, requiring much effort to get back up again. Jake went back often to help one of them get up after they had missed their footing. A chilly mist started to settle all around and temperatures dropped further. Jake called back to them to push them along faster.

A couple of hours passed by the time they reached the inhospitable hut, and Khelvan and Navek flopped down on the cold floor from sheer exhaustion. Eventually, they pushed themselves back up to lean against a wall. They were weak but hopeful and appreciative of the hut and the frugal shelter it offered, and glad to see Jake's zeal was barely diminished by the circumstances. Jake had been useful while they were away – he kept busy collecting timber from old shelves and furniture from both huts. He wanted to have something prepared for them on their return and had built a wood pile in the fire place ready to ignite.

"Let's get some food into ya," Jake said as he undid the ties on their packs then rummaged around for the rations. He knew their hands would be numb. In Navek's pack he came across the small bag containing dried herbs that Lulu had prepared, and held it up, sniffed the unusual earthy smell and tossed it back into the pack. He helped the men open the food wrappings, then squatted on his heels to get rations out from his own bag to eat – it had been a long hungry wait for him too. They savoured the remaining morsels, and then Jake went to the hearth where there was a small pile of dark-brown bats. He had snared them as they had flown from the tunnel at dusk. He held up a handful of them to show the others. "I can cook these but I don't have a light," he said, dropping the bats in time to catch the stone and the flint, as both items came flying through the air toward him. When Jake caught both items, Navek joked, "Just seeing if you are on your toes".

After many strikes, a spark finally ignited the wood shavings Jake had scraped off with his knife. They sat hunched around trying to get warm while the food produced a palatable aroma.

Navek had forgotten about the bag of herbs Lulu had given them till Jake had found them in his pack. He recalled her saying they could be boiled in water and eaten. He picked up the tin billy and went outside and filled it with snow before placing it in the coals to boil. He reached into his pack to retrieve the small cotton bag filled with dried ingredients, and tipped the contents into the tin billy. They all watched on as the strange combination of ingredients sank to the bottom and emitted a strange, but pleasant, earthy smell into the air as the water heated.

The meat had a strong gamey taste, but nobody cared. They ate ravenously till the bats were gone, and then threw the small bones into the coals. Khelvan and Navek were appreciative Jake had their survival in mind and had the skills to catch the winged creatures. They also noted Jake had hardly touched his food supply for three days.

When the billy cooled a little, Navek and Khelvan watched on as Jake poured the contents equally into the three tin bowls. They all looked at each other in surprise to see some of the ingredients had swelled to more than double their size, and the water had turned into a brown soup. There were strips of seaweed, plump pieces of mushroom, small squares of bean curd and other ingredients they had never seen before.

"This stuff is weird," said Jake as he handed them the steaming bowls. As they ate, the different flavours became more and more delicious. The soup filled and nourished their bodies, warmed them from the inside and left them feeling sated.

"That Lulu sure knows what she's doing. This has to be the best soup I've ever eaten," said Khelvan.

The food put the three of them in high spirits, as they sat around the fireplace jostling with each other, enjoying the dancing colours and the warmth. At times the moisture in the wood made the fire pop and a small explosion of sparks landed on them, but they didn't care.

They discussed which way they would go back, referring to the details of the map they had seen in the outpost store. Khelvan and Navek agreed they should head generally to the west which would take them toward Navek's place of birth. After coming down from the mountain range they would turn eastward along the foot of the mountains until they hit the coast, then continue south till they reached Frozia. They knew a ship would sail to the south only once, at the end of every month. They only had a couple of weeks, but they wanted to be aboard the next ship back.

To go this way the trek would take longer in terms of distance, but travel should be easier on relatively flatter ground. None of them wanted to repeat the extremes of the previous journey. It was decided, early tomorrow they would head toward Navek's mountain homelands.

They talked of their underground endeavour, telling Jake about the horror of the tunnels and their encounter with the sorcerer; they knew he was keen to hear about it. It reinforced that they wanted to be away and get off the mountain as soon as possible.

Later in the evening, they all felt a rumble coming up from the mountain like an aftershock. They thought they heard an echoing scream trail off into the night like a wolf howling in the distance; a reminder that Jackyl the sorcerer lay crushed in his self-made dungeon beneath them.

Eventually, the mist cleared to reveal a beautiful yellow crescent moon with glittering stars set against a clear dark blue sky. With the clear night, the temperature dropped to well below zero and was bitterly cold. As evening wore on, chatter around the fire slowed and Khelvan went outside.

He looked up to the constellations and watched awhile as they moved across the night sky, marvelling at the beauty of the magnificent entertainment.

Not long after, the two men covered themselves with the oilskins and pulled their coats up around them, before dropping off easily into a deep sleep.

Jake sat up awhile longer and stared into the coals, poking them with the last of the timber while he considered the strange account he had just heard. He looked up quickly when he saw the whitish image of a tall man standing in the room, but when he looked closely, there was no one there. Jake knew who it was, however, and briefly sympathised with the spirit of the rogue sorcerer. He could feel the utter isolation of the man who had lived a lonely, solitary existence under a mountain – a lost soul. He knew himself how it felt to be on the outside just wanting to join in and be included. Jake went back to poking the fire, feeling sympathy and heaviness in his chest. Without looking up from the coals he said softly,

"Be in peace brother. You are welcome here".

During the night, the weather changed. Clouds came over, rain started to fall and cold sleet blew across their feeble shelter. They huddled together in the night and then the fire went out. They could have slept for days, but eventually, they felt cold to the core and could not sleep anymore.

They decided to get up and travel on through the rain; the nights in the north were not so dark, so they could see their way across the white snow. Such extreme cold would have prevented most ordinary men from continuing and Khelvan wondered how Jake had coped out there alone without fire or food. He saw how tough the young fellow was and what an asset he was to the expedition.

They wrapped scarves around their necks and across their faces, fastened tight their hooded oilskin coats and with packs on, emerged from the icy hut and headed back down the mountain.

They forged on, bracing against the wind and rain with only their squinted eyes showing. Khelvan felt the icy chill, but almost welcomed the sensations of cold and rain after the deathly encounters in the underground chambers which had weakened him. He was now glad to be heading well away from the world of sorcery and on the way home.

For the remainder of the night and the following day, they plodded on over snow covered ground with icy intermittent rain showering down. They sucked on handfuls of snow as they went; the effort and activity helping to generate warmth in their bodies. By afternoon,

Khelvan and Navek were tired. When they did stop to rest, the two men flopped down outstretched on their backs, and remained there with eyes closed, breathing heavily and offering no conversation.

Jake had to travel slower than he wanted as Khelvan and Navek were both depleted of energy. He felt a sense of responsibility for them, and wanted to help them get back. He busied himself tightening up the rope which secured the few pieces of timber he had collected on the way, while he constantly looked around for tonight's dinner.

When it was time to get up, Navek and Jake had to shake Khelvan from a deep sleep to get him going again. Khelvin groaned when they hoisted him up to a standing position. "Common old boy," Jake said stirring him, before ducking to avoid Khelvan's gloved hand from whacking him on the head.

Jake went on ahead of the men, deviating to look for food and firewood. He found one dead tree poking up through the snow, and dug down to break off as many branches as he could, adding them to the others on his back. He kept two sticks out which he left poked upright in the snow for Khelvan and Navek to find when they reached the spot. He knew they could use the support to help them travel in the snow.

When they found the sticks they appreciated his mindfulness, and then lumbered on in silence, each thinking their own thoughts and each feeling very hungry.

They persevered, alone on the tundra without seeing a single animal or bird all day. Slowly they weaved their way along the foot of the mountains where they made good progress on the flat areas. The rain stopped and it was evening when Jake searched for a sheltered place to camp for the night. To the north, layer upon layer of snow covered mountains could be seen in different hues of blue, as the sun went down behind them. Mauve and pink shades spread across the sky to display a beautiful sight.

Eventually they stopped next to a steep cliff wall which gave them relative shelter from a cold wind, but not much shelter from any rain that may fall during the night. After many attempts at striking flint against stone, Jake finally managed to get a smoky fire going with the damp wood, fanning it continuously till it caught. To everyone's surprise he reached into a pocket and brought out the last few nuts as well as three strips of dried beef he had been keeping in reserve. He divided the rations into three and passed a share each to the thankful men, before sitting back to chew slowly on his own portion.

They melted some snow in the billy and drank the heated water to slake their thirst, then sat around the fire saying little , not wanting to think about getting through another day of walking without food. Far in the distance snow wolves howled to each other and communicated across the remote wilderness. The travellers listened for awhile then finally drifted in and out of a fitful sleep, dreaming weird dreams and waking often, as light rain and snow fell on them throughout the night.

The next morning was overcast but the rain had cleared. Jake went off early to scout ahead. He made an arrow on the snow using charcoal from last night's fire, to indicate to the others to follow him.

The men woke unrefreshed, shook off the snow, and reluctantly started off again with their walking sticks. They followed the arrow and also saw Jake's footprints in the snow heading generally to the west as they had planned. About an hour later they saw Jake ahead. They could see him in the distance, stretched out, resting on a large boulder waiting for them.

Khelvan felt dizzy after days without much rest or food, and leaned his back against the boulder, while Navek squatted against it, grateful for the break. The sheer physical effort over the past few days and weeks was catching up with the two men; they became more exhausted each day.

"I know where the hot pools are," said Jake.

Khelvan glanced up to Navek and raised his eyebrows slightly, not knowing what the pools were or how the boy knew where they were. "OK," Khelvan rasped. "I hope you know what you're doing," and gestured with a quick nod for Jake to lead the way. He was almost beyond making a decision or caring, and relied on Jake more and more. He had heard some of Jake's life story from Navek, and would now trust the boy's survival instincts.

Jake headed off enthusiastically, walking ahead with a sense of purpose and pride in his step. He thrived on the sense of responsibility and went ahead till he was out of sight.

Navek wondered again at the boy's tenacity, and sighed

deeply as he pushed himself away from the boulder, helping Khelvan before trudging on doggedly, not caring any more, only wanting to find food.

Later in the morning they again caught up with Jake who stood near an escarpment looking over the edge. The men looked down and saw white mist rising up from the bottom of a rocky gorge. It was coming from a pool of steaming water. Jake hurried down the slope and soon reached the pool, dipping his finger in to test the temperature.

Khelvan and Navek threw the walking sticks over the edge to land at the bottom, and then clambered down over the slippery rocks, hanging on as they went with gloved hands. They had never seen hot artesian pools before, and stood at the edge staring in amazement at the steaming spring, while Jake stripped off his clothes to get in.

"Coming in?" Jake said to Navek and Khelvan, grinning broadly. He waded out naked into the pool, gradually testing the depth with his outstretched foot before sitting on an underwater rock. He splashed water onto his face and arms, rubbed his skin to wash himself, and leaned back to relax in the steaming water.

Slowly, Navek and Khelvan stripped off their clothes to expose formerly muscular bodies which were now gaunt. They shivered when the biting air chilled their bare skin, and hurried to follow Jake into the steamy water, where they sat and luxuriated in the warmth. The heat of the hot pool contradicted the glacial world around them. It relaxed their tired muscles as they washed away the sweat and grime of many days of walking and climbing, as well as the dirt and ash from the tunnels. They sat there submerged till the skin on their fingers wrinkled and they became too hot. Then they sat on the edge and rubbed handfuls of snow against their skin to cool down. Slipping down into the steaming water again, they indulged in the welcoming heat.

After awhile Jake got out and brushed the water from his hot skin, before flicking his head forward a few times to remove water from his hair. Steam rose from his reddened body in the cold afternoon air, and he hurriedly put on his clothes. Jake seemed right at home at the hot pools, as though he had done this all before.

The others stepped out of the water, but were reluctant to leave the hot pool which left them feeling marvellously clean and invigorated, but more hungry and hollow than ever.

As they dressed back into their grimy clothes, Jake whistled from further along the valley to let them know where he was. They whistled back in acknowledgement and tracked him along the bottom of the ravine while light snow started to fall.

The men continued along the snow covered gorge, relatively protected from cold winds by steep rock walls either side. Some of the high walls were worn smooth from centuries of water eroding them away, the signs of past seasons where raging rivers of melted ice and snow flowed. However, it was late spring, and snow still fell in the alpine mountain range where winters had been lasting longer with each passing year.

Khelvan and Navek walked for several hours with heavy legs and hearts pounding as snow started to fall more heavily. They finally caught up with Jake who was busy digging and scratching away on a flat area up behind some rocks. When they reached the rocks, they saw that he had found a pond of frozen water under the snow, and was busy uncovering it. On the snow they glimpsed the small tracks of an arctic fox. This was the first sign of any life they had seen since setting off this way.

Jake lifted a large rock over his head, and then smashed it down hard on the frozen pond, causing shards of ice to fly up. The two men collapsed on the snow nearby, again relieved to have a break as their heads were spinning and throbbing from lack of food. They wondered what the lad was doing and why he was spending his energy that way, though he seemed to know what he was doing.

Jake picked up the rock again and brought it down with a look of fierce determination on his face, and they heard the dry splintering sound of ice cracking. He picked up the rock and pelted it down again and again onto the frozen pool, till finally, the ice gave way. He stepped back so as not to fall into icy water beneath. However, it was solid ice all through.

He kicked out some of the broken lumps of ice to make the hole bigger, and then squatted to peer into the cavity. Jake picked up the rock again, this time hitting the edge of the hole to break off a large chunk. The ice splintered and shattered and weakened under the heavy battering.

Jake rolled the chunk over and inspected it before pushing it out of the way, then again looked into the cavity. Once again he brought the rock down with force, with eyes shut to avoid fast flying shards from hitting them.

Finally, Jake rolled a couple of large lumps of ice over the edge, rolling them down to the men.

Navek got up and kicked one of the shattered ice blocks over with his boot, and was amazed to see the silvery grey side of a decent sized salmon, frozen solid inside the ice.

Jake continued pounding and battering the ice, throwing another frozen fish down to them, then another and another, till he was unable to find any more. He jumped down looking pleased with himself.

"How did you know where to look?" Navek asked in amazement.

"Let's just say the fox showed me where to look," Jake replied, and they looked at him incredulously. "All right, I saw him sniffing and scratching around up here and knew he was onto something under the snow," Jake said, pointing to the fox's disappearing trail in the snow. "He ran off when I got here, but he'll be up there watchin' us still. When I had a look, I found the frozen pool under the snow," he went on. "The salmon swim up these rivers to spawn in spring, but some of 'em get trapped in ponds that freeze over. I've watched hungry polar bears smash frozen pools to dig out food." It was the most words either man had heard Jake speak at one time, and they could see he was in his element when it came to using his survival skills in harsh extremes.

Once again they were heartened by his company and glad they had brought him along.

Jake went to one of the fish and with a swift strike of his boot, broke off the rest of the shattered ice, and then proceeded to do the same with another fish. He took off his gloves and awkwardly picked up the two salmon. He headed over to sit under a rocky overhang, out of the falling snow.

By the time Navek and Khelvan got there, Jake already had his knife out and was cutting into one of the frozen fish.

Navek took out the hatchet and handed it to him to make the job easier. Jake roughly chopped into the fish, exposing the orange flesh inside. He tossed a large chunk of it to each of the men, telling them to take their gloves off first so they would not smell of fish. Polar bears and wolves could sniff out food from miles away.

None of them cared that they were eating icy raw fish that caused their teeth to ache, they were just grateful to have food. The oily meat actually tasted good, and they felt the frozen protein replenish their weakened bodies. On the grey overcast day, they ravenously ate two of the four fish, leaving only the innards and the head. They could easily have eaten all four of them. Afterward, Jake cleaned the hatchet and knife as best he could, and got the men to clean their fishy hands in the snow; they would be heading into bear territory soon.

No one asked how he knew this information, but they trusted he was right and did as they were instructed. Meanwhile, Jake wrapped and tied the other two frozen fish to carry.

After soaking in the hot pool and then eating food, they walked away feeling far more energised and alive than they had for many days.

Jake pointed to rocks higher up saying nothing, bringing their attention to the skinny white fox which sat there watching them. He knew the fox would scavenge through the remains of the fish as soon as they were out of sight, and was glad to have left some remnants for him. In the extreme remoteness, there was not much food available for any animal. "You know those foxes have very good noses and ears too," Jake said. "I have seen 'em race over snow at full pelt, then in mid-stride, dive into the snow using their front paws and nose to break through, then come back up with a mouse!"

Navek looked at the boy who was usually reserved, and saw the vibrancy and the shine in his eyes. Jake was capable of surviving on his own and thrived out here in the remoteness. Navek felt warmth for Jake after all he had done for them these past few days. He reached out spontaneously to put his arm around Jake's shoulders and said, "Well done Jake. Good to have you here."

But Jake, who was not used to such friendliness, shrugged him off and hurried further out in front to hide his self-conscious smile. Navek looked over to see an amused smile on Khelvan's face, and in that moment they were all happy, even as snow continued to fall on them. But there was a long way to go.

For the rest of the day, they wound along the riverbed gully through the mountains. Dwarfed by high rock walls, they walked on in silence, at times feeling the utter desolation of the end of the earth. There were no others around for hundreds of miles. Occasionally they passed shallow caves where the rock face had been eaten out and worn smooth by centuries of rushing water. Jake went into some of them to collect scraps of firewood that had lodged there. It was well after sundown they stopped to shelter in one of them for the night. They lit a fire and cooked one of the remaining fish, then buried the remains along with the last fish so the smell would not attract animals to them during the night.

At first they slept, but during the early hours the temperature dropped and they woke often from the cold. They arose before dawn, dug up the last fish to take with them and set off.

Chapter 22.
The Abandoned Village

Bitterly cold, they continued to the west. The wind intensified and howled through the river valley, stinging their eyes as they struggled on hunched against it. The travellers were encouraged when they started to see leafless branches of shrubs and trees poking up through the snow, as well as the occasional pine tree with branches weighed down by the snow.

The further they walked, the closer they came to Videha clan territory. Navek's former village was not far away, though he had not been back there since the killings years ago. By mid-afternoon the country started to become more and more familiar to Navek. He recognised, not so much the specific mountains, but the lay of the land and the feeling of the place; even the smell of the place, as places do have smells. He was reminded of his boyhood, and recollections started to come back.

By the end of a long arduous day, they had only to pass around one mountain and they would be near the eastern outskirts of his village. Navek was now nearing his birthplace.

He looked toward his old homeland longingly. It was so close. The distant squawk of a familiar bird called out as though beckoning him. They looked up at a large brown eagle gliding effortlessly on the wind.

Apart from the fox, this was the only other sign of life they had seen, and it was an encouraging sign after many days of nothing but snow and ice.

Jake thought of his homeland too, which would have been another day's walk across mountains to the north-west, but he had no desire to ever go back there.

The snow covered river bed came to a bend where another tributary merged in from their right to join the main course they followed. Navek recognised exactly where they were, and could not pass this closely without seeing his old village. He would not come back this way again.

"Let's go via my old village and see what's left," he said, "It's not far, just up behind this mountain."

The other two looked at him surprise, but after a few moments they conceded. With a grumbling stomach Jake asked hopefully, "Any food there?"

They climbed the short distance to reach the abandoned village built on a levelled area on the side of the mountain.

At first they were fascinated to see buildings after days of open expanses in extreme conditions. However, the village was a snow covered ghost town. Most of the rooves had collapsed under the weight of snow and years of neglect and abandonment. Jake went off excitedly exploring, while Khelvan too went to look around with a far-fetched hope of finding food.

Navek wandered on alone, passing the remains of derelict shacks which were once the homes of people he had known. Heaviness in his chest weighed on him and memories of family and friends flooded back as tears welled up in his eyes.

At the far end of the ruins, he came to a hut that was larger and built higher up the slope than the others. He stood there for a few long moments, absorbing the sight of his former home, recalling the days when his father was the revered clan leader. The roof at one end had partially collapsed, but most of the building was still covered, and the rock walls stood solidly. Unbidden tears sprang up and rolled down his cheeks; he was surprised by the depth of the emotions he felt. The deep connection he inherently had with his own roots could never be extinguished, regardless of the past.

Navek wiped away tears and stepped forward, pushing against the stiff door with his shoulder to get it open. He stood in the doorway awhile taking in the familiar sights and smells. He was fascinated to see shambled items and articles which had once surrounded him as a boy, now strewn about the floor by the elements.

At the same time, he grieved at the sharp recollections of a painful past, of nightmares and the acute reminder of his family's death. He stood and witnessed the scraps of a former life, and then it finally dawned on him.

He had just helped to destroy the one who had killed them all! By going on this journey with Khelvan, they had put an end to the dark powers of the vengeful sorcerer – the one who had been the root of all this devastation. It held no joy for him really, only a dim glimmer of achievement.

He entered and looked around. At one end of the living area where the roof was missing, snow piled up against the wall next to the kitchen. Above the rock fireplace was the dusty and faded timber plaque which his mother had spent hours carving out the image of an old spreading tree. Years later she had told him its meaning in a simple verse she had made up:

May your roots forever grow deep in the earth
and your branches reach for the light.
May you give the shelter of wisdom to others
and forever enjoy the fruits of life.

He may not have always followed these words, but he had never forgotten them. His eyes filled with tears again at the memory his mother's gentle wisdom, and also at the loss of his own wisdom when he wasted so much time in the drug dens of Welpecca. He sighed deeply then went over to his old bed, which was a raised platform like a shelf attached to the wall. He touched the dusty old blankets and then walked around behind the wall to see his parents' bedroom. The room was covered in dust and debris and some of their clothes still hung from wooden pegs on the wall, just as they had been left many years ago. Navek touched the stiffened clothes, instinctively smelling them to find any trace of his parents. But there was only the smell of mould and dust.

Khelvan and Jake appeared in the doorway, each holding a few pieces of clothing they had found. Though the clothes were ragged and stiff, they were a welcome change from the smelly ones they were wearing. They looked around the room with interest, noting Navek's grief but saying nothing.

"We'll be staying here tonight," Khelvan said with authority. "We need the break and at least there is some shelter here. Thanks to Jake we still have one fish left, but let's hope we find food soon."

"I'll build a fire," volunteered Jake, uncomfortable with Navek's grief and not knowing what to say. He threw the clothes and his pack against a wall, before setting off to collect remnants of wood from the other houses. Khelvan walked around the tattered hut, placing his hand briefly on Navek's shoulder in silent sympathy as he passed him.

While Jake built a fire, Navek looked through his family's possessions, reflecting on the poignancy of the past. He kept a couple of small items as memoirs, but felt many conflicting emotions. It was difficult to fully grasp being here after all this time, though Navek appreciated the luxury of being in his old house, sheltered from the harsh weather. He too had found a few clothes, but they had once belonged to his father, so wearing them was bitter–sweet. They reminded him acutely of the man who once meant everything to him.

At dusk, light snow fell outside while they all sat around the rock fire place enjoying the warmth of the fire. Jake filled the billy with snow and boiled hot water for them to drink later, while Khelvan cooked the last fish over the coals in a pan he had found. In tin bowls he served each man a portion of the fish. He did not waste the rich salmon oil which had appeared during cooking; they needed all the nutrition they could get for their journey ahead. The fish tasted delicious and they ate slowly, relishing their small portion.

Afterwards they relaxed in the dim room, watching the flames and thinking their own thoughts, as they indulged in the warmth of the fire and frugal comforts of the shelter around them.

After all they had been through their eyes started to become heavy with sleep, but they were brought back to wakefulness when Navek went to the side of the fireplace. He removed one of the rocks, then reached into the cavity and brought out a small wooden box, and sat back down to open it.

Jake sat forward in interest. Navek lifted the lid to reveal seven beautifully coloured opals, each about the size of an unhulled almond.

The deep vivid colours of red, purple, blue and green flashed in the firelight, an amazing spectacle to behold amid the dim surroundings of the hut. They were rare and precious stones, not from anywhere around this region.

Navek remembered his father had revered them highly; they had been handed down for generations from father to son, but that cycle was broken now and belonged to the past. He turned the gems over and watched how the deep colours danced and glimmered, and how the depth of colour was completely undiminished by time. He remembered his father taking them out occasionally to marvel at the colours of the stones that he said, "were jewels made by the earth."

He handed the open tin to Jake, whose wide eyes could not hide his fascination.

"Pick one," Navek offered, and Jake's eyes seemed to widen further.

"No," he said attempting to hand the stones back to Navek.

"Take one," Navek insisted, "I want you both to have one. It's just a token really, a token of this journey together and of better days ahead. Jake looked at the stones, holding them up, turning them over and over in awe of the colourful dimensions and the fiery colours. He had never seen such gems before and finally picked one out, then admired the opal many times before putting it into an inside pocket. He was happy; he had never received such a gift in his life.

Khelvan admired the flickering colours in the firelight and chose one, appreciative of the small gift that would be a keepsake to signify this journey. He handed the stones back to Navek who wrapped the remainder and put them into his satchel with the other items he had wanted to keep.

Around the fire they enjoyed the simple comforts in the old hut, feeling the delicious warmth of the fire, as flames licked and danced around the wood and lit up their faces.

Eventually weariness caught up with them and their tired eyes again became heavy and sleepy.

Navek and Jake opened their eyes instantly when they heard Khelvan's quiet voice beside them. "Psst," he whispered, signalling with a jerk of his chin for them to look over to their left.

Standing quite near were the whitish images of a group of men from the spirit world. Khelvan and Jake sat up in surprise.

Navek sensed his father and the clan warriors were all gathered there. The feeling in the room was magnetic as the images became clearer.

For the first time Navek saw the spirits of his father and the clansmen standing upright and proud, smiling at him. Somehow Navek knew the men were all pleased about his role in the eradication of the sorcerer. His father stood amid the other tribesmen, full of integrity and dignity, steeped in serene happiness as Navek had always remembered him. Clothed in the same battledress he wore on that last day many years before, holding his long wooden staff, Navek's father watched his son with great love and pride.

Then the image of his mother appeared briefly. Her

long dark hair shimmered and her calm smiling face beamed at her son.

Navek felt goosebumps all over him, and a spontaneous feeling of love leaped in his chest at seeing his parents again. He swallowed hard and tried to quell the tears that fell from his eyes.

Hatchiman's regal gaze looked over to Jake and Khelvan, a deep kindness emanating from him toward the two. He nodded appraisingly before his proud gaze went back to his son. He lifted the staff up. When it came back down and touched the floor, the spirits stepped back and were gone.

The three were left in awe at the spectacle just witnessed. None of them moved and none knew how much time had passed by ... a few minutes maybe, but they could not be sure.

Jake and Khelvan looked at each other, feeling the clarity and peace which comes with being brought into the present moment. Nobody wanted to speak or move from the experience; they remained seated around the fire in silence.

Nothing mattered to Navek at that moment, there was nowhere to go and nothing to accomplish. He felt at one with himself and understood his life's purpose. All was at it should be, and without thinking a thought he knew his place in life. All pervading peace, natural and obvious, had been with him all through his life, but unacknowledged it had lay hidden beyond noisy thoughts.

Through unabashed tears he closed his eyes, and

silently thanked his parents and all the clansmen for coming and making him whole again, making life worth living. He was humbled and knew now they had always been with him, existing in a deathless realm where he also would go one day. They had given him a precious gift from beyond this world, and reinforced in him there is no death; we all get recycled back into a power which is bigger than us. A divine hand had reached back in time to before his birth and then weaved his life's story like a tapestry, into a beautiful design that was meant to be: where he was born; the family he was born into; the training he did during his life; the time spent with teachers, friends, mentors; even his painful days at Welpecca were all part of that design.

When Navek opened his eyes, Khelvan and Jake seemed to glow with a divine aura. Navek exhaled a long breath. He now knew his life's journey had been designed and written well before he was born. Nothing had been a mistake or a waste, and every part of his life was valid. A bigger plan had interwoven the three of them together to end the reign of darkness, and he was struck by the enormity of it all.

As Khelvan had said, it had not been by chance he had survived all those years ago. His father had pushed him out of the way so that he would live on to bring about the sorcerer's undoing, and the forecasts of both Sharian and Mancel from years before had now been fulfilled.

Navek lay down to sleep on his old bed that night while the revelations kept coming. He had been transformed from his usual self and felt determined from here on to change his outlook on life and start enjoying it. He saw there was nothing to fear about life ending, except perhaps that he could waste a whole lifetime in ignorance of greater possibilities. His challenge and purpose from now on was to appreciate all he *did* have, not spend his life grieving for what was gone. From here, he would endeavour to accept life, simply as it is, not how he thought it should be. Navek understood the great truth, that the past is gone and the future does not exist, only in the present moment would he find his real freedom. That night he slept peacefully.

The next morning they were up at the break of dawn after a sound sleep. They packed their few belongings and prepared for an early start, and for the first time, the weather was clear and sunny – a pleasant change for the three travellers.

Though they were all hungry, staying in the shelter of the hut and having the divine encounter had enlivened them.

Jake looked around for a scrap of fabric to wrap his opal for safekeeping, while Khelvan watched on, enjoying seeing him like a young boy with a new toy. Jake took the colourful stone out from his pocket several times, fascinated by its array of colours which were different again and more spectacular in the daylight.

Navek was packed and ready, and stood by the door knowing he was unlikely to come this way again. He looked around for the last time at his old home, remembering and cherishing the memory of it. The events from the night before would forever be etched into his heart.

When they left the village, he thought he felt the spirits of the villagers lining the way out of town to farewell him. He could not see them this time, but several times bowed his head out of respect anyway. Then he looked out upon the world's beauty with new eyes.

Chapter 23.
The King of Winter

The three travellers set off down the mountain slope out of town, feeling encouraged and inspired after the previous nights' events. It started off as a beautiful sunny day which warmed them and heralded the beginning of a late spring. Eventually they came down out of the mountains, and instead of heading to the east along the foot of the mountains as planned, they decided to travel south-east across uncertain terrain to hopefully shorten the distance to their destination of Frozia.

They trekked for several hours and saw no tracks or signs of animals but saw another lone eagle, gliding on the air currents high above. The bird watched their movements and called out as it circled.

Gradients were no longer steep, and the ice underfoot became slippery and sludgy as it melted in the warmer weather; but at least it required less effort to walk on.

They came to a small trickling creek where they saw a mother polar bear with two cubs standing in the shallow water. The mother's nose lifted, sniffing the air for signs of food.

Jake saw the bears first and suggested they veer well away. Fortunately, they were downwind from the animals and not detected.

Typical of the mountainous north, the weather changed quickly, and low black clouds drifted across the face of the sun to cast shadows over them. More dark clouds billowed and swirled above the mountain peaks they'd left behind, and cold rain began to fall. They were just under the edge of the cloud formation and the rain did not last long. To the north they could see sheets of grey rain teeming down over the mountains.

With heavy legs they trudged on regardless, arduously putting one foot in front of the other, traversing rough terrain, up and down gullies and along riverbeds.

Khelvan went with his eyes closed at times, and with difficulty tried to hold his mind still and focus, but found it very difficult while his head throbbed and his stomach growled. He sent a silent prayer out to the universe for help, and then could only trust they would make it back.

Trees started to appear on the landscape and at times they saw encouraging hints of spring, even green buds sprouting on bare branches.

However, their bodies grew hungrier and weaker as energy reserves became depleted, and the inspiration they felt in the morning was replaced by the need for food. By late afternoon they had to stop to rest; they were lightheaded and dizzy. Even Jake, who had travelled better than the other two, was now grumpy and solemn as his growing body needed food.

High above and unbeknown to the trio, two solitary figures stood on a mountain peak observing them. With the vast range of snow covered mountains as a backdrop, an old man and a young girl watched their plight.

Jake continued a short distance ahead of the others, industriously collecting firewood which was becoming more available due to the thin scattering of trees. A movement caught his eye; he looked up to see a small white rabbit, oblivious of the travellers.

Jake slipped the firewood from his back. He stealthily crept toward the rabbit, eager for some fresh meat to eat. Nearing the rabbit he pounced, only to see the startled creature bolt into the trees. Disheartened, he felt more drained of energy than he had before.

The other two caught up with him and stopped for a break. They flopped on the ground and leaned their exhausted bodies up against the trees. With hearts racing and heads spinning, they stayed, reluctant to go on.

Eventually they hauled themselves up, as the only alternative was to lie down on the snow and die.

Navek helped Jake tie on his load of wood, then just as they were about to head off, they heard a whistling sound from the trees up ahead. It was a human whistle.

Navek and Khelvan jumped in alarm, annoyed with

themselves for being off guard and unaware of their surroundings. The three travellers banded together to defend themselves; Navek looked briefly at the other two not knowing what to expect.

Again they heard the whistle. Anxiously, their eyes scanned the area. They were astonished to see an old man and a young girl standing quietly among the trees, observing them from about thirty paces.

The old man was short and stocky with a jovial face, a white beard and white eyebrows. He wore a long hooded coat lined with cream-coloured fur, leather boots, and leaned on a dark stick which was shiny and worn from use. Across his back he carried a dark brown leather bag. The man looked like the King of Winter from an ancient tale – formidable and at home in his surroundings, as though he had lived many winters in these mountains.

The girl was almost the same height, but slim and looked about Jake's age. She stood shyly behind the old man, unused to seeing strangers in these parts. She wore a short fur-lined jacket, and boots that were dark brown in colour.

The two groups regarded each other from a distance, until Jake raised a hand in a gesture of peace.

The old man waved back and tentatively edged closer to the three travellers. "Hail my brothers," said the old man sizing them up, noting their poor condition as he approached with the girl close behind.

"Hello," replied Khelvan.

"I am Valery Zoric but they call me Zoric, and this is

my granddaughter Rozelle. We live over there behind that mountain." He gestured toward a mountain to the north.

"I am Khelvan, this is Navek and Jake," said Khelvan, pointing to the others as he introduced them, noting the sharp eyes of the old man that took everything in.

"We saw the smoke coming from the Videha village last night and wanted to see who you were. There have been no travellers pass through here for many a season."

Up close they could see the girl was beautiful with rosy cheeks and shiny dark eyes. She had smooth olive skin and black hair hanging in two long plaits, but seemed very shy and hid behind the old man, looking out with curiosity from behind him at the three strangers.

At first Zoric looked familiar to Navek, then the old man's eyes went directly to him and said: "You don't recognise me Sidewinder, but I was from your clan and knew your father. I can see you are your father's son all right". Navek was taken aback. "H h h how did you know that?" he stammered in surprise.

"I knew you both back then. But first, how about some food, you look like you could all eat a horse," he said, laughing out loudly at his own comment. "Come on, sit around and we'll eat together."

"If you can spare anything, that would be greatly appreciated," said Khelvan politely, welcoming the offer of any food at all, grateful for whatever the strangers could give.

As they unloaded their bags and sat down heavily on the snow, Zoric handed his bag to his granddaughter to serve the food. Delight showed in his twinkling eyes; such an encounter was rare in the alpine wilderness.

"I suppose you are heading to Frozia town," he asked, not requiring an answer.

"That's right," replied Navek. "We're cutting across this way to shorten the journey, though we don't know the terrain."

"Don't worry, don't worry," said Zoric. "We'll come some of the way with you."

Meanwhile, Rozelle took the food out of the pack, revealing a huge leg of roasted goat and several boiled potatoes. She was aware of all the eyes watching as she spread the food out. The food smelt delicious even though it was cold. From her belt she removed a knife from its sheaf and cut into the meat, reaching out to place the pieces on the snow before each man, as well her grandfather.

"Go ahead, eat," she offered quietly, glad to have the attention diverted from her. She proceeded to distribute the potatoes as well.

As starving and malnourished as they felt, each of them thanked their hosts sincerely before eating. They bit into the food ravenously, enjoying each tasty mouthful, commenting several times on the nourishing food as they ate.

"How did you know to bring the food?" Navek asked humbly, seeing that they had prepared all this for them in advance.

"I knew you were coming," Zoric answered with a

shrug, and then picked up the meat and bit into it. He chewed for awhile before adding, "I had a dream a few nights ago, where your father told me to get some food cooking for you," he said, shaking his head and chuckling at the memory of Hatchiman. "In the dream I also saw the three of you all bent over, trudging through a snow storm in great hardship. Last night, we smelt the smoke coming from your old village and saw it hanging low in the valleys. We knew you had arrived and would descend this way out of the mountains, so we came here to find you. You won't remember me Navek, but your father was a great hero around here," Zoric went on. "Everyone knew him or knew of him, and most stood behind his cause to unite all the clans. Since he has gone, I have seen signs of a world changing, and not for the better."

Khelvan looked across at Navek who listened calmly. All signs of grief for his family had gone.

With last night's encounter still fresh in his mind, Navek was unsurprised by such a dream.

Khelvan thought back to their first meeting in that smoky drug den; he felt proud and honoured to know the man who now sat before him. He was a man from such humble beginnings – born the son of a great leader.

"Summer crops have failed and every winter has grown longer. I've known about that sorcerer spinning his evil tricks for years now, but could do nothing about it on my own," said Zoric.

The fact that Zoric knew of the sorcerer and talked about him so casually interested Khelvan and Navek.

"We know something has changed in the past few days. We can feel the shift. The back of the long winter has been broken, the sun is out, so I know you three had something to do with fixing the trouble. Anyway, eat up," the old man said. "We can talk later."

Rozelle got out a container of pickled greens and some flatbreads. She spread some of the pickle on the bread before handing one to each of them, then turned away self-consciously to eat her own food. Though shy, she was pleased to be able to help. She could see their need, but her cheeks flushed red when she caught Jake watching her, before he quickly looked away. They ate till they were full, the first real meal they had eaten in days. Rozelle wrapped the remains and packed it away in the bag, while the travellers thanked their hosts again with genuine gratitude.

"Today my granddaughter and I are celebrating this new day and this new future. We are privileged to provide you with this food. It's the least we can do to help, especially since we know your lives have been in grave risk to achieve this feat. It is only because of your outstanding courage that the wheel of life has been righted and set back on its track."

Several moments went by while they pondered his words, as they had not fully grasped for themselves the magnitude and effect of their recent undertakings.

After the meal their energy began to restore and they felt more enlivened, and the five headed off while there was still daylight.

They had only gone a short distance when Zoric

turned and pointed up to a towering mountain in the distance. He indicated where he and his granddaughter lived, in case they ever returned this way. Zoric's hut was not visible from where they stood, but he told them that once up on the ridge they could see his place on a clear day.

Jake took special note of the outline of the mountain, committing its jagged shape to memory for future reference. He knew he would return one day.

As they travelled on, Zoric's merry chatter amused Khelvan. The old man told them all sorts of stories of survival, old legends of the mountains and many things of interest. Later the conversation became graver when Navek learned about some his father's brave feats which he would never have known otherwise. With the image of his family and clan still fresh in his mind, he appreciated any information and was keen to hear more.

Hatchiman in his wisdom had foreseen the fate of the mountain clans. He had sent an angry and resistant Zoric away to herd goats with his daughter and son-in-law, a few days before that fateful day.

"I cursed your father that day for sending me away to do a boy's task. But eventually I came to see it was out of his great kindness that he protected me and my family. Maybe being around to feed you today was even part of his plan," he chuckled.

"When I returned that day and found the murdered bodies in the village and in the creek bed, I sat down and just wept and wept. For many days after, I felt like my soul was adrift like an untied rope flapping in the wind. It took a long time before I started to live again. I had to learn how to live each day anew, just one day at time."

They all listened to the account as they walked along, touched by the old man's emotion as he recalled the past events. "It was the birth of my granddaughter that finally got me out of my despair and opened my eyes to living life again, and I came to appreciate life's simple joys." He reached out affectionately and put his arm across Rozelle's shoulder before he went on.

"That wasn't to be the end of the loss however. One day my daughter and son-in-law went out to move the goats and never returned. I heard the rumble of an avalanche during the morning, but later when the herd wandered back to the hut on their own, I knew something was wrong. I discovered they had both been killed in the avalanche. I was left with a young baby to look after," he said. "I cursed the gods that day and cursed my lot. But I had to go on ... those little bright eyes looked up so dependently to an old goat like me. Anyway, they say determination and need were born together, so here we are," he added.

Not wanting them to feel bad after his bleak tale, he broke into a silly little song: "Raised on goat's milk by an old goat like me, an old goat like me ..." Zoric laughed out loudly at his own words, wanting to lift the feeling of the group after the serious depiction of days gone by.

Late afternoon shadows from the trees grew longer, and a cool breeze started to blow in from the east. The three travellers felt more grounded and revitalised with full stomachs, and the new company showed the way, giving them confidence.

Jake and Rozelle were both unused to being around anyone their own age, and found themselves awkwardly fascinated by the other. They stole quick glances at each other, which did not go unnoticed by Khelvan and Navek, who smiled knowingly at each other. The attraction was obvious.

To Jake, she was the most beautiful girl he had ever seen. As young as he was, he had already decided she would be his wife one day. He was taking careful note of landmarks and features on the way, and already planned to come back.

Zoric walked alongside Khelvan, leaning on his stick for support and saying nothing while he churned over something, trying to find the right words to say. "Would you consider taking my granddaughter with you Khelvan?" he said quietly. "I am an old man now and won't last much longer. I worry about Rozy living up here alone after I've joined my clan in the afterlife. The winters are bitter and it'll be a harsh life for her, alone up in these mountains."

Not far away, Rozelle heard the words and said emphatically: "I'm not going!" With a defiant gleam in her dark eyes, she glared at her grandfather.

He flinched and frowned, making him all the more worried for her future, isolated in the mountains after he was gone. He only wanted a better life for her.

Jake heard the words but continued on walking behind.

Khelvan turned to Rozelle. He could see from her fiery expression she had no intentions of going with strangers and leaving her elderly grandfather, who had raised her and was all she had ever known. She would never consider leaving *him* alone during his old age.

Much to Khelvan's relief he did not have to answer; he could see the girl would not go. He thought briefly of the rough crew on the ship and the hard trip back, but knew the old man's motives were selfless because of his love for the girl.

Zoric stepped away, raising his white eyebrows and pulling a quizzical face at Khelvan as he did so. He sighed and wisely left the subject alone. He caught up with Navek to tell him more stories about the bravery of his old friends and his father "Hatchi", as he called him affectionately. He chatted away about his boyhood friend, breathing heavily from the exertion in between sentences. Navek was filled with warmth for his father, whose presence he had felt just the night before.

After they travelled another mile or so, Jake sidled up to Rozelle and awkwardly tried to strike up a conversation.

Eventually she set him at ease, talking about their goats and the kid she had rescued from a crevasse last winter. Once the ice was broken, the conversation flowed and Jake related to her easily. He asked many questions about how they survived and how they fed the goats during the long winters; whether they had a barn; and did they manage to store enough fire wood each year.

She told him about their simple life where much time was spent storing food and fuel to survive as the seasons rolled around. They lived in a barn with rock walls and a thatched roof, and had taken some of the building materials from the abandoned village. Her grandfather had not wanted to go back and live there again. "It is a hard life on our own, but we're happy and manage to eke out a living with our few animals. We collect herbs from the mountain in the short summer, but the past few winters have lasted longer, so food is scarcer," she said.

The conversation continued easily, and Navek smiled to himself when he saw the pair chatting away as though they had been childhood friends. He was pleased that the lad finally had someone his own age to relate to. He saw Jake proudly showing her the opal, holding it up to the sunlight and enjoying her fascination with the coloured gem.

A few times when the way became rocky or narrow, the party of five had to spread out in single file. During one of these times, Jake stepped up beside Zoric, who was only slightly taller than him.

He glanced at the old man, who now had his hood pushed back and coat undone as they walked along. Jake saw he was an impressive character with his wild white hair and beard blowing in the breeze. His character was jovial, but he could see too the makings of a once proud and formidable warrior.

When Jake was sure they were well out of earshot from

the others, he looked up at the stoic man ... but words failed him.

Zoric looked back at him, eye-to-eye, and waited patiently for the words to come, as now it was Jake who was finding it hard to speak.

Jake tried to muster up the courage to say something. Eventually, he quietly said: "I'll come back for your granddaughter. In the spring after two winters have passed, I'll return here," he continued, vowing to the old man in a serious tone. Zoric stopped in his tracks and turned to face the lad who had hardly said a word to him before now.

There was a long silence; they could both see Rozelle in their peripheral vision. The old man's sharp eyes searched deeply into the boy, seeking to read his true nature.

Zoric measured his worth and weighed the somewhat impulsive offer, while Jake stood his ground, looking back at the old man with a certainty beyond his years. Beyond the tough, defensive exterior, Zoric saw the resilience of one born to a hard life; the refreshing honesty of youth and the true meaning of what Jake, in his own blunt way was really saying. In the eyes of the youth he saw the earnest and sincere intentions of the offer. Jake really did mean to come back for his granddaughter and was asking for her grandfather's blessings.

Rozelle had stopped further ahead and looked back at them, curious about the conversation and what was going on between the pair. She saw Jake looking up at her grandfather, brazenly holding his gaze. She saw her grandfather's long pause and eventually, the small acquiescent nod, before both turned and continued walking on.

Jake's face was serious and thoughtful; her grandfather had a broadening smile on his ruddy face.

She continued on, then turned back to see her grandfather shaking his head in amusement, displaying a new regard for the youth. He slapped Jake on the back a couple of times. "Sounds good," he said. "Sounds good."

Every now and then a loud outburst of laughter would be heard from Zoric, as he turned over and digested this new information.

The weather remained fair into the evening, and the further they went the more they saw signs of the emerging spring season. The terrain was levelling out and the travellers welcomed the contrast to the high mountain ranges left behind them.

The party maintained a steady pace and covered a lot of ground that eventful day. Not much was said about the sorcerer or how the trio came to be in these remote mountains. Zoric, in his matter-of-fact way, already knew about Jackyl and his recent demise, so the subject was dismissed.

At the top of a hill, a large rocky outcrop emerged from the snow. Zoric stopped the group. "Let's stop here for a rest," he said, as they were all tiring and the temperature was beginning to drop. "Rozy and I will be leaving you soon to head back. You can rest here for the night under the shelter of those rocks. The weather can change quickly around here.

They stood looking out to the south, while on the skyline the colours changed to beautiful evening hues of mauve and blue. "There's an iron ore mine just over there behind those mountains," Zoric said, pointing to the south-west. "If you continue to the south, you'll hit the supply road coming from the mining camp. You can't miss it. Follow it all the way to the port town and you should be there at the end of two days."

They were glad of the break, but felt oddly disappointed to be losing their guides who miraculously saved them when they were depleted, and whose company they had enjoyed.

"Let's eat," said Zoric.

Rozelle got the food out again, as the others took off their packs and cleared a few rocks away to sit down.

Jake went off scouting for firewood which was plentiful. He was soon back striking flint against stone to eventually get a fire started. He glanced over at Rozelle several times as she prepared the food. He wanted to talk to her before they left, though he was unsure of what to say.

Navek found a large log that would burn through the night. The log was too heavy to carry on his own so he called Jake to help. When the boy came over, Navek took out another opal and gave it to Jake.

Jake's eyes widened in surprise. "What …?" He started to ask, but Navek said: "Give it to her".

"But you've already …" Jake stammered.

"Give it to her as a gift for helping us." He pushed it into Jake's top pocket, knowing also if times ever became tough in the future for the pair, the stone could be cashed in to get them out of trouble. "Come on, help me lift this log."

Navek was happy with his decision. They carried the log back, putting one end straight onto the fire to dry out the moisture and get it burning.

They sat around the fire together, gratefully eating the remains of the wonderful food Rozelle shared out, warming themselves as orange flames licked the timber.

Rozelle wrapped a small amount for them to eat the next day, and a small portion for her grandfather on their long walk back to their hut.

When they finished, Zoric stood up and brushed snow from his pants and said: "We fed up the animals before we left, but we have to get back to them. If we leave now, we'll be back by the morning. We know these mountains well, so as long as the sky stays clear we'll use the moonlight to see our way".

They all stood to thank the pair again for all their help. Jake cleared his throat nervously before saying, "We would like to give you something for helping us." He took the opal out of his pocket and self-consciously handed the stone to Rozelle, glancing across to Zoric to include him as well.

Navek could see Jake was nervous, so he stepped in saying: "We have a few stones like this one that came from my father's hut, you may have seen them before Zoric. We would be happy if you would take this one as a small token of our gratitude".

"Ah yes, your father and I used to love looking into those stones," Zoric said. "No one knows where they came from, but they have magic and fire in them. They were handed down to him by his father, and his father before that. Ah, I wished I had more time to tell you what I know Sidewinder. I could tell you many tales, but circumstances are pressing and we must be on our way."

They had only just met that afternoon, but the warm bond of close friendship would never be forgotten. The men touched knuckle-to-knuckle, fist-to-fist, then fist-to-chest in the in the old warrior's way. The hugging seemed to naturally follow.

When Jake shook the calloused hand of Valery Zoric, the old man gave him a knowing wink and then hugged him, slapping him again on the back. Jake went to Rozelle. Not knowing what to say as neither of them wanted to part ways after their brief encounter, they both stood awkwardly. They hugged briefly, and Jake caught the earthy smell of her hair, as her soft body pressed against him. Much to his surprise, she gave him a cheeky kiss on the cheek, and then smiled shyly before turning to leave with her grandfather.

They watched the pair walk away, till Zoric and Rozelle turned to wave before disappearing from sight.

The three travellers were left feeling hollow after the departure; they had all enjoyed their bright company.

Later, Jake thought about new hopes and plans for his

future. An excitement was ignited that had not been there till this day, and a thrill of life's endless possibilities began to race through him.

For Navek, the encounter had been a living link to his family and his clan. They would all hold on to the memories of that day for long after.

Chapter 24.
Coastward

The next morning the trio set off under a cloudy sky, all in good spirits. Their new friends had given them food and inspiration, and new hope for their journey home.

They thought fondly of the pair and hoped they had made it back to their hut. It was a long way for an old man and a girl who had gone on without sleep, and toward the end, much of it would be an uphill climb.

Khelvan, in his mind's eye, was content when he saw a fleeting image of them lying asleep in their beds. "Sleep well," he said. He smiled to himself when it dawned on him he was communicating with the spirit realm again, the first time in many days. He thought he lost this ability in his underground tribulation.

From the time Valery Zoric had pointed out where he and Rozelle lived, Jake had noted the landscape features in his mind – he would remember the way back in two years' time. For many people the scenery looked the same, but Jake would remember particular trees or the shape of a rock, or different landmarks which would become his guideposts when he returned. His good sense of direction had saved him more than once in the past.

At mid-morning they reached the supply road. Jake took out his knife and quickly carved two diagonal lines into the bark of a tree to mark where they came out onto the road. After going a short distance, he turned back to take special notice of their exit point from the forest, imprinting it in his memory. Jake knew he must not miss *this* turning or he may never find the hut again.

They continued along the empty snow covered route without a break. The weather was turning, and they wanted to cover some distance before rain fell. Low, dark clouds gathered and moved across the sky, then hung low amid the surrounding mountains till icy rain started to fall. Under a stand of trees, they stopped for a break and savoured the last of the food. The trees sheltered them for a brief time, then water made its way through the branches and landed on them in big cold drops, rolling from their oilskin coats. The temperature dropped rapidly, but after all they had been through, the conditions did not bother them. They were within two days' walk to the port of Frozia and relative civilisation, where they gambled on catching the supply ship back to the south.

With poor visibility, they headed off along the open road as a biting wind cut into them. Rain stung their faces, forcing them to walk hunched over. They were relieved when it eventually stopped. In the late afternoon, the road finally started to descend toward the coast. There was still a long walk ahead and they were tiring, but no one wanted to stop for the night as there was no dry wood or shelter.

They briefly rested, leaning against an outcropping of large rocks, eating a few handfuls of snow to quench their thirst. They were about to start off again, when Khelvan stopped them. He shoved back his hood and turned back up the road to listen. The others could hear it too.

The distant rumbling of a heavy motor came closer and closer. They all remained motionless next to the rocks. A grey movement disappeared behind trees then appeared again, till eventually a strange vehicle of a type they had never seen before, appeared in the distance, driving straight toward them. As it approached they could see it was a noisy truck with a large steel grader blade used for grading snow off the road, bolted across the front.

They stepped closer to the rocks and watched the odd sight with apprehension. The large vehicle slowed to a stop right next to them, with the noisy engine still running.

The driver's window came down, then an elbow appeared. It belonged to a woman with sunglasses on top of her head. She had knotty blonde hair and sharp blue eyes that peered down at the three travellers with a bemused expression. A few silent moments passed while she checked out the three scruffy looking travellers who were like homeless vagabonds. She wondered what they were doing out here, trekking in isolated wilderness.

"Lori!" exclaimed a surprised Khelvan. "What are you doing up here?" he shouted over the noisy engine.

Navek and Jake looked at each other, taken aback that Khelvan knew the driver.

She leaned forward and squinted at the scrawny, unshaved traveller. "Ha. Not you again," she snorted, recognising him from their trip across the desert. "What the hell are you doing out here at the ass end of the world," she said, more of a statement than a question.

Lori noted the unmasked relief in Khelvan's eyes; he looked like he had been to death's door and back. She could see they were all exhausted.

"That's a long story," Khelvan replied, shaking his head in disbelief at the chances of meeting her again, especially out here in the white wilderness. It was certainly a fortuitous meeting, beyond chance, and he silently thanked his unseen guardians.

"You're still driving. Given up the diamonds, eh?" Khelvan said.

"Well, there's pretty good money in this ice trucking," she replied. She turned off the engine before jumping down to land heavily on the snow. She leaned backward to stretch her back and then tilted her head from side-to-side, clicking her neck. "I run supplies to the iron ore mine once a month in this season. You're lucky to have met me here at all, because I'm actually a day late. And who are these two?" she asked indicating with a jerk of her chin to his companions.

"These are friends. This is Navek and Jake," he

answered, pointing to each of them and absorbing the fact that they truly were his lifelong friends now, after all they had gone through together. "This is Lori," he said in return. "We travelled across the desert together once."

She stepped forward to shake each of their gloved hands, meeting them eye- to-eye and leaving Jake flexing his crushed hand, wondering about the strange girl with such a strong grip.

Casually leaning against a nearby rock with one knee bent, she brought out a pouch of tobacco from her top pocket.

They stood there fascinated by her independence and self-confidence, while she rolled a cigarette with well-practised precision, then lit it. She drew in the smoke deeply, then exhaled, filling their air with the aroma of tobacco smoke. "Need a lift?" she said to Khelvan, still checking out the other two. "A lift would be greatly appreciated," he answered politely.

"You'll all have to squeeze in. Two'll have to stretch out on the bunk bed behind the cabin, and one can ride in the front. But I ain't goin' to that shithole Frozia town," she said. "I'm goin' to Creolleor further south along the coast. It's a shithole too, but slightly less of a one."

She turned to Jake and added, "Excuse the language sonny," causing an involuntary grin to rise to his face. "The road branches off not far down there," she said pointing a bit further along.

"We're hoping to travel by ship back to the south, and they anchor at Creolleor," said Navek.

"Ok. Not a problem," was the reply.

Lori did not seem in any hurry to get back on the road. She leaned back against the wet rocks, arms folded, puffing her cigarette.

"Hungry?" she asked seeing the poor condition of the three travellers and knowing the answer. She pushed herself off the rocks and went to the back of the truck, cigarette hanging from the corner of her mouth.

"You know I always carry food," she said to Khelvan with a wry grin, as she opened the back of the truck. She slid across a wooden box that was covered with a blue and white cotton tea-towel. "You don't get to be this fat without food," she said slapping her plump thigh. "Now throw your bags in the back here, and we'll put this box in the front. It'll be a bit of a squeeze but it'll work out."

Jake was fascinated by the vehicle, having never ridden in one before. He stood beside the passenger door looking up in awe until Lori reached across the front seat and pushed open the door.

Khelvan and Navek climbed up and stretched out at opposite ends of the roomy bunk behind the front seat. Lori indicated to Jake to climb up and ride in the front with her. She could see the captivation on his face, and smiled to herself as he scrambled into the cabin. She started up the old truck, turning the engine over for a while before it finally ignited with a splutter.

With the box of food on the front seat between them, they continued on in the noisy vehicle.

"Help yourselves," Lori said loudly over the engine,

and pulled back the tea-towel to expose the food beneath. "It's only leftovers really, but I'll be restocking at the market in Creolleor, so eat up."

In the warm cabin of the truck, they soon removed some of their bulky clothing, and after eating and drinking, it was not long before Khelvan and Navek were asleep.

Lori rolled herself another cigarette, holding the steering wheel with one knee while doing so. When she checked the rear view mirror, she saw both men asleep.

She tried to make conversation with Jake, but soon found he was not one for small talk. She left him alone to puzzle over the dials and levers on the dashboard, or look out the window at scenery whizzing past.

Jake though, felt fascinated and empowered by the experience of being rapidly carried along inside a machine on wheels. But his thoughts soon went back to Rozelle and all the events of the past few weeks.

At times, the road became dangerous and slippery; sheer drops over cliff edges alarmed Jake when he looked straight down. He gripped on to the door handle with tense, white knuckles. He felt more assured when he saw Lori casually changing the gears up and down to manage the vehicle – she seemed to be an experienced driver.

On a straight stretch of road she called to Jake over the noise. "Oi," she said, indicating for him to slide over to the middle of the seat and steer the truck, while she rolled another smoke. At first he did not know what she wanted, but once he understood he moved over quickly and took the wheel, delighting in the task as any boy would.

Once she finished the smoke, she took the wheel back and continued driving. Jake moved back to his seat, pleased with himself and with a renewed regard for Lori. He thought to himself maybe he would drive a vehicle like this one day.

Occasionally, Lori looked back to make sure the men behind her were alright, but they lay stretched out on the mattress in a deep sleep. It was not long before Jake's head nodded forward, till Lori got him to curl up on the seat to sleep. She smiled to herself, and once again felt good about being useful and helping someone in need.

As they continued slowly in the direction of the coastal town, Lori reflected on the chances of meeting Khelvan again like this. She knew there was something special about this man who had purpose and inner strength.

It was well after nightfall when the lights of Creolleor came into distant view. The three men had managed to sleep through the rough bouncing ride into town, and when they finally pulled into the port of Creolleor, it was the smell of sea air that woke Navek.

He nudged Khelvan and Jake awake. They were delighted to see the town lights and be back in civilisation. It was like being in a dream after all they had been through, a make-believe world of colours and lights. They felt a humble appreciation for simple things usually taken for granted, like colours, lighting, shops, the sounds of people, availability of food and shelter, and many other everyday things. They gazed around at the various shops, some of which were still open. A few people were still out and about.

Lori knew her way around the town and eventually pulled into a dimly lit alleyway behind an old hotel, where she switched off the loud engine and sighed in relief. After the many hours of concentration she sat a few moments with her eyes closed and absorbed the quietude.

"This is where I'll be stayin' for the next couple of nights. I can arrange a room for you three for tonight if you want, and then we can sort out the rest tomorrow. OK?"

"I'll get some money from my bag in the back," said Khelvan.

"Pfft," said Lori, as though the issue of money was a trifling matter to her. "Don't worry about that. Wait here and I'll be back soon."

They got out and stood in the street, stretching their legs, pulling on their coats. The night air was chilly, but it was not as cold near the sea as it had been in the mountains.

The smell of the sea air stirred feelings of excitement in each of them, as it held the promise of adventure and unlimited possibilities. Possibilities of getting back to the beach house where there were no longer huge feats to accomplish, and life could be lived simply.

Lori reappeared and they all got their luggage before she locked up the vehicle and proceeded up the back stairs into the building.

They walked along a corridor, passing several

numbered rooms, till they reached the second last door – number 8. Lori unlocked and reached in to turn on the light.

"This is your room," she said tossing the key onto one of the beds, "and mine is the next one, number 10. They're not much, but the beds here are clean".

They looked in to see a narrow room with a single window, a small wooden table and three single beds.

"Toilets and a hot bath are down the corridor there," she pointed.

"Better than what we've had for the past few weeks," quipped Jake stepping in boldly past the others. He looked around happily before putting his bag on the bed nearest the window. He went over to look through the window to check out the street below.

"Thank you Lori. We all really appreciate this," said Khelvan.

"I know you do," said Lori with a slight heaviness in her chest, pleased at being able to help them. She knew when she picked them up that their circumstances were dire. She had not asked questions but knew somehow they were returning from a dangerous and grave situation. "Just knock on the next door if you need anythin', but I'll be sleepin' in late tomorrow mornin'. I'll see you then though. Watch your back if you go out, there are plenty of thieves around here," she warned, and then left to go to her room.

After facing and surviving all kinds of extremes, they sat around just enjoying the small, clean room, not wanting to leave. They each went off and luxuriated in a hot bath, and then stretched out on the beds, indulging in inactivity.

From time-to-time they got up to look down at the streets below, to simply watch the world go by.

When a sharp knock sounded on the door, all eyes turned to the door not knowing what to expect.

Khelvan got up and opened it to see two of the hotel staff. One held a tray with three covered plates, and the other held a tray with a basket of bread, three mugs and a large coffeepot with a knitted cover over it. "Your order gentlemen," said one, as they stepped into the room and placed the trays on the table before leaving.

Following a hearty meal of beef stew and vegetables, washed down with sweetened milk coffee, they lay in their beds. Through the wall they could hear the muffled sound of Lori snoring, and acknowledged among themselves their gratitude for the tough girl's generosity.

Navek and Jake hoped to hear about Khelvan's previous journey through the desert with her, but he was too tired tonight.

Before drifting off to sleep, Khelvan sent a silent message to Lamaar that it was all over; the mission was completed. He lay awhile listening to the sounds of the night and recalled the recent events.

Words from his teacher came to mind: "On the way you will find others who will help you, though some may seem unlikely companions ..."

He knew he could not grasp it all right now, but over

time he may realise the gravity of their achievement. There had been times when he thought this could be his last day on earth, and it had certainly been the toughest journey of his life. Right now he was content, very fortunate to be alive and humbled by all the help received from both worlds.

Chapter 25.
The True Warrior Way

18 months later …

On the trip back from the icy north, Khelvan told Jake to consider the beach house his home if he wanted. The youth stayed there at times throughout the year, but would go walkabout and be gone for several days, weeks, or even months at a time. Without announcement he would reappear, usually offering no explanation about where he had been or what he had been doing.

Navek returned to live at the beach house, and for the first time since his stay on the islands, he lived simply and enjoyed life's uncomplicated pleasures. In different seasons he collected sea vegetables from the beach or the rocks, and sometimes went up to the mountains with Jake, who had taught him about collecting herbs, roots and mushrooms. Navek learnt which ones were poisonous or toxic, which ones cured inflammation or which ones cured digestive ailments, skills that the lad had picked up naturally from his wanderings through the mountains with Sharian the old healer.

Initially they went together, but often Jake went alone; he was already an expert hunter with excellent bush skills. They collected the produce to eat fresh, but some was dried and stored for cooking or medicines. If there was enough, they would trade with the town folk for supplies, calling in to see the friendly old landlords and give them some of the produce.

The old couple had met Jake a few times and had become like grandparents to both Navek and Jake. They always insisted the pair come in for tea and homemade cakes after their long journey into town, and welcomed their company, grateful for the gifts of food.

When Jake was around, he and Navek enjoyed training together on the sand, exchanging skills and techniques. They often braced wild or cold weather, continuing on in all conditions unless there were electrical storms about. For Navek, these training days honed and polished his old skills and sharpened his reflexes, and the activity helped maintain his life's balance.

He had tasted the downward and self-destructive path of anaesthetising himself to life. He chose never to go back to it. Sometimes though when he was in town, he could hear the ambrosia calling to him; but he would walk on, ignoring the voice of the thief in his mind that wanted to rob him of his peace.

Focused and a fast learner, Jake was keenly drawn to the fighting arts. He thrived on the workouts which helped him define his physical boundaries and limitations. He learned new skills and flexed his growing muscles against Navek – once the best of an ancient fighting style. It was the most direct form of communication they had with each other; he felt sharp and alive.

Jake would also show Navek techniques he had learned from the monks, and they incorporated and perfected their skills together.

Jake regularly returned to visit Sharian in the mountains where he always felt at home. Before Jake's first visit back there, Navek made up a bag of dried seaweed and small dried fish as a healthy treat for the old healer's winter soups. It was a small token of gratitude for all the help and uplifting guidance the old man had given him.

Navek took out the Dragon's Eye amulet he had snatched from the sorcerer's neck. He wrapped and secured it carefully and gave it to Jake, asking him to return it to its rightful owner and send Sharian his best regards.

Sharian was overjoyed at receiving the stone that could enhance his healing abilities, and deeply appreciated the link to his father. He had never expected to see the cherished jewel again. Jake stayed awhile with Sharian, collecting and storing firewood and food for the winter.

In the spring that followed, Jake would return there again on his way back from his winter training with the monks. He would stay a few weeks to help the old man again, not just to repay the debt for saving him all those years ago, but also because it was the first place in his life where he had felt a sense of belonging. He enjoying wandering in the mountains with Sharian; he understood his own purpose when he was around the old man.

Sharian also inspired in him, an intuitive knowledge of healing as Jake learned about the different plants and remedies.

Khelvan returned to the serenity of his teacher's forest dwelling, where he also went back to living the simple existence he had wanted for so long. By choice, he lived in isolation with his teacher and helped tend to the grounds around the house, keeping them trimmed and immaculate for their own enjoyment.

Sometimes he and Lamaar would trek into the mountains, standing at the peaks, gazing out over the mist sitting in the valleys below. In the evenings they would sit on the veranda and look past the elegant clumps of black bamboo that rustled in the breeze and uttered their dry whisperings.

Just maintaining the house and keeping up a supply of food, water and firewood had been enough to keep them pleasantly busy, but now he was ready to venture back out into the world.

He was on his way to the beach house to spend time in the company of friends, enjoy the warm sunlight on his skin, eat seafood, go swimming in the sea and talk of old times around the open fire at night.

Khelvan stood high on the rocks leaning on the stick he had picked up miles back, wearing a serene smile on his face. He was in no hurry and enjoyed the warmth of the afternoon autumn sun on his back. Below him Jake was busy fishing off the rocks. Even at that distance, Khelvan could see that Jake had grown taller, his bare chest and arms were now more muscular, and his dark brown unkempt hair flew around in the sea breeze. It reminded Khelvan of the colour of the bison's winter coat with sun bleached blond ends.

In the distance, a flock of birds flew low over the surface of the sea, feeding on a school of pilchards as small waves rolled in to break on the shore.

Suddenly, Jake, who had been fishing with his back to Khelvan, sensed someone watching him. He turned to look directly up at Khelvan standing on the cliff above.

"Hmmm," Khelvan smiled and nodded to himself. *"He's learning sure enough,"* and they waved at each other before Khelvan continued on toward the house.

Navek was not there, but Khelvan found his bedroom just as he had left it eighteen months before. He dropped his swag before heading down to the sea for a cool swim to freshen up after his long journey.

Just before sunset Jake returned with the catch and both men greeted each other warmly. Even though not much was said, Jake could not hide his happiness at seeing Khelvan again as he went about preparing a fire in the well-used fire pit in the sand. Khelvan leaned back casually on a nearby log just happy to be back, enjoying the ambience of a pleasant evening in familiar territory near the sea.

Jake went on preparing the three large fish he had caught, stuffing the fish with local herbs and slices of lemon. He wrapped them in large leaves and placed them in the hot coals to cook while Khelvan watched on.

Soon after, Khelvan and Jake heard footsteps near the house, and turned to see a healthy looking Navek appear from behind the house after hunting in the forest. He dropped a basket of native plants and mushrooms on the veranda, raising a hand in greeting before bringing over a large bundle of firewood. Navek was gladdened to see Khelvan again after such a long time. "Welcome back stranger," he said happy at the reunion, dropping the fire wood on the sand near the fire before turning to embrace him.

Jake smiled as he went about lightly frying some rock scallops and prawns as an entree, to be followed by mushrooms and fish. They all sat around eating and chatting together, talking late into night and drinking the plum wine that Khelvan had brought for them. Even Jake sipped on the potent wine which loosened him up and made him more talkative and jovial than usual.

During the following weeks, they sometimes trained with weapons on the beach. Jake particularly liked this time, as the intensity of training could become deadly serious, pushing him to his limits. At times, he surprised them both with his own skills.

Khelvan was pleased that the monks and Navek had trained Jake well and the lad thrived on such a discipline. Jake was developing the integrity and good thinking that were important principles of the fighting arts. In keeping with the true warrior way, these skills and techniques would never be used to harm anyone. They would only fight if their lives were threatened.

They all learnt new techniques, polished old ones and sharpened reflexes until their responses flowed automatically. Each with their own strengths, they had been brought together through unbelievable adversity and impossible odds. At the far reaches of the earth they had leaned on each other, worked together and trusted each other.

Jake had not forgotten his promise to Valery Zoric; to go back to the mountains for Rozelle. After his next visit to see Sharian, he would continue on to the north-east to see the girl who was continually on his mind. He would miss the two men whom he now considered to be his brothers. However that is another story ...

Author's notes

The writing of Black Bamboo has been a long journey. It is my first novel, though the outline was started long ago. For fifteen years it was forgotten, then dusted off and brought to completion. I write this tale for those with a love of magic and possibility, and for those who seek a deeper meaning to life.

If you enjoyed the story or would like to comment
Connect online: www.vjstevenson.wordpress.com

About the Author

Vivienne Stevenson is an Australian writer who grew up in rural Victoria. She travelled extensively before living and working in Japan for four years where, surrounded by an ancient and rich culture, the seed of this story first sprouted and took shape.

She has teaching, horticultural and landscaping qualifications, as well as a background in martial arts and meditation – all of which are reflected throughout the story.

Vivienne now lives in Queensland, Australia.